Cairo Circles

a novel

Doma Mahmoud

The Unnamed Press
Los Angeles, CA

For Laila and Zeinab

Cairo Circles

Part
One

1

For almost fifteen years now, Zeina's mother, Salma, had served as housemaid for none other than Madame Alia Abaza, a former actress who starred in a handful of comedies back before Zeina was born, in the mid-eighties.

In Madame Alia's penthouse, there was a small room—originally built as a storage space—reserved for Salma and Zeina. Tonight, Zeina would be locked inside, for it was New Year's Eve and guests would soon arrive for the madame's traditional gathering.

"All right," Salma said. "Are you sure you don't need the bathroom?"

"Just go, Mama."

"I'll be checking on you, in case you do. You need anything else?"

Zeina didn't respond. She was lying down on the mattress that occupied half the room, facing the wall, with her knees tucked into her chest and her long brown hair covering the side of her face. She was eleven and a half years old, but her mother still couldn't trust her to stay in the room. Zeina understood that it was a consequence of her frequent misbehavior, but it was humiliating to be locked inside such a small space like a rabid dog.

"Zeina," Salma said. "I asked you a question."

"It's like I'm an animal."

"Oh, come on," Salma said. "I've told you so many times. I have to."

"Why? Did Madame Alia tell you to?"

"No," Salma said. "It's for me. For my peace of mind. So I'm not constantly worried that you'll walk out into the salon."

It offended Zeina that her presence in the madame's gathering would be considered so scandalous. "What, is President Mubarak coming?"

"See? *That's* the voice in your head I don't trust."

"Khalas," Zeina said. "Just go."

Zeina kept facing the wall and making her disappointment known. She was putting her mother in danger of being yelled at, since Salma ought to be preparing for the guests outside. But it was Zeina's right to be upset, not because she would spend hours in the room, but because it was New Year's Eve, and she would have to sit there, alone, while her brothers celebrated with friends back home. Despite being two years younger, Mustafa and Omar were free to roam the streets under no supervision, simply because they weren't girls.

Salma reached for Zeina's CD player. "Look," she said. "This Walkman is getting old, and I'm sure Madame Alia will realize soon."

Zeina turned around and looked at Salma. "You mean a new Walkman? For me?"

"It's not a promise," Salma said. "But it's likely. She mentioned it a few days ago."

Zeina held her mother's arm. "What did she say?"

"It's best to keep it a surprise," Salma said. "You don't want to hope for something then not get it."

It was early in Zeina's life, when Madame Alia made it known that Zeina's musical talent was remarkable. Zeina would be sitting in the room or kitchen, singing along to the tracks playing on Madame Alia's record player, and then the madame would come across her and clap excitedly, as if she had just stumbled upon a bag of gold. Eventually, she bought Zeina a Walkman, which still worked to this day, and had gifted her album after album ever since. Today, Zeina had dozens of songs memorized.

Zeina held her Walkman close to her chest. "But I still get to keep this one."

"Of course. Yalla, now I really have to go. Listen to some music or draw."

"Can we go home if it ends early?"

"No," Salma said. "It's going to go past twelve."

"Twelve isn't that late."

"What?"

Zeina rolled her eyes.

"What do I always say?"

"Mashy."

"What do I say?" Salma asked again.

"The monsters come out when everyone is asleep."

"That's right," Salma said, before kissing Zeina's forehead. She stood up, walked out of the room, and locked the door behind her.

Salma was meticulous in everything she did, especially in the madame's apartment. What she didn't know, however, was that Zeina often broke her numerous rules. Just a few weeks ago, Zeina had snuck into Madame Alia's bedroom while Salma cooked in the kitchen and spent ten whole seconds lying on the madame's shockingly comfortable bed. A week before that, she opened her son Taymour's tennis bag, which he always dumped beside the front door upon returning from practice, took one of the balls inside, and smuggled it back to her home in Ramlet Bulaq.

One of the rules she had recently broken concerned the room's window. Zeina had always been under the impression that it was locked, but after curious experimentation a few weeks ago, she discovered that it could be opened if the handle was turned completely and pulled with enough strength.

As soon as Zeina heard the doorbell ring, which meant a guest had just arrived and Salma wouldn't return any time soon, she stood up and opened the window. It was just high enough so she could stick her head out but remain grounded inside the room. She looked down at the twenty-one floors of empty space beneath her and was once again captivated by the thought of flying through it. How unfortunate it was that such a thrilling experience couldn't be enjoyed without violent death.

An island in the Nile, Zamalek stood at the center of Cairo, and from the window Zeina had a full view of the city. On the Nile to her left, Zamalek's lights formed a rippled reflection of the skyline, before the dark and flat province of Bulaq on the other side of the river, where Mustafa and Omar were probably preparing to launch Roman candles at midnight. To her right was the rest of Zamalek— the towers, sports clubs, and villa embassies—then the other branch of the Nile and, farther still, a sea of artificial light before the dark Sahara beyond.

Zeina enjoyed the view until the wind became too strong. She feared it would travel through the crack underneath the room's door, down the hall, and into the salon, where Salma was. Indeed, Salma often learned of Zeina's crimes in superhuman ways, so Zeina shut the window, lay on the mattress, and began to draw in her notebook as she listened to Enya's "Caribbean Blue." The lyrics were in English—Zeina had never been able to understand them—but the grandiosity of Enya's voice always drew Zeina back to the album. Today, it prompted Zeina to draw Catwoman—one of the characters from Mustafa's comic books—colonizing Cairo with an army of black cats and murdering all the men.

Zeina's attention was diverted from her masterpiece when the room's door opened. She removed her headphones and was about to tell Salma that she didn't need to use the bathroom, but then Madame Najla's Chihuahua, Boobie, ran into the room.

Boobie hopped onto the mattress and ran into Zeina's arms.

"No way!" Zeina yelled.

"Hi, Zeina," Madame Najla said from behind Salma.

"Hi, Tante."

Madame Najla was Madame Alia's cousin, and together with her son, Aly, who was Taymour's best friend, she was the apartment's most frequent guest. There was probably no woman alive more beautiful than her. Everything from her wavy light brown hair and long eyelashes to the scent of her perfume was simply perfect. Tonight, she was wearing black jeans, black boots, a shimmering gold silk blouse, and a leather jacket. Whenever Zeina prayed, she asked God to make her not only a famous singer but also as charming and gorgeous as Madame Najla.

"Can she stay here?" Zeina asked with regard to Boobie.

"Of course," Madame Najla said. "That's why we brought her."

"Thank you, Tante."

"You need anything?" Salma asked. She was smiling the way she always did when one of the people she served was around: with an innocence that made it impossible to think that this was the same woman who sometimes beat Zeina with a stick.

"I don't," Zeina said.

"All right," Salma said. "Have fun."

"Bye, Zeina," Madame Najla said.

"Bye, Tante."

Salma closed the door and locked it. Zeina's attention shifted toward Boobie, who was now on Zeina's stomach, wagging her tail and licking Zeina's face.

"Is it necessary to lock her?" Madame Najla asked from the other side of the door.

Salma responded as the two women walked away, but Zeina couldn't hear what was said. It didn't matter anymore; her evening had just significantly improved. She had always enjoyed chasing the stray dogs that roamed the streets in Ramlet Bulaq and feeding them, but Boobie was of another species. She was so tiny it was heartbreaking. She was like a toy with a soul, a whole spectrum of feelings and expressions, and it always made Zeina laugh when she froze midplay, stared at Zeina for a moment, then rolled onto her back and requested a belly rub.

Zeina played with her in as many different ways as she could. Eventually, she heard the guests in the salon yell in English. *"Four, three, two, one. Happy New Year!"* And from the red and green fireworks that suddenly painted the dark sky outside, Zeina understood that the new year, 2000, had just begun.

Though she had never gone to school like her brothers, Zeina had been tutored by a service worker a few years ago, a young woman from the Education for the Unschooled organization who came to their apartment once a week for a whole year. Today, she could count to one thousand. She could recite ten chapters from the Quran. She could read numbers in both Anglophone and Arabic and tell time on a clock. She couldn't read words but could, if given enough time, write her full name. She knew the names of fifty types of animals, twenty vegetables and fruits, and six flowers. She understood that the world was humongous and that Egypt was just a small part of it. That December 1999 had just ended, and January 2000 had just begun. That on June 30, she will have lived in the world for twelve whole years. That the reason people like Madame Alia were so rich was not because God preferred them, but because their fathers and grandfathers had worked hard and passed on their wealth; that if she wanted to be like them, she would have to build her wealth on her own.

Zeina wasn't ignorant. In fact, she believed she was smarter than Omar and had recently gotten Mustafa, his twin, to agree, though she could usually get Mustafa to agree with her on anything.

It was probably an hour into the new year when Salma returned to the room.

Zeina held Boobie in fear that Salma had come to take her. "Are they leaving?"

"No," Salma said as she frowned. "Yalla, get up."

"We're going home?"

"No," Salma said. "Madame Alia wants you."

"For what?"

"She wants you to sing for her friend."

Zeina tossed Boobie onto the mattress. "Swear on your mother's soul!"

"Yalla, don't stall."

Zeina reached for her backpack and extracted her black jeans, pink T-shirt, and hairbrush.

"What are you doing?" Salma asked.

Zeina changed clothes with hysterical speed, then ran the brush through her hair as many times as she could, before the urge to leave the room became irresistible. The opportunity to sing for someone besides Madame Alia, Salma, and Mustafa came only once every year or two and would make her night worth remembering. She walked down the hallway toward the salon as the voices of the guests grew louder, until she was just a turn of a corner away.

Salma walked past her. "She's here, Madame."

"Come here, Zeina," Madame Alia said.

The salon looked quite different from the one Zeina helped clean on Saturday mornings. From the outline of the suspended ceiling came a warm light that highlighted the artwork on the walls. On the tables next to each of the three brown sofas were glass vases hosting orchids and roses. On the glass coffee table that stood in the middle of the sofa arrangement were plates filled with finger food: kofta, grilled shrimp, grape leaves, and falafel, all pierced with toothpicks, as well as mini-bowls of dips on the side. Zeina glanced at them and then quickly looked away, because *never stare at food, not even when you're hungry,* was one of the earliest lessons Salma had taught her.

It was also Zeina's first time seeing the salon occupied by so many people. Both Madame Alia and Taymour, the only two residents of the spacious apartment, were always in either their bedrooms, the living room, or the dining room, while the salon remained mostly unoccupied. Now, it hosted seven guests: Madame Alia's best friends Najla and Sherifa, their husbands, Madame Najla's younger brother, and a man with a ponytail and short beard whom Zeina had never seen before.

"Mashallah," Madame Najla's husband, Mister Bassem, said. "She's all grown up. She looks more and more like you."

"Right?" Madame Najla said.

Zeina stood behind her mother's arm. She enjoyed being reminded of her strong resemblance to Salma; she had inherited her mother's olive skin, hazel eyes, and dark brown hair.

Boobie ran out of the hallway toward Madame Najla, who picked her up and placed her on her lap. "Did you guys play?" she asked Zeina.

Zeina nodded.

"Come," Madame Alia said. "Don't be shy."

With a gentle push from Salma, Zeina stepped through the clouds of cigarette smoke floating aimlessly in the air and walked around the coffee table toward Madame Alia, who grabbed Zeina's arm when Zeina got close enough.

"Come, ya habibty," Madame Alia said.

Salma spent a lot of time teaching Zeina how a woman must behave, and Madame Alia frequently contradicted Salma's lessons. Tonight, the full length of the madame's arms and the top third of her breasts were remarkably exposed. Her breath stunk of alcohol, as it almost always did, and her eyes were half shut in a way that suggested she was drunk, which was haram. Indeed, she was a habitual rule-breaker, neither a modest woman nor a good Muslim, and Zeina could never decide whether that was repulsive or heroic. Regardless, the madame looked good; she had light blue eyeliner on her dark blue eyes, and her blond hair curled at the bottom.

Zeina sat beside her.

"This is my friend Mazen," the madame said as she pointed at the ponytailed man. "He's a famous musician."

"How are you, Zeina?" Mazen asked her.

Zeina responded with a smile.

"Ya habibty," Madame Najla said. "She's feeling shy."

It was true. Zeina worried that she would fail to sing for this audience, this gathering of impeccably dressed men and their veilless beautiful wives, who drank and dined and wore gold on their wrists like queens.

"So, let me tell you about this one," Madame Alia said. "She was so much trouble when she was younger. Once, when she was... what, Salma... three or four? She was playing with Taymour out here. I had this little statue of the Buddha that my father had given me as a gift, may he rest in peace. Then this one here gets a hold of it and smashes it on the floor. Of course, I'm yelling at her when I find it. I'm even yelling at Salma. Guess what she says?

"She says, *He was dead anyway. He wouldn't open his eyes.*"

The guests exploded with laughter and the smell of alcohol intensified. Salma was standing beside the bar, smiling in spite of her nervousness.

"My baby," Madame Najla said.

"I guess she made a good point," Mazen said.

"I know," Madame Alia said. "I couldn't be angry anymore. I started laughing. Do you remember, Zeina?"

Zeina nodded her head, though she didn't remember.

"Of course she doesn't," Madame Sherifa's husband, Mister Yassin, said.

"No, I do," Zeina said, immediately regretting it. She didn't need to look at her mother to know that Salma was castigating her with a look.

Never challenge them was also one of Salma's frequent orders.

"Mazen," Madame Alia said. "Yalla?"

"Sure," Mazen said. "Let's do it."

Madame Alia looked at Salma. "Get him the oud."

Salma walked toward the apartment's front door, then returned with an instrument case.

"I'm so excited," Madame Najla said.

Mazen extracted a string instrument from the case. "So," Mazen told Zeina. "Do you know what this is?"

"It's a guitar," Zeina responded, since the instrument resembled Taymour's.

"Not quite," Madame Alia said.

Mazen smiled at her. "It's very similar. Except look"—he extended his arm and brought the oud closer to Zeina—"there are two strings on each note instead of one. It's called a oud. Tell me, who's your favorite singer?"

"Om Kolthoum."

"Ahh," he said. "Bravo. The greatest woman to walk this land."

"Excuse me," Madame Alia said. "But look who you're sitting with!"

"You wish," Mister Bassem said.

Laughter moved through the room and Zeina understood why. Though the apartment was filled with photographs from Madame Alia's brief time as a famous actress, Zeina knew that Madame Alia was ultimately shunned by the film industry. Salma went on an angry rant once, after being yelled at by Madame Alia, and revealed that the madame had starred in six films, that she became famous for her looks, not her acting talent, and that it didn't take long for the public to ostracize her.

"Well," Mazen said. "Besides the women in this room, of course, and our own Zeina right here, who I've heard has a delightful voice?"

Zeina giggled with embarrassment. She felt she might be falling in love with this man, like those women in the movies she always watched with Salma in the kitchen. He didn't only have majestic hair; he had thick arms and a jaw Zeina felt peculiarly compelled by.

"What will you sing for us?" Mazen asked. "Actually, don't answer. Let's do this. I'll start playing a song of hers, and let's see if you recognize it."

"Oh, she will," Madame Alia said. "Trust me."

Mister Yassin extracted a brown kofta-shaped object from his jacket pocket, lit the tip of it as he sucked on the other tip, and then exhaled thick white smoke. Zeina would remember to ask Salma about the kofta-looking cigarette.

Mazen looked at everyone, including Salma, and smiled. He held his pick in front of one of the strings and looked at Zeina. "Ready?"

He stroked into the tune of a song Zeina had probably sung no less than a thousand times: the legendary "Enta Omry." Madame Sherifa sang the first line and Madame Alia silenced her with a snap of her fingers.

"Alia," Mister Yassin said. "Maybe she—"

"Shhh."

It felt as if Zeina's heart were beating inside her skull. She had never been put under the spotlight like this, but she fantasized about it daily. Quite often, she sang in the shower and then bowed and waved before thin air, to thank the imaginary audience she hoped to have when she grew up and became a star. This was her chance to practice now. She stood up and closed her eyes, to get away from the impatient stares coming from everyone around the room, especially Salma's. She heard the first line in her mind, the second, the third, then opened her eyes as the fourth escaped her mouth.

All six guests moved at the exact same time, as if the doorbell had just rung. Mister Bassem put his drink on the table, Mister Yassin leaned back on the sofa, and there was a slight pause in Mazen's playing.

Your eyes took me back to the days that had gone
Made me regret the past and its wounds
The things I saw before my eyes saw you.

Once Zeina found her pitch, there was no losing it. She could take Boobie to the middle of the room and roll around on the floor without missing a note.

I've now just begun to love my life
I've now begun to fear the passing of my time
All the joy that I longed for before you
My heart and mind found it in the light of your eyes.

Zeina mostly looked at Mazen's hands as she sang. When she glanced at Salma, she became confused. Salma appeared awestruck, as if she'd never heard Zeina sing, when in reality she often ordered Zeina to stop singing and shut up at once. It was only when Zeina looked at the guests that she understood why: these were the people Salma served, the bosses who were always right, the madames who could raise their voice at her whenever they pleased, and now they all appeared seduced. Madame Sherifa's mouth was open, Mister Yassin was smiling, and Madame Najla was holding her hands up, as if she couldn't wait any longer to begin clapping.

Mazen hit the last note of the song and Zeina matched it for a few seconds, before the song was brought to an end. For a fraction of a moment, there was a terrible silence, which scared Zeina—perhaps she hadn't quite impressed—but then everyone began clapping and cheering, and Madame Alia went as far as whistling.

"Didn't I tell you?" Madame Alia yelled.

Zeina saw no reason not to bow, so she did, and then the room really exploded with delight. Salma laughed hard and without reservation, as if she were also a madame.

"My God," Mazen said as he looked at Salma. "Your daughter is unbelievable."

"You're so kind, sir," Salma said. "It's a special gift God gave her."

"It really is," Mister Yassin said.

"I have to introduce her to someone," Mazen said to both Salma and Madame Alia. "Nemr would love her. We could get her on the radio?"

Zeina almost yelled, *What?* but trapped the word in her throat and then choked and started coughing. Mazen chuckled and Madame Alia rubbed her back.

There was a lot Zeina didn't have; she didn't have books and friends from school, like her brothers, or friends with houses where she could sleep over on New Year's Eve, like Taymour. She didn't even have a sister. She often wondered why God had cursed her with such circumstances. But if she could sing on the radio, then she would have more than any girl could dream of; she would be happy to be locked inside any room for months to come, if she could sing one track on the radio. How many people would listen? A thousand or thousands among thousands?

"Oh," Salma said. "Walahy, you're so kind, sir. But... her father wouldn't be thrilled with the idea. She's... so young."

Zeina was tempted to protest.

"Forget that," Madame Alia said, before taking a gulp of her drink. "Fathers are the ruin of this country."

"Alia," Madame Najla said. "Easy."

Madame Alia took a drag from her cigarette. Silence took hold of the room and Zeina worried the issue at hand was about to be abandoned.

"He shouldn't have a problem," Mazen said. "It's not TV."

Zeina almost said, *Exactly.* She was tired of being at the mercy of her father's decisions. Though he often gave her kisses and treats he never gave her brothers, Abu Ahmed had been the source of most of her misery. He was the one who had decided, back when Zeina was five, that she didn't need to be enrolled in school and that it was better if she accompanied Salma to Zamalek and learned how to care for a home. He couldn't also be the reason she didn't sing on the radio, as Mazen, this angelic man whom she wanted as a new father, was proposing as a possibility.

"You're very kind, sir," Salma said. "But I'm sure there are many like her."

"Oh no," Mazen said. "Many like *that*? No. That was incredible. She sings with such... with such grace. And she's just a child. The whole country will want to hear this."

"Mama!" Zeina yelled.

Madame Sherifa laughed. "You better not be just saying that."

"No," Mazen said. "I'm completely serious."

"Well," Mister Bassem said. "You know how fathers get sometimes. At the end of the day, she's his daughter. We can all understand. Alia, please, that was wonderful, but"—he looked at the liquor bottles on the table—"it's getting late."

"All right," Madame Alia said. "You were amazing, Zeina. Thank you, habibty."

Zeina understood the exchange that had just occurred and wanted to tell Mister Bassem that he had nothing to worry about. Madame Alia was always surrounded by liquor, Zeina was used to it, and would they like to have another song? Perhaps Dalida's "Helwa Ya Balady" or Fayrouz's "Shadi"?

Salma signaled for Zeina to come to her. "Yalla."

Zeina slowly obliged. As soon as she was within Salma's reach, Salma put her hand on Zeina's back and guided her toward the hallway. But Zeina couldn't leave before she turned to her audience and wished them a good night, an act her mother reprimanded when they reached their room.

"They're not your friends and that is not the way."

"What way, Mama? Every day you tell me that is not the way. They loved me!"

A knock on the door alarmed them.

"Madame?" Salma asked as she opened the door.

"Hello," Mazen said from outside.

"Oh," Salma said.

"Sorry for interrupting, but I just... I had to come over and speak with you. If you don't mind. You know, I would really like to... I wanted to ask if I could come and speak to your husband. About Zeina's singing."

"Yes!" Zeina yelled.

Salma turned around and terrorized Zeina with a look. "Silence," she said, before turning back to Mazen and closing the door enough for Zeina to be excluded. "You're very kind, sir, but my husband works out of the house, and he barely leaves, and I don't think he would—"

"I can be your guest," Mazen said. "At your own house."

Zeina tiptoed to the space behind the door, so she could hear Mazen better.

"Oh, sir," Salma said. "That is... you are most welcome, sir. But the trip would be so difficult. It is far and hard to find."

"Alia tells me you live across the Nile?" Mazen said. "In Ramlet Bulaq?"

"Yes, sir," Salma said.

"Then it shouldn't be a problem," Mazen said. "I'm from a similar neighborhood myself."

"But, sir. It's just so—"

"Please," Mazen said. "I'll see what he says. It's a waste, you know. Your daughter is truly talented."

Salma hesitated to give Mazen a response and Zeina understood why. Salma couldn't simply deny his request; he was, after all, Madame Alia's friend. Nevertheless, the idea would cause Salma great distress. Most of the fights between Zeina's parents revolved around Salma's work, because it required Salma to sleep outside her home sometimes and to remove her veil around men she called "sir" and to serve alcohol.

Now, one of them wanted to come visit.

"You're most welcome, sir," Salma said.

Zeina clapped as silently as she could.

"Thank you," he said. "How can I find you?"

"You might have to write it down, sir."

"Just tell me," Mazen said. "I'll remember."

"All right," Salma said. She took Mazen through the directions, and Zeina followed along to make sure Salma didn't make a mistake.

"All right," Mazen said. "Masaken of Ramlet Bulaq. Fifth street, second building, fifth floor."

"Yes, sir."

"Great! And can I ask you one last thing? Between you and me."

"Of course, sir."

"Does she..." Mazen whispered. "Is it usually like this, with the madame?"

Salma looked down in horror. "What do you mean, sir?" Salma asked, though it was obvious what he meant. The answer to the question was very much in the affirmative; Madame Alia often drank so much when she was alone that she vomited in the bathroom before she went to sleep, making monstrous sounds Zeina could hear all the way from her room.

"Never mind," Mazen said. "Sorry I asked. Can I come Friday, after Maghrib? I'm assuming that's your day off."

"Yes, sir. As you please."

"Great," he said. "Good night!"

Salma waited until he was at the end of the hall before she closed the door. She briefly looked at Zeina, who was overwhelmed with the urge to begin celebrating, before she sat down on the mattress and grabbed her head with both hands.

"Mama, I'm going to sing on the radio!"

Salma grabbed Zeina's hand and forced her to sit down. "Listen to me," she said. "Whatever you heard him say, you don't mention it to anyone, all right? Especially not to your father. All right? Don't bring me trouble I don't need."

"You have to tell Baba. He's going to come to our home."

"Zeina," Salma said, with a tone that indicated that disobeying this order would lead to serious punishment. "Did you hear me?"

"All right," Zeina said. "But you'll tell him?"

Salma stood up. "I have to go back outside. Try to sleep. It's late."

Zeina was locked in the room once again. But this time it was no annoyance; this time she wouldn't need to listen to music or draw. In her mind, she was still in the salon, singing for the guests and relishing in their applause. *Your daughter is unbelievable. The whole country will want to hear this. The radio. Truly talented.* The words played over and over in her head. She wasn't sure why Salma had told her not to mention Mazen's visit; surely she would have to tell Abu Ahmed. And when Mazen visited, perhaps he would convince Abu Ahmed that Zeina was destined to be more than a competent and obedient housewife. She was destined to be a star—a star that he had called *unbelievable*, who sang with such *grace*. What did *grace* mean, anyway? She said it out loud three times, so she could remember to ask Mustafa. She lay on the mattress and reflected on the praise for what felt like hours, desperate to stay awake and keep the night from becoming a memory.

2

The day of the October 8 subway attack, I was living the sort of life that my mother would consider a kafir's. She had always warned me against calling another Muslim a disbeliever. In theory, one does not have the right. But I'm certain that if she had walked into my New York apartment that morning, she would've grabbed the nearest shoe, beaten me with all her strength, and at the very least struggled not to declare me a kafir then and there. This is because when the first shot was fired at 8:39 A.M., I was sleeping beside my girlfriend, Carmen, as bourbon soaked our livers, coke drip lingered in our throats, and her birth control eliminated the risk of getting pregnant on a night we would scarcely remember. As haram of a life as one could live; I might as well have changed my name to Patrick and launched a blog for atheists. But with my mother in Cairo, and me in New York, her belief that I was a good Muslim was as present and misguided as it had ever been.

It was the beginning of my last year of undergraduate studies in New York. My plan was to improve my pitiful GPA, travel with Carmen for Christmas, and try to land an internship at an investment fund or start-up upon graduating. Carmen had gorgeous cerulean-blue eyes, the sort that had me staring so persistently during an accounting class our sophomore year, she eventually stopped me outside the lecture hall and asked what the fuck I was doing. One of the rituals that marked the romantic hysterics of our relationship was when she woke me up on Fridays, before we made our way to campus for class, with a kiwi-and-kale smoothie.

No smoothies were made this morning.

"Sheero, wake up."

I opened my eyes to see last night's eyeliner trickling down Carmen's cheeks.

"Is she all right?" I asked, worried that her grandmother had passed. Abuela was one of her favorite people and was constantly on the verge of death but, given my luck, would probably die on the first day of midterms.

"There was a shooting on the subway," Carmen said.

I sat up. "Did anyone die?"

She nodded.

"How many?" I asked.

"I don't know."

I closed my eyes and let my head drop back onto the pillow; I was lethally hungover. May they all rest in peace.

"Sheero," Carmen said. "It was terrorists."

I looked at her to confirm that she wasn't joking, then hurled the blanket off the bed and rushed into the living room. She pointed a remote at the television and a news anchor arrived midsentence, saying something about a gunman and a SWAT team above the gripping headline: "At Least Five Killed in Subway Shooting, Many Injured." Half the screen was occupied by footage of the scene. Paramedics rushing out of the subway station carrying bloody and wounded victims on stretchers. Panicked civilians in suits being guided by firemen and police officers out from the underground. Street-side witnesses crying on each other's chests and assuring their loved ones on the phone.

"Who did it?" I asked.

"They still don't know."

I began to pray. *Please, God, don't let it be a Muslim. Let it be anyone else. One of those white lone-wolf psychopaths or a suicidal vet with PTSD...*

A Muslim perpetrator would mean more consequences for the rest of us. More scrutiny in JFK's secondary inspection room if, as was my case, you shared a name with a member of Al-Qaeda. Mosques looted in the South. More looks in the subway when you carried a suspiciously full backpack. Kids jumped. Veils torn. Windows stoned. And perhaps even the annihilation of yet another Middle Eastern country.

Please don't let it be a Muslim. And if it is, please make him Malaysian?

"I don't understand who could be capable of this shit," Carmen said.

"And I'm getting word now that we have an eyewitness," the news anchor said.

The screen cut to a blond reporter standing on a sidewalk downtown. "Yes, we have with us here an eyewitness who prefers to remain unnamed."

The reporter turned to her side and the camera pointed at a tall Asian American man wearing a suit.

"Sir, you were getting off the train to go to work. Can you tell us what happened?"

"Sure. Well..."

The man took a deep breath.

"Sorry," he said. "I'm in a bit of shock."

"Of course."

"Um... well. Yeah. There was this guy, I don't know, maybe he was in his twenties or thirties. Everyone was walking out of the station, but he was standing still, in the middle of the platform, you know. Well, I actually didn't see him standing. What I saw was everyone started stepping around something. And then I got close and I saw that it was this guy. And he was on his knees. And he was kind of, like, looking up at the sky and had his eyes closed. And yeah. So I just walked around him and kept going like everyone else. But then I started hearing something behind me. And when I looked back, he had stood up and he was shouting all this stuff. He seemed really aggressive. And—"

"What was he shouting?"

"I don't know if... Sorry?"

"What was he shouting?"

"Oh. Well, it wasn't English, so I don't know."

"Did you recognize the language?"

The man thought for a moment, looking away from the reporter and then looking back at her.

"I'm pretty sure it was Arabic. It sounded like it."

"So this man was Middle Eastern?"

"He definitely looked Middle Eastern."

"Oh, we're fucked!" I said to Carmen. It was going to be Muslims, and though I had been thirteen years old and still living in Cairo in 2001, now I was an Arab Muslim living in New York. Middle Eastern was me: thick-browed and long-lashed, with curly black hair, brown skin, a long neck, and a name impossible to pronounce in English. "We're really fucked," I said again.

Carmen didn't disagree, nor did she try to denounce my fears; she just stared at the television in a complete trance, an expression probably worn by millions around the country. And though the death toll was far smaller than it was on 9/11 and people weren't raining to their death on live TV, America seemed just as vulnerable. Evidently, terrorists could easily target the subway system millions of New Yorkers like myself used every day.

"I could be wrong," the man on TV said.

"What happened next?"

"Well, he started shouting and people started panicking. He opened his jacket up and I believe he had things wrapped around him. So—"

"He had a bomb strapped to him?"

"Well, I don't know. But there was something strapped to him."

"So, people started panicking?"

"Yeah, and kind of rushed away. And I did the same, but then I heard gunshots and that's when everyone really started running. It was so crowded. They really need to do something about these crowded stations. I mean..."

The man ran his hand through his hair as he sighed.

"A lot of people were stomped on, you know. Everyone panicked."

"On the steps?"

"Yeah. Everyone was trying to get out."

"How many gunshots did you hear?"

"A lot."

"Okay."

"The cops were quick, though. By the time I made it to the turnstiles, there was a bunch of them already running in."

"Well, we're glad you're safe," the reporter said. "Please take care of yourself."

"Yeah. Thanks."

The reporter turned to the camera and the camera turned away from the eyewitness.

"So, as you just heard there, Susanne, eyewitness testimony identifying the suspect as a male in his twenties or thirties. Now, one of the points our eyewitness just mentioned is that there was overcrowding. This was due to delays on this subway line this morning, meaning Wall Street Station was completely packed at the time of the accident, or the attack rather, which means that when the panic began—"

"Sorry to cut you off there, Laura, but we've just gotten reports that the suspect has just been arrested and is in critical condition."

"Hopefully that means we can determine a motive soon," the news anchor's male counterpart said.

"It's still to be confirmed, but we do believe that the suspect was acting on his own, so let's pray that this is over and that our civilians are finally safe."

I lit a cigarette and searched for my laptop underneath the pile of clothes on my black Ikea sofa. The target had been the Financial District's Wall Street Station. Eyewitness statements described what looked like explosives strapped around the suspect's torso. Seven people had been confirmed dead and many more were injured.

No information regarding the suspect had yet been released. I still remembered sitting in my grandfather's living room in 2001 and learning that the man who flew a plane into the North Tower, Mohamed Atta, had grown up three miles away from us, right in the heart of Cairo. I hoped the perpetrator wouldn't be Egyptian. It was unlikely, but then there was that knock on my door.

Knock knock knock. "FBI!"

Knock knock knock. "Open up!"

I looked at Carmen and, for a fraction of a second, wondered if I had just spent a year dating a terrorist-aiding, regime-changing Argentinean spy. She did, after all, cowgirl suspiciously well. I tiptoed to the front door and looked through the peephole at the four uniformed men outside. I turned around as she walked toward me and whispered, *"Abre la puta puerta."*

I stepped toward the bathroom, so confused that I considered hiding.

"What the fuck are you doing?" she mouthed at me.

I shrugged my shoulders and pointed at the door, as if to say, *I don't know, but the FBI is outside my door. What is the FBI doing outside my door? Did I buy drugs from the wrong dealer? Did Professor Stockman report my provocative essay on the Iraq War (which was really not a war) to the authorities?*

I remembered the bag of coke on my coffee table and pointed at it. Carmen picked it up, then ran into the bathroom and flushed it. Half a gram of fine powder, gone.

Knock knock knock. "Open up!"

I turned around and opened the door while Carmen stood behind me.

"Sherif El Sherbiny?"

The first officer I looked at was holding an arrest warrant. Another reached for my wrist, stepped to my side, and with a tai chi–esque maneuver handcuffed my hands behind my back. "You're under arrest," he said.

The other two officers began searching the apartment.

"What's going on?" I asked in a panicked whisper.

"You have the right to remain silent. Anything you say or do can and will be used against you."

"I'm not who you think I am," I said, certain that they had mistaken me for someone. "I'm an NYU student. This is my girlfriend."

"What is this?" Carmen said. "He hasn't done anything."

"Please cooperate and everything will be fine." The officer led me out of the apartment and down the hallway with his partner. The other two stayed behind.

Carmen followed us to the elevators. "Excuse me! Where are you taking him?"

"It's okay," I told Carmen over my shoulder. "Sir, this is a mistake."

When we reached the elevators, I looked back and saw that several of my neighbors had opened their doors, some of them looking confused, others looking like they were ready to defend me, like, *No, sir, you must be mistaken. This boy says hi to us every morning and feeds our cats, Lilo and Stitch, when we're gone.*

The old man who had fought in Vietnam, Stanley, seemed to have forgotten the other day when I helped him carry his groceries. "Fucking Arabs!" he yelled as we waited for the elevator. "Get them all out of here!"

Carmen looked back at him. "Fuck you, you racist fuck!"

"Sir, I'm going to ask you to step inside," the officer told him. "You too, ma'am."

"I'm coming with him," Carmen said.

"I'm afraid that's not going to happen."

"Carmen, it's fine," I said.

"What the fuck!" she yelled.

"Don't worry."

The elevator dinged and the doors slid open.

I realized I was barefoot. "I'm not wearing any shoes."

The officer holding my arm looked at my feet and sighed. "We need footwear for the subject," he said into his radio.

"Subject?" I asked.

A third officer brought my pair of sneakers, then returned to my apartment.

"I also don't have my phone," I said. "Or my wallet."

"That'll be taken care of," one of the officers said.

"Can you please tell me where you're taking him?" Carmen asked.

She was ignored as I placed my feet into the shoes.

"Please," Carmen said.

An officer put his hand out to keep her from following us into the elevator.

I wanted to get a hold of my pride and let the officers know that there would be consequences, that I was an American citizen and I would sue, but I struggled to simply tell them that they were making a mistake. "This is..." I said as they both stood behind me, looking forward with the apathy of postal service workers. "This is... I mean this is just... this is fucking crazy."

We arrived at the lobby, and I was once again at the mercy of the officer's tight grip on my arm. I felt so humiliated as I was led out of my building and into the black car outside, under the gaze of several pedestrians, not free to walk away or even conceal my face, that I vowed to leave the country as soon as I graduated, never to return. I had endured a lot of screening at the airport over the years, but this was a crime against humanity, arresting me for no reason on the day of a terrorist attack.

"Do you realize how big of a fuckup this is?" I asked. The two officers had pushed me into the back of the car.

"I suggest you keep quiet for now," said the one behind the wheel.

"What do you mean, keep quiet?" I asked, my voice cracking. "I haven't done a single thing, man. What the fuck is this?"

I looked through the rear window and began to panic as we drove away from my block. "Where are you taking me? What am I being charged with?" I tried to pull my hands away from each other. "Hey! Where are you taking me?" I stomped my feet on the floor of the car. "I'd like to speak to a lawyer!"

The officer in the passenger seat turned around and pointed his finger at me. "How about you shut! The fuck! Up!"

I curled into my seat, silenced like a dog upon the outrage of his owner. If they were arresting me for a legal reason, wouldn't they tell me what it was? I worried I was about to be victim of some secret CIA scheme that needed young Muslims for scapegoats. I remembered the countless images I had seen of prisoners lined up in Guantánamo: fully grown men brought to their knees, blindfolded and chained to the rubble under the Caribbean sun. Many of them had never had a trial, and what if it was all true, that they weren't in fact terrorists but innocent men like me, and I was scheduled to join them by dawn? What if the media was about to be fed a gripping, fictional narrative regarding my history as a terrorist-aiding bearded Arab? What if I was never allowed to see my mother again? My best friend, Taymour, often told me, *Bro, you're always tripping about the what-ifs.* But surely this was valid enough reason to fear that my life as I knew it was ending. When the officer turned onto the Westside Highway, I thought that was proof; he was about to leave Manhattan and take me to some secret military base where I'd vanish into political imprisonment.

"Please tell me where I'm being taken," I said again and again. We took a left toward the Financial District a few minutes later and I began to feel nauseous. "I haven't had any food," I said. "I don't feel well."

We drove into the underground parking lot of the Jacob K. Javits Federal Building and stopped in front of an elevator, where two officers were waiting to escort me inside. They were handling me as if I were a figure of great importance, Charles fucking Manson, when in fact they were wasting their precious time.

On the twenty-third floor, I was led through an empty hallway and into an interrogation room, where I was forced to sit down before a metal table in the corner of the room. One of the officers uncuffed my left wrist and cuffed my right hand on to a ring attached to the table.

"Sit tight," he said before they both walked out.

A bright light hung above me while a camera stalked me from the corner of the ceiling. A buzzer sounded off and a bald African American man wearing glasses and a black suit walked into the room.

"Mister El Sherbiny," he said as he uncuffed my right hand. "Take it easy. You're all right."

He sat down on the chair beside me and placed a folder on the table.

I held my returned hands against my chest. "What?"

"I'm Special Agent Lewis. FBI. We just want to ask you some questions. Now, I need you to know that you do have the right to remain silent. All right? You also have the right to consult an attorney. Anything you tell us can and will be used should you see your day in court. If you decide..."

Mention of attorneys, rights, and court seemed to propel me over some edge. This was not a dream or a mistake. This was fucking *happening*. I was sitting in a ten-foot-square room with horribly cold lighting in the FBI headquarters, on a chair that had probably been occupied by money launderers, drug smugglers, human traffickers, and actual terrorists, a lot of whom were probably in prison right now.

"Do you understand?" the agent asked me.

"What is happening?" I asked, beginning to slightly tremble. "This is crazy."

"It's a yes or no question," he said. "Do you understand?"

"What's going on?"

He sighed. "All right," he said. "Let's do it again."

"Yes, yes," I said. "I understand. I have the right to remain silent and the right to an attorney."

"Great," he said. "My partner said you weren't feeling well. Do you need to eat something?"

"I want to know what I'm doing here. This must be a mistake."

"We'll get to that. I asked if you would like to eat anything. We have bagels. Chips?"

"A bagel is fine."

"Cream cheese?"

It took a moment to realize that he was being genuine. I nodded.

He stood up, left the room, and quickly returned with a bottle of Poland Spring and a cream cheese bagel. I looked at the bagel and realized the absurdity of my accepting it. As soon as I articulated the fact that I had just been victim of the single most outrageous misarrest in the agency's history, I would be free to go home and eat whatever I pleased.

I slid the plate away from me. "Sir. Can I speak for one minute? Is that my right? Can I just speak for one minute without being interrupted?"

"You don't want to eat first?"

"No. I'd just like to speak for one minute."

"Sure."

"All right. Thank you, sir. Listen, you're going to be shocked when you realize how big of a mistake this is, all right? I don't know what happened this morning in the subway, but I woke up thirty minutes before you guys showed up at my place. I'm just an NYU student, man. I know I share a name with some people you guys have been looking for—maybe that's what's going on? It causes me problems at the airport, but I'm an American citizen. I was born in Oakland and lived there until I was seven. I'm about as nonreligious as an Arab can get, man. I'm not even... I'm not even really Muslim."

The words tasted sour as I said them—*not even really Muslim*—but the pressing matter was to convince Agent Lewis and his peers that I was one of the Good Ones." I was, after all, not really Muslim. Not religiously, at least. Over the past couple of years, I had developed serious doubts about Islam.

He placed his hand on the folder. "You have *no* idea why you might be here?"

"I don't."

He stared at me for a long and silent moment.

"What?" I said.

"You moved here on August 13, 2006, correct?"

"Yes, sir."

"And you grew up where?"

"In Cairo, sir. From the age of seven to eighteen. Before that, we were in California."

"Who's we?"

"My parents and me. My dad died, and then my mother and I moved back to Egypt."

"And were you close to your extended family? In Cairo?"

"What?"

"Your extended family."

I looked at the folder on the table and wondered why he would ask such a question. The answer slowly approached, got closer, bigger, clearer, like an object falling from the sky, until he opened the folder and the certainty that I had been mistaken for someone was sucked out of the room. Despite my capacity for logic-transcending imagination, I hadn't thought of my cousin Amir.

"Were you close to this young man?"

A photograph of Amir was placed in front of me. Black dots instantly began floating onto his face from the corners of my peripherals.

"Amir El Kafrawy. We believe he was your first cousin?"

"What... what was? Yes... why? Amir's my cousin, yes. Why?"

The agent cleared his throat. "Well, I'm afraid I have some bad news. Amir was the gunman behind this morning's attack. He was in critical condition when the arrest was made, but he's been declared dead as of..." He looked at his watch. "Twenty minutes ago."

I became incapable of completing a thought. Amir, subway, me, the FBI. Amir, religious. How did he... ? Where was... ? Die? No, he didn't live. How could... ?

Agent Lewis reached for the Poland Spring and opened it. "Here."

I took a sip. "Illinois," I said.

"Sorry?"

"He lives in Illinois."

His right eyebrow curled with suspicion. "You weren't aware that he's been living in New Jersey?"

"No," I said. "He lives in Illinois."

"You weren't aware?"

"What was he doing in New Jersey?"

"That's what we're here to figure out."

I didn't shed a tear for Amir's life. Not a single tear for the man who had once been my closest friend, only to become a stranger over the years. The most urgent issue was not his death but the disaster he might have just bestowed upon my life. I remembered the last time I saw him, two years ago, and all the conservative rhetoric he had harassed me with. I remembered our cousin Habiba telling me that he had messaged her on MSN and told her to change her profile picture, which featured two of her male friends. *You're not a belly dancer,* he had sent her. *This isn't how you were raised.* I thought of his expulsion from flight school, which he told our family happened because of a fight with a classmate. Had he met the wrong people there? Was it possible? I tried to imagine what it would do to my family and failed. I failed because it was not, in fact, possible. Amir was an idiot, yes, and a little strange—he always had been—but he would never be capable of such a crime. Our mothers were twins. He was my blood. He must have moved to Jersey for a job opportunity and was in New York for an errand. He must have been in the wrong place at the wrong time.

"Now," Agent Lewis said. "I want you to tell me what you know about Amir."

"This is a mistake," I said as I glanced at Amir's photograph. "Amir... Amir isn't capable of this sort of thing. You have the wrong person."

He sighed. "Just tell me, Sherif."

3

On the first day of the year, Mustafa sat among forty-two boys and took his official mid-year history examination for the fifth grade. The nine-year-olds wore black pants, red polo shirts, and navy-blue sweatshirts. Each wooden bench was occupied by double the number of students it was meant to hold, and a curvy layer of dry chewing gum covered the underside of each desk. The history teacher, Miss Nesma, an overweight and middle-aged woman whose patience for the young boys was drained entirely at least five times a lesson, stood at the front of the classroom between two Ministry of Education employees, who were there to administer the exam.

The ministry employees finished going through the guidelines before telling the students that, though they would step outside the classroom, they would be watching the students closely, which they never did. As soon as they left the room, Miss Nesma turned to the class and said, "To those of you who need to use your books, go ahead and do so. But remember and beware: cheating is haram."

Mustafa giggled and looked around the room, wondering if anyone else saw the irony. But everyone was staring at the exam with dread, as if copying answers down was going to be of serious inconvenience.

A couple of years ago, Mustafa's mother had given him a pair of Adidas running shoes that her boss's son, Taymour, had outgrown. After wearing them for more than a year and witnessing their impeccable durability, he discovered just how fake and inferior the Addidos shoes he had worn all his life were.

The Rud El Farag School for Boys was no more legitimate than Mustafa's Addidos. Without being allowed to cheat, most of the students would fail to move on to the next grade, which would lead to an array of problems Mustafa suspected the school would rather avoid. And so the students exchanged preemptively drafted cheat notes, and when one of them arrived at a question he couldn't find the answer to, Miss Nesma went as far as encouraging him to open his textbook to page thirty-seven.

Mustafa paid no attention to the disgrace. In spite of the collective cheating, he was confident he would score higher than everyone in his class with only his knowledge. He had always been serious about his education, fraudulent and discouraging as the school was. He took care of his books, never doodled in them, understood the material, and always hurried to school in the morning to reserve his seat at the front of the classroom. Among hundreds of boys, only a few of his kind managed to survive; others were quickly intimidated and forced to participate in the mainstream anarchy. But no one bothered Mustafa; he had the rare privilege of being as nerdy as he pleased, simply because he was protected by the worst vandal of all: his twin brother.

Despite reaching the fifth grade, Omar was still partially illiterate. As always, he was relying on Mustafa to finish his exam ahead of time, then replicate the answers on Omar's paper with altered handwriting. Meanwhile, he walked around the classroom, poking his classmates with a nail that had fallen out of one of the desks.

"Omar Ahmed!" Miss Nesma yelled, as she did daily. "Sit down!"

"Why are you so loud?" Omar yelled back.

Miss Nesma walked up to him, whipped his back with her long wooden ruler, and grabbed his ear. "Give it!" she yelled as she took the nail out of his hand.

Omar waved his arms to exaggerate his pain and fill the room with drama, but his usually interactive audience was unresponsive, too busy with the exam.

She grabbed his hair and led him to the front of the room. "Sit next to your brother," she said. "I don't want to hear another word, you understand?"

Omar forced a boy off the bench and sat beside Mustafa. "All right then. Akhooya, habiby," he said as he put his arm around Mustafa's shoulders. "My brother, my love."

"Will you shut up?" Mustafa asked.

"How's it going?"

"I'm not going to do your test if you keep making noise."

"Khalas, sorry. Everyone shut up!"

"You're the only one making noise, you donkey," Miss Nesma said. "Keep behaving like this and see where you end up. Your brother, inshallah, will become a lawyer while you look for food in the trash."

Mustafa chuckled. It was, indeed, perfectly possible for the scenario to play out, if Omar kept up his antics. Without a doubt, Mustafa and Omar were unidentical in almost every regard, even in looks. Mustafa had hazel eyes and pale skin like his mother, whereas Omar was brown on both fronts, like their father, and had hair so frizzy and rarely washed that it had brought lice into their home three times.

"Actually!" Omar stood up. "I'm going to be the president of the Arab Republic of Egypt. President Omar Ahmed Abdellatif."

Miss Nesma laughed, then abruptly stopped. "Sit down, you disgrace of a boy."

"And not only will I—"

Mustafa pulled Omar down and forced him to sit. "Stop."

"Fine," Omar said. He put his arm on the desk, rest his forehead in the pit of his elbow, and fell asleep.

Mustafa filled Omar's paper only to the extent that ensured Omar would pass. It was only fair for Mustafa's scores to be considerably higher; Omar was the superior one in almost every other regard. Last week, he had managed to get one of the girls who lived in the building beside theirs to give him a kiss on each cheek. He was one of the best at football too, whereas Mustafa had been told that he kicked like a sharmoota. It was Mustafa's right to be the one who thrived in school, and Omar never questioned the disparity between their scores. *If I put down all my answers onto your paper*, Mustafa told him once, *the markers might have proof that we cheated.*

When Miss Nesma announced that time was up, Omar took his exam from Mustafa, handed it in, and rushed out of the room with the rest of the class.

Mustafa stayed back to ask about upcoming material.

"The history of the Arab Nation," Miss Nesma said.

"The Six-Day War too?" he asked, to show that he had read ahead in the textbook.

"Yes. But yalla, go now, Mustafa. I have to prepare for the next class."

Outside the school, Omar was standing among older boys, some as old as fourteen, smoking a cigarette. Mustafa knew better than to lecture him about it in front of them, so he waited until Omar said goodbye and they began walking home.

"It's bad for you," Mustafa said. "You'll be coughing all the time like Baba. Don't you want to be a football player?"

"Yeah, yeah," Omar said. He put his arm around Mustafa's shoulders. "But listen, you rat. I have something important to tell you."

"What?"

"You know... today... I'm thinking today there's a new champion, you son of a bitch!"

Omar pushed Mustafa and began running.

"Yabnel eh!" Mustafa yelled. "Cheater!"

The last one to touch their building would buy the other a bag of sugarcane juice. If he didn't have the money, he would pay with a fully powered afa, an open-handed smack on the back of the neck that often left you light-headed.

Mustafa chased Omar for a few hundred feet along the sidewalk on the corniche, while cars, motorcycles, and overcrowded buses sped past them on the adjacent freeway, until he eventually passed him and took the lead. Omar was good with a football, yes, but Mustafa was faster.

"Told you to stop smoking!" he yelled over his shoulder.

"Fuck you, you ugly bastard!"

To avoid the tunnel that cut under the Embaba Bridge, they turned left away from the Nile, then right into the rubble field that led to the border of Ramlet Bulaq.

Mustafa led the race as they entered the eshash, the slum within the greater slum, where the alleys were only as wide as it took for a motorcycle to drive past a donkey cart without getting scratched. The one- and two-floor huts in the eshash created a labyrinth of redbrick, but Mustafa and Omar knew their way around it just as well as anyone.

Omar shortened the distance between them. "You're getting tired, aren't you?"

"You wish!" Mustafa yelled, though he was. Playing football every day meant Omar had better stamina.

Mustafa dealt with the dozens of turns by slowing down, pivoting on the dust-covered ground, and changing direction at the right moment. Omar, on the other hand, was crashing hands-first into huts and pushing himself in the new direction.

"Watch out!" Omar yelled.

Mustafa ignored him and kept his eyes on the ground, cautious of the hurdles that were splattered all over the alleys: the endless piles of trash, abandoned baskets, pet chickens, and, most importantly, the donkey shit that lay every few dozen feet. One step into the dark green piles of shit and a bunch of flies would gather for a feast on his damaged Addidos.

It certainly didn't make anyone happy, the boys racing this early in the afternoon. At this time of day, most of the slum's inhabitants were working elsewhere, and those who remained—mostly the elderly—were napping and keeping warm in their huts. Mustafa and Omar's frantic races made the stray dogs bark and the malnourished donkeys bray. But it was part of the excitement, this disturbance; they didn't only race through the eshash, they made a show of it: they kicked things, insulted each other, and ran along before anyone could give them trouble. It was one of the few activities through which Mustafa could behave as recklessly as Omar and have fun. Mustafa was often ridiculed for being a nerd, but during these races, he felt no less daring than his twin.

There was someone, however, whom Mustafa preferred to avoid while running home. Am Kahraba was Ramlet Bulaq's designated madman. Just last week, he joined Mustafa and Omar's race. *Run!* he yelled as he ran beside Mustafa, smelling like a goat's corpse. *Run from the devil or he will fill you with the thirst for sin!*

He usually passed his time in the narrow alley between the two wells where people from the eshash collected their water, speaking to his imaginary wife and two daughters. And though it was a shortcut to his home, Mustafa chose to run around it. Omar, on the other hand, ran through it and took the lead.

Mustafa had always imagined that when God created Omar, He ordered whoever was in charge of heart construction to make Omar's incapable of fear. Sometimes Mustafa envied this; other times he was certain that it would lead to Omar's death.

"Fucking crazy," Mustafa said, as he tried to run faster and catch up. "Don't run through the butcher's alley!"

A few months ago, the butcher's daughter had been playing in front of his hut when Omar tried to run around her but knocked her down with his knee instead. The man caught Omar, beat him for a couple of minutes while Mustafa watched helplessly, and warned them both that if they ever ran through his alley again, he would hang them by their feet until their blood dripped out of their eyes. Whether it had been an exaggerated threat or a frank promise, Mustafa didn't want to know, and thankfully Omar avoided the alley entirely.

When they ran out of the eshash, flying into the more developed masaken where they lived, they were so exhausted that the race turned into a show of desperate speed-walking, with short episodes of running that Omar triggered but failed to commit to.

The five-floor yellow buildings of the masaken, which had been built by the government in the fifties and rented out to low-income families, were spread along wide and paved roads, with cars parked on both sides.

As they turned into the street where they lived, Mustafa watched Omar nervously, then catapulted himself into a sprint. Omar got a hold of the strap on Mustafa's school bag, tried to pull Mustafa back and claim the win, but then Mustafa grabbed on to Omar's arm. They yanked each other and spun in circles right in front of their building.

"Let me go, you fuck!" Mustafa yelled. "You're going to rip my bag!"

"Fuck you!"

"You lost! Accept it!"

"Fuck your mother!"

A window jolted open five floors above them, the wooden shutters opening with such force that they crashed against the wall on each side.

"Ento ya welad el kalb!" a man yelled. "You sons of a dog! I can hear you shouting all the way from my fucking dreams!"

They looked up. "Sorry, Baba."

If Abu Ahmed ever warned them about something and they did it again, they could expect no further forgiveness and a belt lash on their backs. Still, Omar tiptoed toward their building and placed his hands on it, taking advantage of the fact that Mustafa wouldn't risk upsetting their father.

Mustafa shook his head. He was drenched in sweat and his shoes were covered in dust. "You can never win without cheating," he said.

"And you can never lose without complaining."

They entered the building and walked up the stairs, arguing over Omar's win as they passed Am Ibrahim's two baskets of chicks on the second floor and the stray cat that had recently given birth to nine kittens on the fourth floor.

Mustafa's father, Ahmed Abdellatif, commonly known as Abu Ahmed, owned both apartments on the fifth and highest floor. One of them was the maktab, the office, where he worked and slept, and all three children were forbidden from entering it. Why? Because children didn't belong in a place of work. What type of work? Abu Ahmed was supposedly a "Business Man." And though the title had always satisfied Omar's and Zeina's curiosity, Mustafa had recently become skeptical and questioned his mother on the matter. *You're too young to understand,* she said again and again, but that was nonsense, and it had become obvious to Mustafa that she wasn't proud of Abu Ahmed's work.

The other apartment was where Mustafa lived with his siblings and Salma. As soon as they walked in, he took off his uniform and hung it on one of the nails that were drilled into the cement wall, so it could dry out. In the bathroom, he was surprised to see that the water had returned, so he washed his face and flushed the urine that had sat there since the morning.

Outside, Mustafa joined Omar for a nap on the only bed in the apartment, where Salma and Zeina usually slept. The boys usually slept on the carpeted floor, and any opportunity to seize the bed was much embraced.

When Salma and Zeina arrived home later in the afternoon, Mustafa woke up and rushed to see what they had for lunch. Every day, they returned from work with delicious food that their boss's family had failed to finish. He was a big fan and often ate whole dishes without knowing what exactly he was putting into his mouth.

Today, however, they brought a dull combination of tomato soup and black beans. Salma was heating it up on the knee-high stove in the corner of the apartment while Zeina washed plates in the bathroom for the family to eat on.

"I don't understand why rich people would ever eat beans," Mustafa said.

Zeina came out of the bathroom. "Because it's healthy. But you should've seen it. Today there was leftover veal atayef from the party. Mama, tell him how you made them. She put these small slices of veal mixed with mayonnaise and mushrooms and onions in between these small pancakes, and, Mustafa, you wouldn't believe—"

"Oh, shut up!" Omar yelled as he turned on the bed. "I'm trying to sleep."

"You're always sleeping, you pig," Zeina said. "I wasn't talking to you."

"Don't start now," Salma said. "I don't want noise."

"She's the only one making noise," Omar said. "Always talking and talking and singing and snoring."

Mustafa and Salma laughed. It was true, Zeina snored.

"Oksem Belah, I'll slap you so hard you won't know up from down," Zeina said.

Mustafa and Salma laughed harder.

"Where did you learn to speak like a thug?" Salma asked.

"It's the only way of speaking to this type of person," Zeina said.

"*This type of person*?" Omar asked. "Is she stupid or what? Dumb bitch."

"Omar!" Salma yelled.

"You're my sister, you idiot," Omar said. "You're a piece of shit."

"Silence," Salma said, despite chuckling. "Mustafa, set up while I get your father."

Salma left the apartment. Mustafa fetched a newspaper from the third drawer in the dresser, then laid a few pages down in the middle of the apartment to protect the red carpeting from any food stains as the family ate on the floor.

Abu Ahmed was wearing shorts despite the cold, the thick hair on his meaty brown legs keeping him warm, and a white sleeveless shirt, on which he rubbed off the boogers he was picking from his nose as he followed Salma into the apartment.

His gigantic feet made the floor vibrate just like one of Mustafa's favorite comic book characters, the Hulk. Indeed, Abu Ahmed was almost as big as their front door and could, in theory, grab Mustafa and Omar by their necks, pick them up, and bang them together like cymbals. Zeina and Omar frequently angered him, but Mustafa was good at avoiding the man's outbursts. He had great instinct for distinguishing between the right and wrong moment to ask him for something. Right now, for example, having just woken up with an empty stomach, and having had his nap disturbed by Mustafa and Omar earlier, any wrong move carried great risk.

Abu Ahmed sat on the floor and crossed his legs. "Where's the food?"

Salma placed the meal on the newspaper: a bowl of tomato soup, a plate of beans, and a plate of sliced cucumbers and tomatoes. Zeina fetched eight pieces of balady bread from the plastic bag hanging from the handle on the front door. Everyone grabbed a piece, then they all took turns using small pieces of the bread to scoop up the food.

Abu Ahmed's open mouth chewing was the only sound made until he addressed Mustafa. "You had that exam," he said. "How was it?"

"It was good," Mustafa responded. "Elhamdolelah."

Abu Ahmed looked at Omar. "And you? A donkey like you've always been."

Omar laughed with a mouth full of food.

"You're laughing?" Salma asked him. "Come spit on my face if you ever make anything of yourself. Keep like this and you'll be a garbage man."

"That's exactly what Miss Nesma said," Mustafa said.

"No," Abu Ahmed said. "Don't say that."

Mustafa was surprised to see Abu Ahmed defend Omar.

"Don't insult the garbage man," Abu Ahmed continued. "God willing, inshallah, your son will be *the garbage man's assistant*."

Salma, Zeina, and even Omar laughed, while Mustafa wondered from what position his father was speaking. Abu Ahmed was an illiterate orphan who somehow moved out of the eshash and managed to rent two apartments in the masaken. He owned a motorcycle. The only sort of business that Mustafa imagined an illiterate orphan with Abu Ahmed's temperament, appearance, and background could lead was an illegal one. Mustafa didn't doubt that Abu Ahmed smoked hashish; often his maktab smelled just like when the neighborhood's teenagers smoked peculiarly shaped cigarettes. If Mustafa had to guess, his father was not a businessman but a hashish dealer. Nothing else could explain the men who sometimes came to his maktab in the middle of the night. And as far as Mustafa was concerned, there was more honor in collecting garbage than in selling hashish. If smoking it was haram, as Mustafa's religion teacher at school had reiterated several times, then selling it must be haram too, which meant Abu Ahmed would be going to Hell after death. This was a source of great angst for Mustafa, who couldn't imagine how the family would fare without him in Heaven. Abu Ahmed had a temper, one Mustafa sometimes had nightmares about, but he was also the family's leader. When an electric socket exploded or a rat entered their home or Omar injured his ankle, Abu Ahmed's wisdom was often required.

"Well," Mustafa said. "Garbage men go to Heaven."

Everyone looked at him.

"What?" Salma asked.

"It's not haram to be a garbage man," Mustafa said reluctantly, afraid that he wasn't being implicit enough with his message.

Abu Ahmed giggled. "This one," he told Salma as he pointed at Mustafa. "What are you trying to say, my son?" he asked Mustafa as he looked at him.

Mustafa looked down at his lap and shrugged.

"Well," Abu Ahmed said. "Would you like to hear a joke?"

Zeina nodded and Omar said yes.

"On Judgment Day, God asked a man, *What did you dedicate your life to?* And the man said, *Cleaning garbage.* And God asked him, *Where?* And the man said, *Egypt.* So God looked down at Egypt and said, *What about all that garbage that's been left in your own home?* And the man said, *That's not garbage, God, those are my wife and children.*"

Salma, Zeina, and Omar broke into laughter, and Mustafa couldn't help but giggle.

"You crazy man," Salma said.

"So God said, *What are their names?* And the man said, *That's Omar. He smells like a dead cow because he showers once a year. And that's Zeina. She wakes up the whole neighborhood with her snores. And that's Mustafa. He only likes to urinate on his bed.*"

Salma and Omar were laughing hardest, while Zeina protested her part.

"Baba, I don't snore!" she yelled.

"And I haven't wet the bed in almost a year," Mustafa said.

Abu Ahmed laughed and grabbed Mustafa's ear. "I'm only joking, you donkey."

Mustafa wasn't comfortable with the joke. He had struggled with bed-wetting for as long as he could remember: years of disappointing his mother almost every night and forcing her to wake up and wash the plastic bedding on which he slept. After years of trying remedies suggested by doctors and neighbors, he had finally managed to get rid of the habit and had hoped not to hear about it any longer.

"You should be able to take a joke," Abu Ahmed said as his expression became serious. "Only women are so sensitive."

"Wait," Omar said. "If that man is a garbage man and those are his children, then *you're* the garbage man!"

Zeina's laughing became all the more hysterical.

Abu Ahmed slapped Omar across the face with only a fraction of his strength, but still with enough of a swing for the laughter to come to a halt. "Don't lose your respect."

Silence filled the room, and Omar appeared on the verge of tears, more because of the humiliation than the physical pain.

"That was a bit hard," Salma said.

"I swear to God, if you cry," Abu Ahmed said. "I'll force you to take a shower."

Zeina and Mustafa broke into laughter once again. And Omar smiled.

"You need to know that there are limits to what you can say to your father," Abu Ahmed told Omar. "Understood?"

"Fine," Omar said. "I'm sorry."

For a few minutes, the family recovered from the laughter in silence and continued eating their meal.

"Mama, aren't you going to tell him?" Zeina suddenly asked Salma, without offering much context to the rest of the family.

Salma looked at Mustafa. "Did you see the kittens feeding from the cat?"

Mustafa nodded.

"Tell me what?" Abu Ahmed asked.

"They're so little," Salma said. "It's unbelievable. I just want to eat them up."

"I think we should name them," Omar said.

"Tell me what?" Abu Ahmed asked again.

"Mmm?" Salma responded.

Abu Ahmed burped so loudly Mustafa almost choked on his food. "She's saying you have something to tell me," he said.

"Oh," Salma said. "Nothing. You know how your daughter runs her mouth. Mustafa, try to feed them whenever you can. Last time all her kittens died. Every single one."

"All right," Mustafa said.

Abu Ahmed looked at Zeina; Zeina looked at her plate.

"I remember that," Omar said. "They would go outside the building and just lie beneath a tree, waiting to die. It was *weird*."

Abu Ahmed looked at Salma. "Are you going to speak or what?"

"What?"

"There's something you need to tell me?"

Salma sighed. "We were entering the neighborhood and this boy was high," she said. "Tried to grab my bag out of my hand. But I pulled it away. That's all."

"What street?" Abu Ahmed asked. "What did he look like?"

"Walahy, I don't remember," Salma said.

"What street?" Abu Ahmed asked again.

"Aboul Farag," Salma said.

"Just now?"

"As we were coming home, yes."

Zeina was staring at her plate nervously.

"Do *you* remember what he looked like?" Omar asked Zeina.

Zeina shook her head, which meant she was lying. Whenever she resorted to nodding, shaking her head, or clicking her tongue, you could be certain Zeina was hiding something. She was a raghaya, the type to always speak far more than was necessary. If she really didn't remember what the man looked like, she would've said something like, *No, I wish I did. I want to say he was bald, but I think I might be imagining it, and I can't really remember if he was tall or not. I was so scared. He must've been big because I was so scared.* Instead, she was staring at her plate and avoiding eye contact with anyone, and Mustafa suspected the entire handbag anecdote was false.

"Well," Abu Ahmed said. "That's just fucking stupid."

"Calm down," Salma said.

"You didn't look at the man who tried to rob you," Abu Ahmed said. "I mean, she's a child. But you?"

"It all happened so quick," Salma said.

"Well, then don't come telling me!" Abu Ahmed yelled.

Everyone stopped eating.

"Don't come telling me someone tried to rob you and not describe him! What the fuck am I supposed to do with that?"

"I'm sorry," Salma said.

Abu Ahmed resumed eating.

Salma gave Zeina a look, which confirmed that a beating was now due for Zeina.

The rest of the meal was had in silence, and then Abu Ahmed stood up and walked to the bathroom. "Someone come pour," he said on his way.

Mustafa stood up and ran over. He opened one of the big bottles they had preemptively filled up (the water was once again gone), then poured some onto his father's meaty hands over the sink, while the man washed them with soap.

"Fucking can't remember what he looks like," Abu Ahmed said to himself. "What can you say to that? You can only say that you married an idiot."

Abu Ahmed dried his hands on the towel hanging from the nail above the sink, then walked out of the bathroom and apartment to his office across the hall.

Mustafa returned to his spot on the floor. Salma was still staring at Zeina; Zeina was still looking down at her plate.

"We can't tell you," Aly said.

"They're idiots," Sheero said.

"And I might be singing on the—"

"Khalas ya Zeina!" Salma yelled.

Taymour and Aly stopped laughing when they realized Salma was angry.

Alia entered the kitchen in her black silk pajamas, smoking a cigarette. "Why are you yelling?" she asked Salma.

A few weeks ago, Taymour and Aly were walking through the Gezira club when Aly pointed at a woman across a huge, crowded playground and said, *That's my mother*. They approached the woman, and it did, indeed, turn out to be Tante Najla. Aly bragged about how he had always been able to recognize his mother's walk from a mile away, a comment that saddened Taymour, who realized that his equivalent to Aly's skill was being able to instantly determine just how drunk his mother was.

Right now, for example, given the smirk on her face, the slight (but not too long) pause between her steps, and the sideways tilt of her head, Taymour knew that she was one or two drinks in: drunk enough to be kind, but not enough to be inappropriate or become enraged for trivial reasons. Indeed, his favorite mother was not the sober, miserable one, but the one who had just opened a bottle of wine, so he managed to relax as she hugged him and kissed the top of his head.

"How are you?" she asked him.

"Good."

"Come give Tante a kiss," she said as she put her arms out.

Aly and Sheero approached her and allowed her to kiss them on both cheeks.

"If you keep yelling at her all the time," Alia told Salma. "She's going to hate you."

"Of course she won't," Salma said. "Right, Zeina?"

"Of course I won't," Zeina said.

Alia laughed. "Always repeating your mother's words."

"She's saying she sang for my parents," Aly told Alia.

"She did," Alia responded as she smiled at Zeina. "She was great."

"*Sheero is in love with her,*" Aly said. "*He wants to marry her.*"

Aly looked at Taymour and expected a laugh, but Taymour knew his mother wouldn't be receptive to the joke, so he ignored it.

"*Are you stupid?*" Alia asked him. "*Don't make jokes at her expense.*"

"*She doesn't understand,*" Aly said.

"*Still,*" Alia said. "*That's not funny.*"

"*Okay,*" Aly said. "*Sorry.*"

"*Tante, I swear I never said anything,*" Sheero said.

"*I know, habiby,*" Alia said. "*It's this little devil, always.*"

Zeina was facing the television but looking at them from the corner of her eye, probably aware that they were talking about her.

6

I didn't tell Agent Lewis the truth about the night Amir had spent at my home. I told him that Amir came to my apartment, we had a quick chat, and I set up the sofa for him. I went to the Halloween party and came home to find that he was gone. When I called him, he thanked me for hosting him and told me he was making his way to Illinois earlier than he had planned. We hadn't spoken ever since.

"That's it?"

"Yes, sir."

I took a second bite of the cold bagel as he watched me. I probably shouldn't have lied, but it was essential for me to stress that Amir and I hadn't had anything resembling a relationship for upward of four years.

"So he left your place before you got home?"

I nodded. "That's right."

He nodded slowly as I struggled to determine how many seconds of eye contact I should hold. I reached for the water bottle once again and then he sprung to his feet, which startled me to the point that I dropped the bottle.

"You okay?" he asked as I picked it up.

I nodded.

He grabbed the door's metal handle and waited for a buzzer to let him out.

When the door closed behind him, I pulled Amir's photograph closer and was pained to see resemblance of my family all over it: Gedo Zenhom's thick, boomerang-shaped eyebrows; Teta Safeya's pointy nose; and the same cleft chin both our mothers had. Somewhere in my grandmother's photo album in Cairo, there was a photograph of our mothers on their twentieth birthday, holding a cake and staring at the camera with eyes similarly shaped to the ones that looked at me now. In that photograph, they looked delighted, beaming with youth as my grandfather captured the celebratory feel with his new camera. In this one, Amir looked utterly exhausted and unamused, as if he had lived an entire century and encountered nothing worth seeing.

"What have you done?" I asked Amir in Arabic, and then I remembered I was being watched. I slowly slid the photograph away from me and wondered how many people were watching me, wondered if they had captured my speaking to the photograph and if there was any chance it would be leaked on the internet.

The buzzer sounded off again and Agent Lewis returned to his seat beside me.

"All right," he said with a regretful tone, glancing at the photograph before looking at me. "Here's the deal."

"I'm sorry," I said. "I lied."

"Okay then," he said. "Why did you lie?"

"I lied because I'm scared."

"What is it you're scared of?"

"I don't know!" I said. "Yesterday I was getting drunk. Today I'm here. I've been arrested. There was a shooting. And Amir... I mean... he lives in Illinois. I didn't even know. I had nothing—"

I felt as though there was something in my chest obstructing my breathing.

"Hey," he said. "You want to try to breathe for a minute?"

I slowly inhaled through my nostrils and then remembered that the assailant was alive when he was taken to the hospital.

"What did he say?" I asked as I exhaled. "Before he died? Did he say anything?"

"Just... take a moment."

"No!" I yelled. "I—"

I could no longer speak.

"Hey," he said, lifting his hand into the space between us. "Try to calm down."

I exhaled.

"Good," he said. "I'm just going to ask you a few questions, okay? But I need you to calm down first."

I closed my eyes and tried to do something I sometimes did to relax after a heavy coke binge. I tried to remember my grandfather's farmland in Denshawai, where my family and I spent every Eid of my childhood. I tried to recall the fresh air and silence that surrounded the mango trees, the bleats of the goats that roamed around the farm at all times, but none of the images came, because the same boy with whom I had played hide-and-seek on that farm was now, according to this FBI agent, not only dead but also guilty of murdering innocent people.

I succeeded in taking a few deep breaths.

"Better?"

I nodded. "Am I being charged with a crime?"

"Listen," he said. "You say you lied, I'm giving you a free pass. But it can't happen again, and if you're not guilty of anything, then you have nothing to worry about. Will you cooperate and answer my questions truthfully?"

I nodded. "Yes. I promise."

"Great," he said. "Let me ask you something. Do you like living here, in New York?"

I nodded.

"What do you like about living here?"

I felt like I was being asked a trick question.

"You like going out? Going to the park? Walking down the High Line?"

"Yes, of course."

"Well, you know. That's what we all like. That's what I work day in and day out to preserve, you know? And guess what? No one's going to be going to any park today or walking along any river. A lot of people are going to stay home because they're afraid. I mean, someone might pull a gun on them or a bomb might go off any second, is what they're all thinking. Now, my job is to keep those people safe, to try and make sure this doesn't happen again. Does that make sense to you?"

I paid attention to his eyes and saw that he was exhausted. "Absolutely, sir."

"Good. So you say you lied. Now, what's the real story here?"

"Well, he did fall asleep early. And I did go out. When I came home, he was asleep. Then, in the morning, he was upset because I had brought a girl over to my apartment. Because, you know, he saw her naked and stuff. So he packed his bag and left."

"He walked in on you?"

"No. She went to the bathroom naked."

"Okay. And why was he upset about that?"

"Well, he got pretty conservative, I guess. In Illinois. I just... But I still don't see how this is possible. Amir would never do anything so horrible."

I sounded more unsure of myself every time I said it. The truth was that I didn't know much about who Amir had become. I didn't know what his life in Illinois had been like, where he had lived, or how he had spent his time. I didn't know how or why he had become so conservative. I hadn't cared enough to ask.

"He felt like what you were doing with this girl was wrong?"

"Yes."

"He was intolerant with these things?"

"I hadn't properly spoken to him in years. That's what you need to understand, sir. Besides that night he spent in my apartment, I really haven't spoken to Amir in four years now."

"Let's stick with the questions."

"I just... He had become intolerant, yes."

"Okay. It's a relief to be honest, isn't it?"

I nodded because it was.

"When you say he had become intolerant, what else did he say or do that makes you say that?"

I told him about Amir's remark on the girls in my elevator.

"All right," he said. "What else?"

I shrugged. "That's it. It really was like a five-minute conversation. I know that sounds ridiculous, but you can confirm with that girl."

"Did you hear him talking on the phone to anyone?"

I shook my head.

"Anything about friends? The people he was hanging out with?"

"No," I said. "Was someone else involved?"

He ignored the question. "I'm going to play a tape for you and see if you can identify one of the men speaking. I have a script of it here, translated, and then I'll ask you some questions."

He gave the camera a thumbs-up, and suddenly two speakers on the opposite corner of the ceiling, right behind me, began to hum.

"Alo," a man said in Arabic.

"Hello, brother," another said in Egyptian dialect.

"Hi, brother," the man said. *"Where are you?"*

The dialect was from somewhere around the Levant.

"I'm heading to the airport now," the Egyptian said. And though I hadn't heard the voice in a couple of years, I was certain it was Amir's.

Agent Lewis raised his right hand and the recording was paused.

"You recognize—"

"It's him, yes."

He raised his hand again and the recording resumed.

"All right," the man said. *"When you get to Bassem's, call me, all right?"*

"I will."

"What's wrong? You sound discouraged."

"Not at all," Amir said. *"I feel very relaxed."*

"Good. Good. You should be. New York is a beautiful place. You're going to love it. You'll find all the birds you like there. And you can collect as many as you want."

"I know."

"And I'll see you there soon, yes?"

"Yes," Amir said. *"I'm excited."*

"Remember to call me once you've tried the bagels."

"Yes. Don't worry."

"All right. Salam, brother."

"Salam."

The recording stopped.

"So," he said. "First things first. Do you at all recognize the voice of the other man? Maybe it was a friend of Amir's? Or someone he had mentioned?"

I shook my head. "Not even a little bit. That's not an Egyptian."

"When Amir left your place, that morning after Halloween, did he at all say where he was going?"

I shook my head. "Just that he was visiting a friend in New Jersey."

"He didn't mention the name?"

"No."

"You sure? It seems weird that you wouldn't ask."

I shook my head and glanced at Amir's photograph. It was impossible to imagine him planning and orchestrating such a violent plot, and harder still to imagine that he thought the murder of innocent people could be justified with religious reasoning. We had learned about Islam together, growing up, and violence had never been described as something God supported. I could, however, imagine Amir being manipulated and deceived by someone far cleverer than him.

"Fuck," I said under my breath.

"What's that?" Agent Lewis asked.

"This is crazy."

Agent Lewis nodded. "Do you recognize the voice?"

I looked up at him. "That is the first time I have ever heard that man's voice," I said. "And I have absolutely no idea who he is or who he might be."

He nodded. "Okay."

"That is the truth," I said.

"I believe you. What do you think they were talking about there?"

I was confused.

Agent Lewis looked at the translated script. "He said, *New York is a beautiful place... You'll find all the birds you like there. And you can collect as many as you want.*"

"Amir was always obsessed with birds. He studied them."

"*You'll find all the birds you like there?*"

I realized what he was implying: that New York and birds were code for something. But Amir had always been obsessed with birds. He helped our grandfather breed pigeons and collected encyclopedias on all the bird species.

"Let's play it again," Agent Lewis said as he waved at the camera.

The hum returned and my heart started racing.

"No," I said. "Please. I've already heard it."

"We just want to make sure that—"

"I'd really like to go home."

He looked down at the script and then back at me. "Just... take a second."

I shook my head. "You said I have a right to an attorney and I have the right to remain silent. I want to exercise those rights."

"This is time sensitive," he said. "If your cousin was working with someone, and it looks like he was, we need to be as quick as possible in our investigation."

I remained silent.

"Well," he said. "Let me ask you this. Which family members was Amir interacting with?"

The question was provocative: a clever one to ask to get me to keep talking. Most likely, Amir was still in touch with his parents, Khalto Heba and Uncle Ashraf. But if he had really been plotting to murder innocent people, there was no chance they would have had a clue. Today would probably be their worst day on record, and the last thing they needed was an FBI agent and a translator knocking on their door.

He stared at me and waited for a response, but I remained silent; it was my quickest ticket out of the building.

"No?" he asked.

I shook my head.

He sighed and stood up. He waited for the buzzer, opened the door, and left. After at least two hours of sitting around and waiting, they gave me my phone (which had run out of battery) and wallet and let me go.

When I walked through my door, I found Carmen lying on the sofa. She jolted up onto her feet as I walked straight to my bedroom.

"What happened?" she asked as she followed me.

In my bedroom, my dresser drawers were open. Clothes had been tossed all over my carpeted floor and the school material on my desk was no longer organized. My phone charger, which was always plugged into the socket beside my bed, was also missing.

"Where's the charger?"

"Sheero!" she yelled. "What the fuck?"

"I need to call my mom."

"It's outside," she said. "I've been trying to call Taymour and Tamara, but they're not answering. I think they're still asleep."

I plugged my phone into the charger and then directed my attention to Carmen, whose puffy eyes revealed all the crying she had done. For reasons I was often unsure of, she loved me deeply, and though I loved her too (or at least told myself I did), I wasn't inclined to tell her the truth. She would ask me at least a dozen questions I didn't have the answers for, and I didn't know how I would begin to explain who Amir was.

"What do you think happened?" I asked in a sarcastic tone as I walked to the kitchen. "They mistook me for someone else."

Growing up with my mother had made me a highly skilled liar.

"What?" she asked. "How?"

"I told you. I share a name with a guy."

I poured myself a glass of bourbon and took a big gulp.

"They don't have pictures of these people?" she asked.

I shrugged and took another sip. "Apparently not."

I walked back to my phone and saw that it was yet to turn on. I sat on the sofa and opened my laptop, which I used to message my mother.

Hi Ma. I'm okay and safe. My phone is off, but I will call you in five minutes.

I searched for my chat history with Amir.

Happy birthday Sherif, he had sent me on my birthday back in July, and I hadn't responded, like I responded to everyone else—not even with a simple *thank you.* I had been drunk and then forgotten about the message. I hadn't cared enough to show him the same courtesy I had shown people whom I had known for a year or two. Frankly, I had perceived Amir as a burden since we were children, as the lame and less fortunate cousin whose envy I had to constantly make sure not to exacerbate. The troubled kid with whom I always had to sympathize. Looking back, it was beginning to dawn on me just how many warnings our family had had that his issues were serious.

Growing up, certain experiences introduced me to a degree of pleasure so great that the burden of life—boredom, sadness, and such—almost ceased to exist entirely for weeks or months on end. The first time my friends and I got high, for example, we were in such awe that we bought a brick of the stuff and spent every moment outside school plummeting again and again into that marvelous headspace, wherein everything that previously felt good now felt divine, everything from film, music, and laughter to sleep and food—even water too.

Another magical episode occurred in the seventh grade, when my friend Aly gathered the boys in our class and gave us the life-changing instructions. *Listen to me,* he said. *Listen to me right now. Go to the bathroom, spit into your hand, and then rub the tip of your penis until you quiver like a retard.*

The only thing that had a similar effect as my introduction to hashish and orgasms was the first portable gaming console I ever owned, the Game Boy Light, which my mother gifted to me one morning during the sixth grade.

My life was forever changed. I no longer needed to be home and finished with homework to play video games. I could play them everywhere, at all times. I no longer needed to read a book or chat with friends to pass time on the bus. I could *Super Mario* on the way to school and *Tetris* on the way back.

Today, I no longer needed to dread Khalto Nermeen's mandatory fifty-second birthday party. I could simply bring fresh batteries and equip myself for the three-hour event.

Khalto Nermeen was my oldest aunt and had recently been diagnosed with breast cancer. Naturally, the party remains the single most awkward social gathering I've ever attended. We had been told that it was unlikely that she would die, but nevertheless she was bald, for reasons I didn't understand, and looked like she hadn't had food in weeks. In spite of the collective effort to smile, there was someone sobbing in some corner of my grandfather's apartment throughout the whole evening. And when it was time to clap, cheer, and sing "Sana Helwa," multiple people excused themselves from the dining room.

There were, however, those of us who managed to drown out the sadness with the "Sana Helwa" lyrics. There was my grandfather, who spent the whole party kissing my aunt's bald head and saying, "They'll all feel stupid when you recover." There were all my uncles-in-law, who wouldn't cry in front of so many people if the whole family had cancer, simply because they were men, and this was Egypt, the Land of Strong Men. And then there was a selection of teenagers and children, myself included, who lacked enough attachment to my aunt to be able to enjoy the chocolate cake.

I was severely familiar with the prospect of death and somewhat glad to see the rest of the family getting a taste of it. Only three years had passed since I had walked up to my father's corpse in our Oakland kitchen, touched his cold cheeks, realized that he was no more alive than the chicken wings in our freezer, and began to grasp that my favorite person had just vanished from existence. Three years had passed, but I still yearned for the refuge of running up to him as he arrived home from work and hugging his thigh. I could still close my eyes and trick myself into feeling his big hand rubbing my hair; I could still remember the sound of my mother's laugh as he spun her around to the songs of Elvis Presley. I often resented my cousins for having two parents, so much so that, on several occasions, I found myself wishing Khalto Nermeen would die so my cousin Habiba could know the pain I had suffered.

It was a malevolent feeling I knew I wasn't supposed to have, one implanted in my head by the shetan. After the candles were blown, I decided to show Habiba my Game Boy. While most of the family sat around the salon, we snuck away to the living room and I taught her how to play *Super Mario*.

Amir was on his way back from the bathroom when he noticed us. "What's that?"

Habiba's Mario was avoiding trouble. I prepared myself for the onslaught of questions I knew Amir was sure to harass me with.

"It's my new Game Boy."

"What's a Game Boy?"

"It's a video game console."

"When did you get it?"

"Today."

"Where did you get it?"

"I don't know," I said. "Ma did."

"Was it expensive?"

"I don't know," I said. *But there is no chance your parents will get you one*, I thought. *We both know that.*

"Does it come with many games?"

I ignored the question.

"What are you guys doing?" Mariam asked as she walked into the room. Despite being a few days younger than me, Mariam was my least favorite cousin. She was the type of person to enter a room with the intention of being as irritating as possible, and I often suffered the urge to slap her across her face.

Habiba's Mario died and I took the console from her, knowing that Amir and Mariam would likely ask for playtime.

"That's so fun," Habiba said.

"Can I play?" Amir asked.

"No," I said. "I want to play for a bit."

"Can I play after you?" Mariam asked.

"I said no."

Our fourteen-year-old cousin Tamer, the oldest, walked into the room with Mariam's little sister Nesma.

"What about me?" Amir asked.

Tamer sat on the armrest beside me. "What's that?" he asked.

"It's my Game Boy," I said as I started playing.

"Can I play?" five-year-old Nesma asked, placing her hand on my forearm. The cuteness of her tiny fingers and high-pitched voice was hard to ignore, but I couldn't grant her a round on the console without doing the same for everyone else.

"Don't ask him," Mariam told her sister. "He's selfish."

"Yes," I said. "I'm selfish. So are you."

"Stop it," Tamer said.

Amir poked my shoulder. "Can I play after you?"

I ignored him and tried to focus on keeping Mario alive.

He poked me again. "Sheero. Can I play after you?"

I barely managed to kill three incoming bees before I had to jump over a levitating platform, which I almost reached, before I fell to my death.

"Shit," I said.

"Can I play?" Amir asked once more. "Please."

I restarted the game. "No."

"Why?" he asked.

"Because!" I yelled as I stood up. "It's *my* Game Boy."

Mariam, Nesma, and Amir looked at me with disgust.

"I told you he's selfish," Mariam said.

"Sheero, you're so selfish," Nesma said.

Nesma always repeated whatever her sister said.

"Shut up," I said to Nesma. "Come up with your own words."

"I have my own words," Nesma said.

"Forget it," Amir said. "I don't want to anyway."

For a moment, I felt guilty, but then I quickly became irritated. It was my Game Boy and I ought to do with it as I pleased.

I escaped to my grandfather's bedroom, Game Boy in tow, but then realized my mother would soon come looking for me and order me to spend time with the family. Maybe she would even threaten to confiscate the console, so I placed it on my grandparents' bedside table and left the room.

In the salon, the adults were sipping on tea while the kids ate biscuits and baby Enas fed from Khalto Nahla's breast. Everyone was listening to Gedo tell Uncle Hamza a story, so I sat between Habiba and Teta.

"And Baba was a young boy at the time," Gedo said. "Probably younger than your daughter. How old are you, Habiba?"

"Eight."

"Yes. About her age. And so, at the time, I mean, our pigeons were family. Really, you know how this one is obsessed?" he asked as he pointed at Amir, who was sitting between his mother and Tamer. "That's how everyone felt about our pigeons. And so, one day everyone finds these officers, the British, standing at the end of a field shooting at some pigeons for sport. And of course they got upset, so a few men approached the officers. *Why are you doing this?* they asked. A fight broke out and an officer's gun went off. He shot one of our women, so, of course, the fight got worse. My gedo was one of the men involved. At this point, dozens of men surrounded these officers, so they got scared and ran away, back to their base twenty kilometers from our village. But one officer didn't make it back."

"The men killed him," Tamer said.

"No," Gedo said. "He died because of heatstroke! You see, the white Englishman had no right to roam our villages and kill our pigeons. So? The sun killed him."

Multiple people laughed.

"And what happened after that?" I asked.

My grandfather looked at me and smirked. "That couldn't be the end of it."

I shook my head. My grandmother smiled and kissed my head.

"Well," he said. "One of our men found his body. And then, a minute or two later, a group of officers came and found this peasant holding their dead British friend. So..."

"They thought the peasant had killed him," Tamer said.

"Yes," Gedo said. "So they shot the peasant. The next day, dozens of soldiers arrived and arrested fifty-two men, one of whom was my gedo."

"But aren't *you* Gedo?" Nesma asked.

"*His* gedo, you idiot," Mariam told her. "His grandfather."

"Bent," Khalto Nahla said. "Don't speak to your sister like that."

"Should we wrap up?" my mother asked. "It's getting late."

Within a few minutes, everyone stood up and began to gather their belongings. Recently, Amir had asked me a good question: *Have you ever realized that your mother makes all the decisions for our family?*

I had noticed every day since.

"How many pigeons did they kill?" Amir asked.

My grandfather laughed. I also had a question to ask and hoped if the three of us could share a moment, Amir would forgive me for being rude to him earlier. He was the only cousin who I felt was my close friend.

"What happened to the fifty-two men?" I asked.

"Not that many," Gedo told Amir. "I think just a few."

"What happened to the fifty-two men?" I asked again.

Amir walked away without looking at me.

"Well..."

"Baba," Ma said from behind me.

I turned to see that she was shaking her head at Gedo.

"It's a long story," Gedo told me. "Another day."

It was only years later that Ma told me the rest of the story. A few of the fifty-two men were sentenced to death—one was hanged outside his home—and the remaining four dozen, including Gedo's gedo, were flogged.

I went to the bedroom to fetch my Game Boy but didn't find it there. I assumed my mother had taken it, so I returned to the salon and asked if she had put it in her bag.

"Put it in my bag how?"

"Didn't you take it from Gedo's room?"

"No," she said.

"It's not there," I said.

"Go look again."

I returned to the bedroom and searched every reachable corner of it. When I went back outside, the entire family was gone. Gedo and Teta were finishing their tea.

Ma and I spent the next half hour searching the entire apartment for the console. With every room we covered, I became all the more confident that someone, almost certainly Mariam, had stolen my Game Boy. Now they had all gone home and there would be no way to prove it.

When we had only the bathroom left to search, I started crying. I was almost certain someone had stolen it. It was an incredible console, so fresh off the market that it almost appeared extraterrestrial. It made sense that someone would want to take it. None of my cousins owned a Game Boy or PlayStation or VHS player, and I was familiar with the feeling of having less. In our family I was the pampered one, yes, but my best friends' families owned beach houses and luxury cars my mother could never dream of having. I was the only one whose mother hadn't gone to a French school, the only one without a driver, the only one not living in either Zamalek or Mohandesin. Recently, I had lied to my close friends and told them that my mother owned an apartment in Zamalek, and we lived in Haram only to be close to our family.

"Stop crying," my mother said. "Crying isn't going to help us find it."

"Fee eh ya Amany?" my grandmother asked from down the hall.

I was about to shout, *Someone took my Game Boy!* But my mother pointed her finger at me and threatened me with a look.

"Nothing, Mama!" my mother answered before closing the bathroom door. "Listen," she said as she turned to face me. "You need to stop crying. I'll get you a new one if we can't find it, but... you can't accuse anyone of theft, all right? Not unless you have proof. Because if you accuse them of stealing, and it turns out they didn't, you're going to feel really bad. You understand?"

I nodded.

"I'll figure it out."

"What are you going to do?" I asked.

"Just let me deal with it. You'll have your Game Boy, all right?"

It took me longer than usual to fall asleep that night. As I lay in bed, I imagined Mariam lying in hers, playing with my Game Boy under her blanket, maybe beating my high scores.

I worried Ma was going to accuse her sisters of having raised a bunch of thieves. I always worried for my mother. She was a tough woman and a successful dentist, yes, but my father's death followed her everywhere, not as a tragedy of the past but an absence of the present, one you could notice in her excessive daydreaming and the two pillows she had to hug to fall asleep. Recently, I had walked into her bedroom and caught her dancing alone. I worried I had put her in a situation that could only lead to bitter quarrels with the only family she had besides me.

For years, Friday morning followed the exact same routine, so the next day Ma bought breakfast from the local market: balady bread, cheese with tomatoes, and a box of ful. Once finished, I went to my bedroom and played video games until Teta called our landline and announced that Sheikh Anwar had arrived. And since I was, in many ways, my mother's slave, her personal Make a Human project, I would be ordered to go downstairs and join my cousins for an hour of religious lessons and Quran recital, before we made our way to the masjid for Friday prayer.

"What do you mean?" I asked my mother, tilting my head at a please-have-mercy angle as I stood between her and the television.

"What?"

"Did you forget about what happened yesterday?"

"No," she said. "I told you. I'm dealing with it."

"Well, can't I skip—"

"Sherif!" she yelled as she looked behind me. "I told you, you'll get your gamer."

"But—"

"I'm not going to say it again."

I rushed out the front door and slammed it behind me, then ran down the stairs in fear that she would come after me with a slipper. In my grandfather's apartment, Sheikh Anwar was already on his designated seat at one end of the dining table, wearing his usual white gown and head cap, both of which matched his long white beard perfectly. I walked toward my seat beside Amir, grabbed a Quran from the middle of the table, and opened it to a random page.

"You're late again," Amir said, and I was glad to see that he had forgiven me for the night prior.

Right across the table was the thief of the family.

"What are you looking at?" Mariam asked.

I looked away.

"Young boy," Sheikh Anwar said. "What did we say about being late?"

"Sorry, Sheikh."

"Look happy to be in the presence of God's words."

"Okay, Sheikh."

"Now," he said. "Let's all open to Suret El Bakara."

Sheikh Anwar was a kind, noble man whom our family consulted for anything religious and who was largely responsible for the development of our morals, but no one had ever denied me as much joy as him. Growing your hair long as a boy? Haram. Wearing a necklace? Haram. A bracelet? Haram. A pet dog? Haram. A hamster? Haram. Music videos on TV, wherein pop stars like Britney Spears moved their butts in breathtaking ways? Haram. American films that showed characters having premarital sex? That was so haram the mere suggestion that it could be halal was haram.

Nevertheless, I had become accustomed to the Friday ritual. Sheikh Anwar read a verse, with a voice as deep and precise as the one he used to call prayer from the masjid, then all six of us read it. We tried to emulate his pace and pronunciation, until he shouted, "You!" and we looked up to see where his kofta-thick finger was pointing.

"What?" Mariam asked.

"You're skipping verses."

"Sorry, Sheikh."

"Close your book."

Mariam closed her Quran and sighed. She had probably been preoccupied fantasizing about the Game Boy hidden in her bedroom.

"Recite Suret El Nas."

"In the name of God, Most Merciful, Most Compassionate," Mariam began.

"Recite," said the sheikh.

"Say, I seek refuge in..."

The urge to giggle spread around the table, as it did at least once every lesson we had with Sheikh Anwar. This time, however, I found nothing amusing; I only wanted my Game Boy returned.

"Habiba," he said. "Remind us how old you are?"

"Eight, Sheikh."

"And how old is Mariam?"

"Ten, Sheikh."

"Recite, girl."

Habiba recited the first of the sura's five pages with the precision and confidence of someone narrating her Sunday afternoon. She had always possessed incredible ability when it came to recital and was often used as a tool to embarrass those of us, mostly Mariam and I, with more secularly inclined personalities.

We finished reading the sura and Sheikh Anwar asked us to close our books. He put his hand into the plastic bag on his lap and extracted one of the branches of sugarcane he always chewed on for his diabetes.

"So," he said as he began to peel the branch with his teeth, spitting the exterior into an empty plastic bag on his lap. "Today I want to talk about the subject of theft."

First, I was shocked at the coincidence, but then I quickly realized my mother likely stopped by the masjid and spoke to Sheikh Anwar on her way home from the market.

I made eye contact with Mariam and she wasn't the first to look away. Amir, Habiba, and Tamer were looking at Sheikh Anwar, seemingly unaware of why the subject could be unnerving. Nesma was picking her nose.

"Let's say I'm walking down the street," Sheikh Anwar said. "And I'm wearing these shoes that are ready to be thrown in the garbage. And on the side of the road, suddenly I see a pair of shoes that look completely new. They're shining. And they appear to be my exact size too. What do you think the shetan would tempt me to do?"

He spat into the plastic bag and wiped his juicy beard with a napkin.

"He would tell you to take the shoes," Habiba said.

"That's right," Sheikh Anwar said. "*Take them,* the devil would say. *Look at them. They look so new and comfortable. No one is around. No one will ever find out. Do you really think anyone needs these shoes more than you?* What should I do in such an instance?"

Habiba put her hand up.

"Someone besides Habiba," he said.

Nesma put her hand up.

"Tell us, young girl."

"Go clean your shoes?"

Everyone except Amir and I laughed. When I looked at him, I saw that he appeared worried and was deliberately avoiding eye contact with me.

"Yes," the sheikh said. "But what else? You tell me, Mariam."

"You should disregard the shetan and leave the shoes where they are," Mariam said with a monotonous tone. "Because you don't know who might've dropped them by mistake. And you don't take anything that's not yours unless it's being gifted to you. Anything else is considered theft."

Sheikh Anwar pointed his branch of sugarcane at Mariam. "That's right. Except maybe say it with a little liveliness."

"All right, Sheikh."

"But let's say that I do succumb to the shetan," the sheikh said. "And I go and take the shoes, and I run away. What happens next, Amir?"

"You ask God for forgiveness and try to amend for your sin," Amir said.

"That's right," the sheikh said. "Because why, Sherif?"

"Because you can't expect God or anyone to forgive you unless you first ask for forgiveness," I said. "Unless you show that you regret what you've done."

"Absolutely," the sheikh said. "So I command you, my sons and daughters, if you have sinned, if you have lied, if you have stolen, don't be afraid to admit it. For that takes great courage. Most importantly, God will, in His own way, begin to forgive you. Now, I've been told one of you took something that wasn't theirs yesterday. I encourage you to come forward, if not now, then later, to whoever you trust, and admit to your wrongdoing. After all, you're family. Everyone will be forgiven."

I looked back at Mariam and saw her looking straight at Sheikh Anwar.

"I'm sorry, Sheero."

It took me a beat to realize that it was Tamer who had spoken.

"What?"

"I hope you can forgive me," Tamer said. "I got jealous. I'll give it back."

I was embarrassed for all of us. Tamer was our oldest cousin, the one Amir and I always attempted to emulate, the one whose keepy-uppies and breakdancing skills we were continually in awe of. "It's fine," I said. "It's really okay."

"Good," the sheikh said. "You see, this was good. You must understand that you are still young. This is how you all learn. You make mistakes and you learn. Tamer, my son, remember that to admit to wrongdoing takes courage, and that's what you've just done here. A proper man." The sheikh patted Tamer's shoulder twice.

"Oh, enough," Amir said as he stood up. "Enough of this."

Habiba pulled his arm. "Sit down."

He pulled it out of her grip.

"Sit down, boy," the sheikh said.

"I'm sick of all this stupid talk," Amir said. His voice was calm and his expression appeared unmoved, but his words were nothing short of insane; to call the sheikh's words "stupid talk" was as reckless as it would be if one of us assaulted Gedo.

"Sit down, boy!" the sheikh yelled.

Nesma started crying and I almost did the same. I feared all the sheikh's talk about the shetan had activated the one in Amir's brain.

"What's going on?" Teta asked as she entered the room. "Is everything all right?"

"No, it's not," Amir said as he dug his nails into the tablecloth.

"You've lost your mind!" the sheikh yelled.

I stood up. I wanted to go home.

"Toz feek," Amir told the sheikh before he walked away, into the hall that led to the front door, and out of the apartment.

"You son of a dog!" Teta yelled.

Tamer returned the Game Boy as soon as we were dismissed, but it took me a few hours of reliving the event to realize what had actually occurred: Amir had stolen the Game Boy and Tamer had only tried to cover for him.

I didn't see Amir that whole week, not even in the mornings when we all stood under our building and waited for our buses to take us to school. He finally reappeared when he came downstairs the following Friday and extensively apologized to the sheikh, who hugged him and kissed his forehead.

Amir and I never spoke of the fact that he had been the true culprit, but there was a mutual understanding that all was forgiven and nothing of the sort would ever happen again. He was remorseful; he was extra nice to me for months, evidently grateful for my forgiveness, and made sure to ask for permission every time he touched one of my belongings. I was familiar with the rotten feeling that had driven him to steal the Game Boy and felt sorry that it did.

"Sheero," Carmen said as I stared at Amir's birthday message. "Why aren't you talking to me?"

I closed my laptop as she sat beside me and rubbed my back.

"What's going on, amor?"

I cringed. Part of the reason Amir and I had become strangers was reflected in this moment: I lived abroad with an Argentinean girlfriend who called me "amor." I spent most of my time chasing overpriced brunches, drug-fueled parties, and nap-inducing orgasms. Traces of my Egyptian middle-class roots had become scarce. In fact, the thesis of my life was to erase all such traces. When I imagined my ideal life fifteen years down the line, I saw myself eating prosciutto and Camembert on a boat off the coast of El Gouna, telling my kids to take it easy on the cherry clafoutis. Never did I picture any kids munching on my grandmother's mahshy with their second cousins. No, I would cut the cord with every member of the family except my mother. And wouldn't I be perfectly within my rights? Once upon a time, my mother had taught me the importance of social duties: that I should regularly check on my family members and spend as much time with them as possible. That it's important to perform labor for the benefit of others, in spite of the inconvenience it causes you. Lessons that would've ensured I responded to Amir's message and sent him one on his birthday too. Lessons that would've made me feel obliged to cancel my plans on Halloween and spend it with him instead.

"They announced the guy's name?" I asked Carmen.

She nodded. "Why?" she asked with growing apprehensiveness.

I looked away. "He's my cousin."

"What?"

"Amir. He's my cousin."

Carmen didn't make a sound. When I looked back at her, she was just staring at me and holding still, without blinking or moving a muscle. And the perplexity drawn on her face was so reflective of how I felt that I burst into laughter.

"You asshole," she said with relief as she smirked. "That's not funny."

When I saw that she thought I was only kidding, I laughed harder and harder.

"I'm not joking," I said as I laughed. "I'm actually being serious."

Suddenly, questions about Amir's corpse popped into my mind and brought the laughing to a halt. What would be done with it? Did criminals lose their right to a proper burial? Would they cremate him? I pictured the diener placing the corpse into the crematory chamber, unmoved and lacking hesitance, as if he were placing dough into a brick oven. I saw Amir's skin burning until his bones were revealed. I thought of the smell. I leaped toward the trash can beside me and vomited the bourbon out.

Carmen rushed to the kitchen and returned with a glass of water.

"You all right?" she asked as she handed me the glass. "You need to eat."

"I did," I said. "They gave me a bagel. With cream cheese."

"What do you mean he's your cousin?"

I reached for my laptop and opened it, hoping to find an empty seat on tonight's EgyptAir flight to Cairo. It would probably look suspicious to law enforcement and the general public—who I figured would learn of my name sooner or later—if I left the country within hours, but I needed to be with my family as soon as possible.

7

The night before Mazen's scheduled visit, Zeina didn't enjoy much sleep. She woke up what felt like every ten minutes, hoping to see sunlight piercing through the shutters, so she could finally prepare for his arrival. She visualized the day ahead time and time again. God willing, Mazen would arrive before Abu Ahmed left for his nightly business. They would sit in Abu Ahmed's office, drink the tea that Salma would make them, smoke some cigarettes, and come to the conclusion that, without a doubt, Zeina ought to be featured on the radio for people across the country to hear. That it was a tremendous opportunity that could benefit the whole family. Abu Ahmed wouldn't be overjoyed, but he would give his consent, and then Salma would naturally become just as excited as Zeina. Right before leaving, Mazen would provide them with additional information regarding Zeina's prospective performance, and then, for the first time in a long while, Zeina would have something to look forward to.

In the end, Zeina overslept, and Mustafa woke her up after returning from Friday prayer with Omar and Abu Ahmed.

I'll be there after Maghrib, Mazen had told Salma. After the third prayer. With four hours to spare, Zeina did everything she could to make her home as presentable as possible. She washed the dishes, changed the bedsheets, sorted the cushions that made up a seating corner on the floor, covered the doodling that Omar had inflicted on the cement walls with one of Salma's veils, murdered the family of cockroaches living behind the closet, and, when nothing else could be done with the apartment, filled a bucket with soap water and mopped the building's filthy staircase. Meanwhile, she hoped Abu Ahmed would wake up and inquire as to why she was cleaning so arduously, and then Salma would be forced to explain. But he had gone into his office after Friday prayer and presumably fallen asleep.

Right before Maghrib, Zeina aired the apartment and lit a stick of incense to eliminate the accumulated smell of feet and farts. Salma watched her and made sarcastic remarks. "Oksem Belah, I should have someone come every day," she said. "Mister Mazen and Mister Magdy and Mister Moussa. This is just wonderful."

Ever since the party, Salma had repeatedly mocked the prospect of Mazen's visit, and Zeina wasn't sure if it was because Salma was convinced he wouldn't come or afraid he just might. Regardless, Zeina had a feeling he would. He hadn't asked if he could visit in passing; he had been genuinely moved by her singing and took it upon himself to walk over to their room during the party and ask to meet with Abu Ahmed. When Salma made it seem like a nuisance, he insisted, as if Zeina's voice was of serious urgency.

When the sheikh from the masjid finally said, "God is great, God is great," through the loudspeakers that reached the entire masaken and called the neighborhood's men to come pray Maghrib, Zeina jumped up and down on the bed.

Salma was sitting cross-legged on the carpet, knitting a pair of black socks and shaking her head.

"Mama," Zeina said. "Aren't you going to wake him up?"

Salma snickered. "You live in another world."

"Mama!" Zeina yelled.

"Don't give me a headache!" Salma yelled back. "If anyone comes, I'll wake him up. If you don't like that, go and wake him up yourself. See what happens."

Zeina wanted to grab the half-finished sock in Salma's hands and throw it out the window. Salma was tarnishing the most important day of Zeina's life.

If Mazen arrived, he would have to be kept downstairs until Salma woke Abu Ahmed up and explained that they had a guest. Zeina considered going downstairs and waiting to receive Mazen herself, but it would be inappropriate, so she turned to the only person she could rely on.

Mustafa was lying on the carpet, his face almost touching the inside of a comic book, which Zeina yanked out of his hands.

"What are you doing?" he yelled.

"Yalla, go downstairs," Zeina said. "He has a long hair and a belly. You'll recognize him. Keep him downstairs until Mama wakes Baba up."

Mustafa pointed at the comic book. "But they're about to rescue Rictor and Boom Boom from Genosha," he said, as if he hadn't read the book many times before.

"They can rescue them later," Zeina said. "Or here"—she gave him the book—"take it with you. But keep an eye out."

Mustafa snatched the book out of Zeina's hands, put on his slippers, and went downstairs. Zeina opened the window right beside the bed and looked at the western end of the road, from which Mazen would be arriving, as per Salma's directions.

It being a Friday, the street was relatively empty. Stray cats napped on top of cars, Am Ramzi fanned his corn stand, and Omar and his friends pleaded with one another, over and over again, to pass the fucking ball.

Zeina had heard the saying: *If an Egyptian says seven, he won't be there before eight thirty.* But every minute that Mazen was late carried great danger. Abu Ahmed could wake up at any moment, put on his clothes, and simply depart to wherever it was that he went for work. Salma certainly wouldn't stop him. And if Mazen arrived after Abu Ahmed left, what would they tell him? That he was too late? That they had no idea when Abu Ahmed might return? Zeina was afraid such complications might arise. She knew the customs. Mazen couldn't enter their home and wait for Abu Ahmed with Salma. It would be inappropriate. Why? It was here that Zeina always hit the wall: because that was *the way it was.* Apparently, people had always acted a certain way. And although she didn't understand this way, neither the logic behind it nor why it changed so drastically whenever they went to Zamalek, she understood that the way was her enemy. The way granted Madame Alia permission to yell at Salma whenever she pleased. The way prohibited Zeina from entering Taymour's and Madame Alia's bedrooms if she wasn't helping clean them. The way forced her to spend the majority of her time in a tiny room despite the massive and always empty salon under the same ceiling. The way discouraged her from asking Madame Alia and Taymour any questions, even something as simple as how they're doing. The way had allowed Abu Ahmed to keep her from getting an education and to sentence her to a life of taking orders. A life without any prospect of change. The way her life would turn out, apparently, was similar to Salma's. She would live with a man of her father's choosing, for whom she would do laundry, cook, and birth children. The way was entirely abominable. And Zeina's yearning for an alternative, for the luxury and freedom enjoyed by everyone on the other side of the Nile, often overwhelmed her to the point that she struggled to fall asleep at night. Perhaps Mazen was being sent by God to put her on another path. All she could do now was pray that he arrived soon and that Abu Ahmed remain in the office until then.

Half an hour after the prayer calling, she remained optimistic despite Mustafa's impatience. "I don't know," Mustafa said after coming upstairs. "Maybe he's busy, Zeina. And I really can't read. There's not enough light."

"Enta, you're stupid," Salma told him. "Doing whatever she says, always. Just sit and spend your day as you wish."

"Mama, can you please go to the call center and call Madame Alia?"

Salma chuckled without removing her eyes from the black sock.

"Mama, I'm serious," Zeina begged. "Maybe he got lost or something. Please."

"I gave him very—"

Zeina heard a whistle that resembled Omar's: the same whistle he used to call his friends down from their homes to come play. She looked at Mustafa and saw that he also recognized it. Another one followed, and then Omar's voice: "Mustafa!"

Zeina ran to the bed, jumped onto it, then stuck her head out the window so fast that she almost fell over. She saw Omar talking to Mazen on the road and screamed with relief. "Mama, he's here!" she yelled, so loud that Mazen spotted her and waved. He was wearing bright blue jeans, a white shirt, and a brown leather jacket. She waved back and turned to tell Mustafa to go downstairs, but he was already gone.

Salma had dropped the sock, and was on her feet now, staring at Zeina.

"Mama," Zeina said. "He's here. I told you Mama."

Salma approached the window, peeked at Mazen, then retreated into the apartment. "In the name of God. Most Merciful, Most Compassionate."

"Mama, you have to wake him up."

Salma turned her back to Zeina and looked down, scanning the floor with her eyes as if searching for a written answer.

Zeina saw that Salma was shaking. "Mama," she said. "What's wrong?"

Salma took Zeina's hand and led her to the front door. "Yalla, go downstairs. Tell him to wait for a moment until I tell you to come up."

"Mama, don't worry," Zeina said. Abu Ahmed was an ill-tempered man with a lot of pride, Zeina knew that, but there was no reason to be so horrified. Mazen was here only to ask if she could sing on the radio. If anything, it was a cause for celebration. Everyone in the masaken would hear of it, Zeina's prospective performance, and tune in, and then praise Abu Ahmed and the family for making them proud.

Still, Salma mumbled prayers under her breath. "Yalla, go," she said as she pushed Zeina out of the apartment. "I'll tell you when he's ready."

Across the hall, Zeina stuck her ear on the door of her father's office and heard nothing inside. She hoped Abu Ahmed would get ready in a timely manner.

Downstairs, Mazen and Mustafa were standing on the sidewalk. Zeina wanted to run into Mazen's stomach and hug him, but she was so nervous that she struggled to so much as greet him. His arrival in Ramlet Bulaq had the potential to change her world overnight, and all she could do was pray that her father would let it happen.

"Hello," Mazen said when he saw her.

"Hello," she said back.

He put his hand out and she shook it. She was so distraught by his kindness that it almost hurt. She had envisioned his arrival dozens of times but couldn't believe that he was actually here in real life, couldn't fathom that he had come all the way just for her sake. Who was he, the Prophet? She was restless, couldn't look at his eyes, so she stared at the window of her apartment instead. When Mustafa awkwardly opened his comic book and began reading, while the three of them stood in silence, she wanted to grab it out of his hand and smack it across his face.

"I see you like reading," Mazen said.

Mustafa didn't respond or take his eyes off the pages.

"Mustafa!" Zeina yelled, so loud she scared both of them.

"What is wrong with you?" Mustafa yelled back.

"He asked you a question!"

Mazen laughed.

"Sorry," Mustafa said. "What was the question?"

Mazen smiled and rubbed Mustafa's hair.

"He likes reading, yes," Zeina said. "I'm sorry you have to wait. Baba is waking up. He should be ready soon."

"That's fine," Mazen said. "I just woke up from a nap too."

Zeina looked at her window for the fourth time and was relieved to see Salma signaling for Mazen to come upstairs.

"Go up," Zeina said. "Fifth floor. He's awake."

"Oh," Mazen said. "All right."

He walked into the building and Zeina was glad she had cleaned the staircase. She hoped the stray cat wouldn't hiss at him on the fourth floor and that none of the neighbors would open their doors and say something classless as he passed them.

She waited something like a minute before she walked into the building and peeked up through the spiral of the staircase. She heard Salma greet Mazen, saying something about how he was most welcome. When the door to either their apartment or Abu Ahmed's office was closed, she skipped outside and interrogated Mustafa.

"Did he mention that he was here for me?"

"What do you mean?"

"What did he say? When you came down here?"

"That he was looking for Mama."

"And?"

"And what?"

"What did *you* say?"

"I told him to wait until she woke Baba up."

"And?"

"And?"

"And!"

"You're scaring me," he said.

"Why?"

"Because."

"There's nothing to be scared of," she said. "This is great. He's here, Mustafa." She punched his shoulder again and again. "He's here! He's here, he's here, he's here!"

He pushed her. "Enough!"

She closed her eyes; she was getting dizzy.

"You've gone crazy," he said.

"Do you think Baba will agree?" she asked.

"I don't know," he said. "Where *is* the radio anyway?"

"We don't have one. But we have one in the kitchen at Madame Alia's."

"No. I mean, is there a radio building? That you're going to go to?"

She had no idea. "I wonder how many songs I will sing."

"You should sing 'Shadi,'" he said. "You sing it really well."

She smiled and hugged him: her favorite person by far. "I'll dedicate it to you," she said. "Before I sing it, I'll say, *I dedicate this to my brother Mustafa.* Sometimes they dedicate songs."

He smiled.

She remembered there was a chance Abu Ahmed would reject the idea. "Mama was scared," she said. "I don't know why."

Mustafa opened his comic book and resumed reading. Zeina ran into the building to check for any sign of Mazen on the staircase. She wished she could go upstairs and eavesdrop on the conversation but wouldn't dare. When she returned outside, she glanced at Omar, who was mid-football game, and saw that he was restless about the meeting too. He was looking up at their window between every pass and play. Perhaps he was realizing just how stupid he had been for dismissing Zeina's dreams.

They heard a door being opened and closed. Mustafa closed his comic book and Zeina stood behind him, as if a threat were approaching. Mazen's footsteps got louder and louder until they saw him turn at the last set of stairs, which led to the entrance.

As soon as Mazen looked at her, Zeina knew the meeting hadn't gone well. Nothing was stretched with excitement on his face; his mouth was shut and his eyebrows were compressed into displeased zigzags. Nevertheless, she remained hopeful. Perhaps he was frustrated by something else. But then, as he got close, he smiled at her in that terrible way she was all too familiar with: the same way Taymour, his friends, Madame Najla, and Madame Alia's neighbors often smiled at her. A smile that said, *I'm sorry for your dreadful circumstances, little girl.*

She looked away from him. He put his hands on her shoulders and knelt down to level his face with hers. "Little star," he said. "You just keep singing with that voice of yours, all right? Don't let it get away."

She became frustrated when she came close to tears. "What did he say?" she asked.

Mazen stood straight and shook his head. He sighed and squeezed her shoulders, then said goodbye to Mustafa and walked away.

"Thank you for coming," she said.

He turned around, said, "Of course," then continued on his path.

Mustafa hugged Zeina, but she quickly pushed him off. Perhaps she had been foolish for expecting something out of the norm, but that wouldn't be the case forever. As soon as she was an adult, she would leave this rotten place and sing on whatever radio station she liked. She would build her *own* path and do everything within her power to make sure no one pitied her. And when she became a famous singer, she wouldn't share her wealth with her father, wouldn't even acknowledge that she was related to him. She watched Mazen walk away down the road and wished she could follow him. As he turned the corner, she heard a piercing scream behind her and quickly recognized Salma's voice.

Omar was the farthest from the building but somehow the first to rush up the stairs, with Zeina and Mustafa running close behind.

"You bring a man into my home!" Abu Ahmed yelled. "He wants to buy my daughter! You fucking whore!"

"I had no choice!" Salma yelled back.

"No choice! Why? Are you his fucking whore?!"

The neighbors opened their doors as Zeina and her brothers ran past them.

Zeina's legs were shaking. "Please help," she said between breaths. "Please!"

On the fifth floor, she was horrified to discover that her parents were in Abu Ahmed's office and that it was locked. Omar banged on the door with his fists and she did the same.

"Baba, stop!" she yelled. "Baba!"

"You had no choice!" Abu Ahmed yelled from inside. "That's because I married a whore! I was wrong for ever letting you go work."

"Enough of it," Salma said. "Don't be crazy."

There was a moment of silence and then the sound of a hard slap. Salma let out a wail not unlike that of the stray dog that was crushed under a passing car last week. Hearing it, Zeina closed her eyes and screamed as loudly as she could, for as long as her lungs allowed, hoping it would cause enough alarm for someone, hopefully one of the neighbors, or God, to bring the beating to an end. When she opened her eyes, she saw that Mustafa had fallen to the floor, an expression of utter shock drawn on his face as a dark stain spread through the legs of his blue jeans.

Omar kicked the door. "Ya Baba enough!"

Glass shattered against something inside—perhaps one of Abu Ahmed's ashtrays, thrown at the wall. For a moment, Zeina feared he was going to kill their mother, and so she screamed again, hoping her voice would make it through her father's anger and reach what little heart he had.

The door finally swung open and Omar fell into Salma's arms. She shoved him aside and walked right past her children into their apartment across the hall. Zeina ran around her to examine the damage; tears were streaming out of Salma's eyes, while a cut on her lip and another one on her hairline leaked blood. Zeina began to weep and wrapped her arms around Salma's waist, holding her as tightly as she could.

"Mama," she said. "I'm so sorry."

Mustafa wept even louder and hugged Salma too, a vigorous smell of urine following him into the apartment.

Salma rubbed their backs. "Fucking coward," she mumbled through her panicked breath. "Fucking coward of a man. I wish my father could see the filth he left me with. God take you and burn you in Hell, you coward. I'm going to fucking kill you."

"Mama, cover your cut!" Omar yelled. He had fetched some toilet paper from the bathroom and was placing it in Salma's hand.

Abu Ahmed walked into the apartment. His eyes were wide and his bald head was shining with sweat. He was the most evil man to have ever lived, a living relative of the monsters from Mustafa's comic books. What had they done to deserve such a father? Just a few minutes ago, Zeina had fantasized about which song to sing on the radio; now her mother had been humiliated and beaten, called a "whore" before the neighbors.

"You fucking listen to me," Abu Ahmed said as he approached them, pointing his finger at Salma's face.

Zeina closed her eyes and held on to Salma. "Please," she begged. "I'm scared."

Omar stood in front of Abu Ahmed and pushed as hard as he could on the man's big stomach. Abu Ahmed grabbed both of Omar's shoulders and pushed him aside, sending Omar tumbling onto the carpet.

"You coward!" Salma yelled, as she took a few steps back and held on to Zeina and Mustafa. "Enough of this!"

"You listen to me," Abu Ahmed said, this time with a lower voice. "Starting tomorrow you stop working for that woman. Do you understand?"

"Baba," Mustafa begged as he wept. "I'm sorry."

Omar stood up and pulled at the back of Abu Ahmed's shirt.

Abu Ahmed turned and pushed Omar aside again. He picked up a metal tray from the kitchen counter and threw it at the wall, making a loud bang as it bounced back and landed close to his feet.

He kicked it away from him and returned to his office.

Salma sat on the bed and noticed the urine on Mustafa's legs. She kissed his forehead as Omar held toilet paper against her bleeding lip. "Go," she said as she grabbed Zeina's arm and looked at Mustafa's legs. "Go clean him up."

Zeina fetched a clean pair of Mustafa's pants from the closet and took him to the bathroom, where she made him wash his legs under the shower and change. She was desperate to relieve her mother of any burden she could. "Stop crying," she kept telling Mustafa, though she was crying as well. What if she could put poison in her father's food, like some of the neighbors did when a stray dog barked too loud during the night? Abu Ahmed had hit Salma before, twice: once during Ramadan, when Salma told him that his not fasting would guarantee him a place in Hell, and another time, when she accused him, in front of the children, of spending half his money on prostitutes. Surely his death would only be good riddance, and God would have no choice but to forgive Zeina.

8

Outside Cairo International Airport, four taxi drivers approached me and began with "Welcome, welcome home," and "The city has lit up," and "What a sweet face you've brought us," before they offered to carry my suitcase and argued among one another about who would take me home. I rebelled against their unsophisticated system and demanded to ride with the oldest man, who was losing ground in the dispute. I figured he would be the most likely to let me sit in silence until I arrived home, but as we waited in line to exit the parking lot, he asked me where I had returned from, and it turned out he had numerous opinions to share about America.

"It's all their fault," he said. "They burned Iraq to ashes, thinking that they could spill that much blood and get away with it. But that's not how the world works, is it? They're lucky they haven't had more attacks. Do you know, my son, what it means to have a foreign man come into your land, kill your neighbors and relatives, and imprison you in your own jails? They will suffer the consequences for decades. It's good you came back to your country."

I performed a smile. "There's a lot of kind people there, you know. And to attack innocent civilians is just wrong."

He looked offended. "Of course it's wrong. Do you not know the chapter from the Quran, 'The Disbelievers'?"

"I do," I said, hoping he wouldn't recite it.

"*In the name of God, Most Merciful, Most Compassionate. Say, Disbelievers. I do not worship what you worship. I will never worship what you worship. You will never worship what I worship. You have your religion and I have mine.*"

"*Ameen.*"

"*Let there be no compulsion in religion. Attack only when attacked.*"

"Yes."

"Of course it's wrong," the man said again. "These same terrorists kill their own Muslim brothers in Iraq. On the day of days, they will meet God, who will hand them the worst punishment."

"Right."

"But so will the Americans."

I sighed. On a regular day, I would have spent the rest of the journey trying to explain to the driver, regardless of how stubborn he was, that there were millions of Americans who accepted and loved Muslims as their fellow citizens, and that their main intention was to get by, not to wage war against Islam. I would have emphasized that for every million men who believed that America was at war with Islam, one man would be successfully convinced to sacrifice his life for that war. But now my own cousin had become that man, that fool, and I didn't have the will to argue with the driver.

I lit a cigarette as we made it out of the airport and onto Salah Salem Street. On the surface, Cairo was a shock to the unaccustomed eye. Buildings originally painted in different colors were covered with so much dust that they had evolved into similar shades of grim. Drivers swerved in and out of lanes with no regard to order, honking every few seconds for no reason, as if to contribute to the mandatory *peep peep peep* that never ceased. Vendors whipped at the legs of malnourished horses so their carts could be dragged faster. Stray dogs and cats scavenged for food around the piles of trash that were dumped every mile or two on the sides of the road.

I usually began to appreciate Cairo's aesthetic within a few days of my return. Instead of being agonized by the constant honking, I would enjoy the sha'abe music blasting from the speakers of different cars and maybe even clap along to the tablas. Instead of being disturbed by the children who begged, the scars and zits and despair on their faces, I would notice the luckier children behind them, doing tricks with their bicycles on the sidewalks. Instead of fixating on the restrictions of religion, I would see just how profound it was that, five times a day, every day, millions of people gathered to pray and meditate together. This, however, was far from a regular homecoming, and I feared I was at risk of losing whatever affection I had for my hometown.

At a stoplight, a man with no legs dragged his torso through the spaces between the cars and asked me for change. I stuck my arm out the window and gave him a five-dollar bill. "You have to get it exchanged at the serafa," I said. "It's worth thirty pounds." He kissed it, tapped it on his forehead, and then looked up at God.

There was no traffic on the 6th of October Highway, an unusual occurrence that punched my chest with anxiety. We would be downtown in minutes, and I would have to withstand what could be weeks of family arguments, breakdowns, and mourning without being able to have a single drink.

As we drove through Zamalek, I thought of what would happen if Amir was identified by someone who knew him as my cousin. It would be one of the relevant topics of conversation for weeks to come. *Did you watch the game last night? Did you go see that movie? Oh, you know that terrorist on the news, the one who shot up the train? Well, that's Sheero's cousin.* What would it do to my reputation here in Cairo? Would people assume I came from a family of fanatics? Would any respectable man ever let me marry his daughter? I already came from an inferior lineage. My grandfather hadn't been a basha with European blood; he had been a businessman, and a peasant too. He had never learned how to eat with a fork and knife and could speak only one language. Now, my cousin had become a terrorist, a murderer, and not only would people claim to know someone who knew him, but my high school friends would remember meeting him, the day my mother forced me to take him out on his birthday.

Amir's eighteenth birthday was on a Thursday toward the end of my junior year of high school. Over the past few years, we had become increasingly distant. He was busy with his studies, I was busy with mine, and we were becoming seriously different people. More and more, I was becoming a product of Cairo's bourgeoisie. I spent most of my free time in Zamalek, watched American TV shows, read Stephen King novels, and drank alcohol on weekend nights. During the summer I traveled to the North Coast and spent months living at Taymour's beach house. I had covert make-out sessions in swimming pools; I had received my first hand job the month prior. Amir, on the other hand, had two friends who lived down the street from us and spent most of his time either smoking shisha at the local ahwa or studying for his sanaweya a'ama. His sole sexual experience had occurred on Chatroulette, where a few foreign girls had apparently shown him their breasts over webcam.

I rarely spoke to Amir about my life; I felt ashamed that a simple egg-split in our grandmother's womb had led to the great imbalance of fortune between us. I always felt like I could've easily been Khalto Heba's son, and he, my mother's; when he spoke to me about his life, I often felt the urge to apologize, as if every one of my life's blessings had been robbed from his.

Still, I saw him at least once or twice a month. My mother often called him to see if he was hungry and wanted to join us for dinner. And it was during one of such dinners, as we ate rice and black-eyed peas, that he revealed to us that it was his eighteenth birthday, and all twenty-six members of our family, including Gedo, had completely forgotten.

My mother put her fork down and smacked her chest. "Ya habiby! How could I forget? April tenth, of course! How could we forget?"

"Shit," I said. "Happy birthday, Amir. I don't know how I forgot either. I'm sorry."

"It's all right," he said. "I shouldn't have even mentioned it."

"Oh, stop it," my mother said.

"If I didn't have plans," I said. "We could've gone to the cinema or something."

"Don't worry about it," he said.

"Well, why don't you take him out with you?" my mother asked me, knowing precisely why but having never accepted it as a good enough reason.

Amir and I made brief eye contact. He took a bite of his food and waited to see if I would summon the courage to say yes. Like my mother, he was aware that regardless of how often I assured them that it was his discomfort I was trying to prevent, it was primarily mine. Under the elitist gaze of my friends, I would be too embarrassed to be associated with Amir. They would quickly see him as bee'a, as fundamentally inferior, given his clothes and background and weak English.

It would be cowardly and selfish to abandon him on his birthday, but I struggled to present a genuine invitation.

"Maybe," I said. "If you really want to, Amir."

"No, it's fine," he said. "I'm a bit tired anyway."

I glanced at my mother, who was slowly shaking her head. The rest of the meal was eaten in silence and Amir was the first to go wash his hands.

"You're taking him with you," my mother whispered the moment he shut the bathroom door behind him.

"*Ma.*"

"Please. Do it for me."

"But I don't—"

Amir walked out of the bathroom.

"Amir, habiby, go out and celebrate your birthday with Sheero," Ma said as she smiled. "It'll be fun."

I imagined throwing my fork at her.

"No, it's fine, Tante. I don't think he wants me to."

"It's not that," I said. "It's just... my friends aren't, like, Egyptian."

"What?" Ma asked. "Of course they are."

I put my fork down and slid the plate away from me. It was pathetic that I needed to include my eighteen-year-old cousin in my social life because he didn't have one of his own.

"I just don't know if you'll like them," I said.

"Well, take him and see," my mother said.

I imagined throwing my whole plate of spaghetti at her.

"Fine," I said. "Can you be ready in half an hour?"

He looked down at himself. "I'm ready now."

I looked at his maroon shirt, which had 'Ferocious Charisma' written across the front of it.

"I can lend you one of my shirts."

"Why?" he asked as he looked at his chest. "What does it mean?"

It means the opposite of what it claims, I wanted to say. "It doesn't really mean much," I said. "Or it does... but... just take one of mine."

"All right, Mister Fashion Guy."

In my room, he tried on a few different shirts until he settled for a light blue button-up. "It's actually nice," he said as he looked at himself in my mirror.

"It is."

"Amir El Kafrawy," he said as he shook my hand. "Lawyer. Man of business. Romance enthusiast."

I laughed at the perfectly executed movie reference. Amir and I shared enough memories to be able to do that: crack a joke and remember our childhood. During such moments I was reminded that he was family, that if I ever got admitted into a hospital, he would probably be among the first to visit me. Still, the sentiment was always fleeting, and I only had to catch him picking his nose, as we sat in the taxi on our way to Zamalek, to feel burdened by his company once again.

Please don't pick your nose in front of my friends.

Thankfully, the plan wasn't to go to a party or bar but just to have an a'ada in a café, where we would smoke shisha and hang out. Amir's usual a'ada was with his two friends in the ahwa down the street, where a cup of tea, three coals' worth of shisha, and a soda cost no more than ten pounds. Café Le Caire, on the other hand, had a minimum charge of a hundred and twenty pounds. My mother had given me enough money to pay for Amir, of course, so I told him not to be shocked at the prices on the menu.

As we walked into the café, I hoped there wouldn't be too many people in the room we usually reserved on Thursday nights. All would be fine if it was only my closest male friends, who would have a few things in common with Amir.

To my misfortune, we found more than a dozen people crammed in the room, both girls and boys, sitting on the chairs lined up against the walls.

"Sheero!" a few people said as Amir and I walked in.

"Heyo," I said. The room was thick with cigarette and shisha smoke. "How are you guys even breathing in here? This is my cousin Amir."

One of the Egyptian social norms that I always despised was the need to greet every single person in the room with a handshake or a kiss. It always seemed like a waste of energy when you could just say hello with a wave of your hand aimed at the collective. But even Amir knew that if you did that people would be offended and go as far as saying matsalem: *Why don't you greet us properly?* So he followed me around the room as we performed the chore. Halfway through, I realized that he was shaking hands with the girls instead of following my lead and kissing them on both cheeks. He was also doing it in this official hold-my-hand-and-really-shake-it diplomatic way, instead of simply tapping their hands like any regular teenager.

I winced a little but held my cool. If I was going to survive the night, I couldn't be hyperaware of Amir's actions and wonder what everyone thought of him. As we finished the greetings, I saw Farida and Lara watching him and giggling.

"Dakhel masged dah wala eh," Farida said. "What is he, walking into a mosque?"

A few people giggled as Amir turned around and looked at her.

"*Shut the fuck up, Fifie,*" I said in English.

"Don't mind her," Taymour told Amir. "It's nice to meet you."

"You too," Amir said.

"*She was just joking,*" Lara said. "*But he can give us a kiss. We don't bite.*"

"*Maybe he doesn't want to touch your ugly ass face,*" I said.

A wave of *ooohhhhhh* moved through the room.

Amir was smiling, but I knew he was out of his element, not only because we were speaking English but because there were girls.

The girls in my class were some of the most sexually adventurous teenagers in all of Cairo, along with the girls from the Lycée Français and the American School. If you were a high school boy in any other private school, with an ever-growing sex drive you could no longer satisfy by masturbating daily, one way you could *possibly* have your penis touched was to first meet the girls from the British School. Here they sat, wearing tight jeans and tank tops, smoking shisha, and giving a stranger a hard time for not greeting them with a kiss. Meanwhile, Amir had recently told me that every single girl in his class had become veiled by the time they were in the ninth grade. *That* was Egypt, this was not, and at least now he would know what I had meant.

I found two empty seats in a corner beside Taymour and Khadiga, whom I trusted to be the kindest to Amir. The room was silent; we were the center of attention.

"We've actually met before," Taymour told Amir as we sat down. "A while ago."

"No, you haven't," I said.

"We have," Taymour said. "Years ago."

"I remember," Amir said. "We played football together."

"Oh, right," I said, remembering my tenth birthday at the sports club.

"You were pretty good," Taymour said. "But then again, you were bigger than us."

"I was," Amir said. "Now Sheero is almost taller than me, the bastard."

Several people laughed and I was thrilled. I was more than willing to be made fun of so Amir could be liked.

"A tall bastard, yes," I said to kill the silence.

"You're the first of Sheero's cousins that I've met," Khadiga said.

Amir smiled and said, "The rest of them are idiots," which prompted more laughter. I had mistakenly assumed his sense of humor wouldn't translate. A couple of conversations resumed around the room as a waiter took our order.

"I'll have a watermelon shisha," Amir said.

"I will too," I said. "And a Coca-Cola. Do you want to drink anything?"

"I'll have a raspberry Fanta," he said.

"Wait," Khadiga said. "You like raspberry Fanta too?"

"Of course," Amir said. "Who doesn't?"

"No one!" Khadiga said. "No one here drinks it. They all say it's disgusting."

"I don't think it's disgusting," I said. "I just think it's inferior to orange Fanta."

"You're inferior to orange Fanta," Khadiga said.

"What?"

"You know why I don't like orange Fanta?" Amir said. "Because it's piss next to orange juice."

"Oh my god, yes!" Khadiga said, as she pointed to Amir in agreement.

I couldn't believe my eyes.

"Whereas raspberry Fanta," Amir continued, "is way better than raspberry juice. Raspberry juice tastes like sewage water."

Taymour and Khadiga laughed and I felt like applauding Amir's performance so far. We continued on the subject of Fanta flavors, until, from the corner of my eye, I saw Farida walking over to us, ridding me of the comfort I had begun to gather.

Farida DuPont and I had a turbulent history. Four years prior, my friend Ibrahim and I were searching the school's premises for a spot to smoke cigarettes, when we found Farida, the half French girl in our class, getting fingered behind the swimming pool's underground filter by a boy three grades above us. Shocked at the sight of the eleventh grader's forearm so deep up her skirt, Ibrahim and I screamed, ran away, and were told later that day by Maged and his crew that if anyone heard of what we had seen, we would suffer the consequences. We took the threat seriously and kept the secret, until Ibrahim moved to Beirut later that year and spilled. It took only a few days for the story to spread across the entire school, and I made sure to tell Farida right away that it was Ibrahim who was culpable. But someone was going to pay for the new reputation bestowed upon Farida and Pedophile Maged. Regardless of my honesty, I received a beating later that week, which was so unnecessarily violent that my mother was summoned to school along with Farida's and Pedophile Maged's parents. During a meeting with the principal, it was revealed to all involved that I was innocent of any wrongdoing. Sixteen-year-old Maged had engaged in sexual activity with thirteen-year-old Farida; Ibrahim told multiple friends on MSN Messenger; people took the liberty of adding fictional elements to the story, claiming that Farida was screaming, *Fuck me, Daddy*—because someone gave our generation limitless access to an ocean of online porn—and I lost half of my front tooth.

Maged was expelled for beating me up. Farida was forced to apologize to me, but from that day on we regularly took jabs at each other. She was the shortest person in our grade, a fact I reminded her of almost weekly, and in our shared science, history, and math classes, I sometimes followed up her answers with a correction or disagreement, so as to expose her stupidity.

Now she was within arm's length of my Achilles' heel.

"What are you guys talking about?" she asked Khadiga.

"Raspberry Fanta," Khadiga said.

"You're so obsessed with raspberry Fanta," Farida said.

"He is too," Khadiga said as she pointed at Amir.

Amir nodded his head.

"She drinks it every day," Farida told Amir. "They shouldn't even be selling Fanta at our cafeteria."

"Why not?" Taymour asked.

"I don't know," Farida said. "A school's cafeteria should be selling juice or something."

"That's boring," Khadiga said.

"Do they sell soda at yours?" Farida asked Amir.

"Juice would definitely be a better idea," I said in a voice louder than usual, in an attempt to override Farida's question.

"Sorry?" Amir asked.

"Your school's cafeteria," Farida said.

"Oh," Amir said.

"You know it's his birthday today," I said, but I was practically talking to myself, and though half the people in the room were engaged in their own conversations, Khadiga and Taymour were following Farida and Amir's exchange.

"We don't have a cafeteria at my school," Amir said.

"Really?" she asked. "Where do you go?"

"The Nefertiti School of Prosperity," Amir said. "About to graduate, thank God."

Farida chuckled. "Wait," she said. "The what?"

"*Oh, fuck off,*" I said.

Amir looked at me, then back at Farida. He had no clue what could be amusing about what he had just said. "The Nefertiti School of Prosperity," he said again.

Farida hit her knee and released a storm of laughter. I looked at Taymour and Khadiga and saw that they were doing their best to refrain from laughing too.

Khadiga held back her smile and said, "*Fifie, stop.*"

"Please!" Farida said louder, successfully grabbing the rest of the room's attention. "Please say that again."

Farida and I made eye contact for a brief moment, and I tried to communicate that, though she was about to score a good win, I would do everything in my power for as long as it took to make sure she became a school-wide joke.

"I don't understand what's funny," Amir said.

"Just ignore her," I said.

Farida was bent over on her seat with laughter.

"What's so funny?" a couple of people asked.

She briefly contained her laughter and held Amir's forearm. "Please, please say that again. I beg you. Which school?"

"The Nefertiti School of Prosperity," Amir said in all seriousness, looking at me while I looked at the floor. "Why's that funny?"

Farida became hysterical again and a few people chuckled.

Khadiga was covering her mouth and laughing as discreetly as she could manage.

"Nefertiti!" Farida exclaimed, as if finally finding the answer to a question she'd spent minutes pondering on. "Where is that, Bulaq?"

"*Cut it out,*" Taymour said.

"*Seriously,*" Khadiga said. "*It's not funny.*"

"*All right, all right,*" Farida said as she began to calm down. "I'm only joking."

"You're joking?" Amir asked as he looked at her.

Farida stopped laughing as Amir stared her down. The room was silent for a few seconds as they looked at each other. She looked at me, then looked back at Amir, who was still staring at her with eerie persistence. "Yes," she said. "It was just a joke."

Amir barely moved. He was sitting still on his chair, head tilted to his right, as he stared at Farida. I was about to tell him to forget it, that Farida's a bitch. I was also trying to think of a rebuttal that would leave her speechless.

He finally looked away, and the tension in the room slowly began to dissipate.

He reached his hand and inspected his shisha.

"*You're unbelievable,*" Taymour told Farida.

"*It's really not—*"

Amir detached the bowl on top of his shisha and tossed the hot coal onto Farida. She screamed and fell to the floor. I stood up and grabbed Amir's arm, but it was too late. The hot coal had slipped into Farida's shirt and she was on the floor, kicking and screaming, flapping like a fish out of water. "*Oh my god!*" she yelled as she pulled her shirt over her head.

People fell to their knees and brushed their hands against her dark red bra and stomach. Small pieces of coal bounced off on the floor. Soda cans fell from tables and a glass shattered against the floor. Farida's screaming got louder. A few waiters arrived in the room and asked what happened. "Ice!" someone yelled. "Get ice!"

I turned around and saw that Amir was still sitting there, his face devoid of any feeling, as if he had simply sprayed her with a few drops of water.

He shrugged as he looked at me.

I walked up to him and grabbed his throat. A waiter wrapped his arms around my chest and pulled me away, while another two escorted Amir out of the room.

"Kos mayteen omak!" Aly yelled, as he grabbed a Fanta and threw it in Amir's direction, missing him by only a few inches.

Farida had been pulled to a corner and put on a chair, while all the girls held ice against the pink spots on her stomach and below her neck. Several people were looking at me and shaking their heads.

"*What the fuck, Sheero?*" Khadiga asked.

The scent of spilled watermelon tobacco took hold of the room.

I followed the waiters escorting Amir out of the café.

"Let go," Amir told them as they led him onto the sidewalk. "I'm leaving."

There was heavy traffic on Hassan Sabry Street; dozens of cars were honking to try to get past the stoplight. I walked up to Amir and looked at him. I wanted to slap him—less so because I wanted to hurt him but more to get a reaction—to have him realize the insanity of what he had done. I knew he'd hit me back, though, so I walked up to him and pointed my finger at his face instead. "Are you fucking crazy?"

"Fuck off."

"Fuck off? Fuck off! You fuck off!"

He completely ignored me and continued to search the block of traffic for a taxi.

"Are you insane?" I asked him with genuine curiosity.

He looked at me. "Go and check on your pretty friend."

"Fuck you," I said as he entered a taxi.

I walked back into the café as everyone walked out. Farida was crying, as if grieving a close friend, and Taymour was yelling at his driver on the phone.

Khadiga shook her head when she saw me.

They walked past me and I followed.

"I'm really sorry," I told Farida, and almost began to cry. I was terrified of what would be said at school on Monday, how this night would be transcribed and narrated.

Taymour took her to a clinic where she was treated for—thankfully—first-degree burns. Strangely enough, Farida and I became good friends after that night. I apologized several times, and she was rather kind about it, assuring me that it hadn't been my fault. Because of my popularity at school (which I often felt existed only because of my close friendship with Taymour), the incident was quickly forgotten, but in my family's building it caused significant noise.

When I got home, I told my mother what had occurred, and she was so upset that she walked downstairs and asked to speak to Amir. When she began yelling at him, Khalto Heba got upset. *You don't let anyone yell at your son, so don't come down here and yell at mine!* They had a loud dispute in our stairwell. My grandfather got involved, forced them to make peace, and asked to speak to Amir and me in private. He lectured Amir on all the catastrophes that could've ensued as a result of what he had done. *If her parents go to the police you could go to jail,* he told him a few times. *And what will I do if her father comes knocking on my door, ha?*

The lecture went on for a long time while Amir and I sat in silence and avoided eye contact. My grandfather ordered Amir to apologize and instructed me to shake his hand, which I did, since I was obliged to do anything he asked of me.

I didn't speak to Amir again. I didn't congratulate him when he graduated from high school a month later. When I came across him in our staircase, I walked past him without so much as making eye contact. When we had fetar at my grandfather's dining table during Ramadan, and he asked for a dish in front of me to be passed, I continued eating as if no one had spoken. Almost every single member of the family attempted to persuade me to forgive him, but I didn't want to, not only because I was spiteful but also because the separation between us had been somewhat of a relief. I was no longer obliged to spend time with Amir or ask about his life. I no longer had to endure the existential angst born from our relationship. It was only on the day of his departure to Illinois, five months later, that I suddenly thought how lamentable our rift had been. There was no telling when he would return, and even if he did in a few years, I would likely be abroad for university.

The old taxi driver requested a ridiculously high fee for the ride, one he hoped I would accept because I lived in America and didn't know better. I was too restless to bargain, so I paid him the money as we turned the corner into my street, where my four youngest cousins were having a beatboxing competition as they sat on the trunk of my mother's car.

The oldest among them, Enas, was the first to spot me. "Eda! Sheero!"

I got out of the taxi. "Hello. Why aren't you guys in school?"

"It's the Prophet's birthday," Enas said. "What are you doing here?"

"What am I doing? I'm visiting my family."

On the phone, Ma had made sure to tell me that news about Amir's crime and death were still to be shared with the oldest and youngest of the family: Teta and her preadolescent grandchildren.

I took my suitcase out of the trunk and hugged the rest of the boys, making sure not to hold Amir's six-year-old brother, Youssef, for too long. "Look at you," I told him. "You've gotten so much taller. Do you remember me?"

He nodded. I realized he was wearing an orange Lacoste sweatshirt that had belonged to me when I was his age. My whole life, Ma had given my younger cousins my clothes as soon as I outgrew them, which I always felt distanced me further away from them. When my cousins accepted my clothes knowing that they had been mine, it was a direct acknowledgment of the fact that I was the one in the family with more, the only one with clothes made abroad that could last up to a decade. My mother always disregarded my complaints, though, and for the first time I began to see why. Looking at Youssef, it dawned on me that the convenience of being gifted a durable sweatshirt was worth more than the slight discomfort it caused me.

"Amir and Sheero and Tamer used to hang out in the street like us keda all the time," Enas told the rest of them. "Right, Sheero?"

I rubbed his hair. "That's right. But we weren't as cool as you guys."

They laughed.

Youssef poked my hip. "Did you come from America?"

"I did."

"Where's my brother?" he asked.

If I looked at Youssef and really thought of the question, I might have sobbed, so I quickly looked at Enas. "Is my mother at Gedo's or upstairs?"

"Why didn't he bring my brother with him?" Youssef asked Mohamed.

"You don't even remember your brother," Mohamed replied.

"She's at Teta's," Enas told me.

I was surprised to hear someone refer to the apartment as Teta's and realized Enas probably didn't remember Gedo.

Eight months after Amir left for Illinois, my grandfather went to Denshawai to look at some land he still owned. His first night there, he either slipped or fainted in his cousin's bathroom and hit the back of his head right on the edge of the sink, which killed him within minutes. It was then, at seventeen years of age, that I first witnessed just how much of a mark a single person can leave on others. Not only did my mother, five aunts, and grandmother mourn his passing as if it marked the end of the universe, but the funeral in Denshawai (which Amir didn't come back for, since he had overstayed his U.S. visa) was shockingly crowded. Hundreds of men showed up: Gedo's numerous cousins, nephews, childhood friends, as well as peasants, carpenters, contractors, and drivers he had worked with over the decades, a lot of whom felt the need to tell Tamer and I—the oldest two grandsons present—just how much admiration they had for our Gedo. One man in particular, who worked on the same cotton farm as Gedo when they were both children, told me that Gedo had paid for the hormone therapy that had, after five desolate years, finally blessed the man and his wife with a son. And then the son himself gave me his condolences, and then the son's son, who appeared my age, shook my hand and went for a kiss on each cheek, after which I woefully contemplated the oils he had just transferred from his face to mine—a concern that I realized, without a doubt, made me a disgrace to my entire lineage.

It was also then, on my first trip to Denshawai, that I realized my mother's family was actually quite fortunate relative to many Egyptians, not only the beggars on Cairo's streets and the drivers, maids, guards, and waiters who served my friends and me across the city, but also the millions of low-wage workers scattered across the Nile Valley.

I walked into the building's ground-floor entrance, where Amir and I had once made stray cats fight over a can of tuna. Chocolate wrappers, juice boxes, and empty plastic bottles were scattered on all corners of the entrance, and the floor's white ceramic was smeared with enough dirt to become slightly sticky. On the first floor, I stood outside Teta's apartment and heard her arguing with Ma and Khalto Nahla.

"Stop treating me like a child!" Teta yelled. "I want to speak with her."

"She's asleep, Ma. Why should I wake her up?"

I rang the doorbell.

"Is that her?" Teta asked.

"Who is it?" my mother asked as she approached the door.

"It's me, Ma."

She opened the door, nodded in silence, then looked above her, to tell me that I should go straight upstairs.

"Is that Sherif?" Teta asked from inside her living room, though I wasn't within her peripheral.

I slowly retreated as silently as I could.

"It's Sherif," Teta said. "I heard him!"

Ma bulged. It was too late to pretend. "Come in, habiby," she said.

I stepped into the apartment and then she hugged me.

"She still doesn't know," she whispered to me about Teta.

I left my suitcase beside the door and walked down the hallway that led into the living room.

"Teta!" I said with performed animation. "I've missed you."

"Sherif?" she asked, as she sat on her designated chair and eyed me with suspicion.

I shook her hand, knelt down, and kissed her twice on each cheek, trying to hide from her gaze for as long as possible.

"What brings you here?" she asked as I stood straight again.

"I'm surprising you," I said as I turned to Khalto Nahla, who, as if on cue, smiled to appear surprised.

"No," Teta said. "Something is wrong. What's going on? I knew it."

I sat down beside Teta and took her hand in mine. "How are you?" I asked her. "I've missed you."

She took her hand away. "Tell me what's wrong," she said.

"Nothing is wrong, Teta."

"Is it Amir? Has something happened to him?"

Her precise guess surprised me. I looked at Ma, who discreetly shook her head.

"He hasn't called in months," Teta said. "A year, even."

Behind her, a display of wedding photographs hung on the wall. One was of Khalto Nahla's wedding photograph from 1995, wherein Amir and I walked in front of the bride and groom and threw flower petals over our shoulders.

"Amir is fine," Khalto Nahla said.

"So then call his mother!" Teta yelled. "Tell her I want to see her now!"

The doorbell rang; we could hear the four boys outside.

"Enas, go upstairs!" Ma yelled.

"We just want some water!" he replied.

"Upstairs!" she yelled back.

"Why?" he asked.

She cursed under her breath as she walked toward the door.

Teta took the opportunity to catch my eyes.

"Tell me the truth, son," she said under her breath.

I felt I was at risk of breaking down, so I stood up and announced that I needed to go to the bathroom, then walked into the hallway that led away from the living room.

"The boy's lips are quivering!" Teta yelled.

"Mama, *please* calm down," Khalto Nahla said. "Your heart won't take all this yelling!"

"Why are you crying, Sherif?" Teta asked as I walked into a bedroom.

Because Amir is dead, I wanted to say. Because I abandoned him. Because when I come here, I'm reminded of how much I love you all, but in New York I'm able to forget you quickly. Because I don't know if this family will ever recover from this; because I fear I will abandon you too.

I sat on the bed and tried to think of a way of telling Teta the truth.

Ma entered the bedroom and sat beside me.

"Are you all right?" she asked as she took my hand in hers.

I nodded.

"Yes?"

I nodded some more and bit down on my tongue. *Be a man,* I thought. *They're going to need a man.*

"So, what happened?" she asked.

On our phone call the day prior, I told Ma that I had been arrested but that I would give her details when I arrived in Cairo. There was no way for me to be sure that my calls wouldn't be listened to.

As was customary in our family, I told her a fictionalized version of the truth. They had arrested me but without handcuffs. They took me out the building's back door, not the main entrance, and none of my neighbors had seen me being arrested. In the car, they made sure to inform me that I was only being brought in for questioning and was in no trouble of my own. They were quite cordial and sympathetic. All in all, the experience was only distressing once I was informed of what Amir had done.

She sighed. "Did they have to kill him?"

"He had a gun."

"Your grandma will want to bury him."

"I don't think that's possible, Ma."

She shook her head and looked at the ceiling. "Why?"

The last time I had seen her speak to God like that was after my father's death.

"I don't know what to do about your grandmother," she said.

"We'll figure it out."

"Your aunt's a mess."

"It'll be okay."

"And the kids," she said. "How are we supposed to tell the kids?"

"Ma," I said as I rubbed her back. "We'll do this together. You don't have to take full responsibility with this."

"So who will?" she asked.

I had no answer. Indeed, Ma and Gedo had always been the designated heads of the family. The ones who could think critically and make informed and logical decisions for the rest of us. It was Ma who had succeeded in selling Gedo's land in Denshawai without being deceived into unnecessary losses.

"I'll be here," I said. "I'll stay for a month if I have to."

She shook her head. "You have school."

"I can still drop my courses."

"Some men came to take Ashraf this morning. I'm worried about him."

"Why?" I asked.

"We should go back outside."

"He'll be fine. He hasn't done anything."

She sighed. "Do you remember Ibrahim Refaat? That kid Amir used to hang out with? From the building around the corner."

I didn't. "Sure."

"His father paid a visit to your aunt and uncle two weeks ago. Showed them a bunch of messages Amir had sent their boy. Israel this, America that. Videos of wars and God this, God that. The boy was losing his mind. We tried every way to reach him, but we couldn't track him down."

"What?" I said.

She nodded.

"Why didn't you tell me, Ma?"

She shrugged.

9

Sometimes, when Abu Ahmed was in a charming mood, he would tell Omar and his siblings some part or another of the story of how he had come to marry Salma. Whenever he missed a detail, Salma would interject, and Mustafa, being as curious as he was, always asked the right questions, which meant that, over the years, the three children had become well informed on their parents' story.

Salma moved to Cairo from the countryside in 1986, after her aunt and mother died of hepatitis C within one year, and her father became convinced that someone from their village had cursed them with the evil eye. After months of settling into the eshash of Ramlet Bulaq, the only neighborhood in Cairo they could afford, her father's second cousin Fathy, who worked as a bawab in a Zamalek building, recruited Salma as a potential housemaid for a wealthy couple who had just married and moved into the penthouse. Salma went to Zamalek, met with Alia Abaza, and with God's blessing was hired to work the next week. She was seventeen.

Abu Ahmed was beginning to develop his business, which Omar had recently come to suspect, through Mustafa's observations, might revolve around hashish.

A few months ago, Omar had asked Abu Ahmed, as they returned from Friday prayer, if hashish was haram, and Abu Ahmed told him that it was not. Nevertheless, it was embarrassing for Omar to consider that his father could be smuggling drugs. In the streets, to call someone a drug dealer was to insult him, to call him a thug, and Omar still hoped there was a chance Mustafa had been entirely mistaken.

In any case, while Salma learned how to serve as a maid, Abu Ahmed was generating decent money and looking for a wife to start a family with. His only problem was that everyone in Ramlet Bulaq knew his story: he had grown up in an orphanage and was a homeless teenager for some time before saving enough money to rent a hut in the eshash. Unfortunately, most men married their daughters if not to a nephew or nephew-in-law, then to someone from a verifiable lineage.

Still, when Abu Ahmed came across Salma entering the eshash one summer evening, he swore that no other man from their deranged neighborhood would have her as his wife. He began waiting for her arrival at the entrance of the eshash every night and prepared what Salma once told the children was *street poetry*.

"Watching you walk into this slum is like watching honey being poured into the sewers," Abu Ahmed would say. "I swear on the father and mother I never met that you're the most beautiful woman to have ever graced this damn neighborhood."

Hearing it years later, Omar became hysterical. He could never imagine his father uttering such words, but apparently Abu Ahmed recited them for Salma every day, despite the fact that, for a whole month, she didn't respond with a word; she just walked past him as if no one had approached her. When Abu Ahmed realized the flattery wasn't working, he began to beg Salma, every evening, for a chance to buy her a bag of termes, fresh roasted lupini beans, on the corniche. "One bag," Abu Ahmed said. "We'll have it and part ways. And if you never want to see my ugly face again, you never will."

Eventually Salma accepted the persistent invitation. After all, she loved the salty termes, and if there was a chance she could stop Abu Ahmed from approaching her every day, she would pursue it. It had been about a month and a half of the ritual, and it was becoming so ridiculous that the people residing close to the entrance of the eshash looked forward to witnessing Abu Ahmed's daily rejection.

To Salma's surprise, Abu Ahmed was a fool but not the one she had imagined. He had a wild sense of humor (which Omar felt he had inherited) and managed to entertain her for two whole hours. As they ate termes on the corniche, he pointed at the passengers on the feluccas and speedboats that cruised along the Nile and constructed comic but also entirely plausible narratives for their whole lives. He made her laugh to the point of pain, and she agreed to meet him again the next day.

He paid her father a visit the week after that and surprised them both by announcing that he was renting two apartments in the masaken, one for himself and another for his prospective father-in-law. And that he would like to ask for Salma's hand. The masaken meant dignity; it meant toilets and sinks and running water and proper cement walls and enough space to have a closet and an oven. It meant less cock-roaches on your bed and no rain dripping through the cracks in your ceiling. Her father accepted, held Abu Ahmed's hand, and read the opening chapter of the Quran. A humble wedding was organized for the following month.

If Abu Ahmed was a drug dealer, Omar had no idea whether Salma or her father had been aware of it. What he did know was that, today, Salma often mumbled about the regret she often felt for having married him.

A little before midnight, Salma was lying stomach-down with her face pressed into a pillow, keeping silent despite Mustafa's requests for assurance that she was fine. Zeina lay on the bed beside them, still crying over the fight she had caused.

Omar was in his designated sleeping place on the carpeted floor, trying to get warm under a blanket and fall sleep, so the night could finally end. He despised his father's senseless rage, especially because he sometimes saw it reflected in himself too. Just yesterday, one of his friends insisted on taking a penalty during a crucial game and then missed it, and Omar became so frustrated that he kicked the boy's legs out from underneath him. When the boy fell on his back and began to cry, Omar felt a brief urge to apologize, but then became so infuriated with the boy's hysteria that he considered kicking him again. Nothing repulsed him as much as weakness and self-pitying. He cowered at the thought of being the type to sob with such ease, and many of his fights with Mustafa were concerned with exactly that.

Right now, for example, Mustafa was entering his third hour of crying.

"Mama, maybe you need to go to the clinic," Mustafa said. "Cuts can get infected. Please answer, Mama."

Omar stood up and walked to the light switch beside the front door. "Enough," he said as he turned the light off. "She's fine. Let her sleep."

"No, she's not fine," Mustafa said.

Zeina sniffed, as she had done every few minutes since the beating. "Mama, are you angry with me?" she asked for what felt like the hundredth time.

Omar had to refrain from telling her to shut her mouth at last, to grow up, and to realize that nothing would have happened if it hadn't been for her nonsense. He didn't know what had been said between the visitor and Abu Ahmed, but he could discern that the man had offered Abu Ahmed money. And though Omar resented his father and would have protected Salma and hit him back if he was strong enough, he understood why Abu Ahmed had lost his temper. A man doesn't simply visit another man and offer to buy his daughter's services. Zeina was ignorant of that, of course, since her mind had always been littered with romantic fairy tales.

"Just go to sleep," Salma said. "All of you."

Omar lay down again. "I'm about to," he said. It was so cold he had to wrap himself with two blankets despite the thermal underwear. "It's freezing."

They heard the door to Abu Ahmed's office being opened. Omar sat up and saw light leaking into their apartment from the office across the hall.

Abu Ahmed approached their door and opened it. The whole family made no sound or movement, hoping Abu Ahmed would think they were asleep and leave.

"Are you awake?" he asked with a calm tone.

Perhaps what was most disturbing about Abu Ahmed's episodes was that, after enough time passed, he always tried to pretend as if nothing had occurred; he would yell at Salma, insult and degrade her, and then come back with a joke or compliment, which she was somehow supposed to embrace.

"We're sleeping," Omar said.

Abu Ahmed turned the light on. "What's all the drama? Khalas, I got a little angry. It's normal."

"She was bleeding," Zeina said, before sniffing again. "That's not normal."

Abu Ahmed took a few steps toward their sleeping corner. "Bleeding where?"

Omar removed the blankets from on top of him. "Baba, let us sleep."

Abu Ahmed ignored him and walked up to the bed. Omar stood up and Abu Ahmed smirked at him. "Come on," he told Omar. "Tell them they're overreacting."

Omar couldn't stand looking at him. Abu Ahmed was powerless against his demons and it was distressing to witness. Omar placed his hand on the man's big stomach. "Leave it for tomorrow. We have school."

Abu Ahmed looked at Salma. "And what if I was one of those husbands that *really* hit their wives? *Ha?* That punch them and break things on their heads?"

Zeina began crying again.

"Why can't you not hit her at all?" Mustafa asked.

"Sometimes I get angry," Abu Ahmed said, as if it were a fair answer. "It happens. You don't need to make a soap opera out of it."

Zeina turned to her side so she could face away from him. Mustafa copied her, as he so often did. Omar knew their reasons but wanted them to show the man some mercy. Abu Ahmed obviously regretted it.

"Salma," Abu Ahmed said as he touched Salma's back. "Answer me."

Salma lifted her head from the pillow, just enough to be able to speak. "If you have any respect for my father's soul, you'll get your hands away from me."

Abu Ahmed snickered and walked away, as if Salma were being melodramatic, and perhaps he actually believed she was. He had always had his own outrageous beliefs. In his eyes, the food and shelter he provided for Omar, his siblings, and Salma were a blessing they should be eternally grateful for, one that justified, or at least made up for, his frequent mistreatment of them. *I never even had the blanket you sleep under* was something he often reminded them of. *I found my meals in the trash.* And though Omar didn't see it as enough to forgive the man's behavior, he did believe that his father, underneath all the complications, had a kind heart.

Omar turned and faced the bed. "Mama, khalas, forgive him," he said. "You know he doesn't mean to—"

Zeina turned around. "How are you defending him?" she yelled.

Omar slapped her hand away from him, harder than he had meant to. "Shut up," he said. "None of this would've happened if it weren't for you."

Mustafa turned around. "Stop."

"It's true," Omar said. Just in the past week, Zeina had caused three instances of conflict between their parents. An argument because Zeina wanted to spend New Year's Eve in Ramlet Bulaq, but Abu Ahmed wouldn't be around to keep an eye on her. An argument because Zeina urged Salma to tell Abu Ahmed about their visitor. A fight because of the visit and Zeina's delusional wishes. If Zeina needed to be made aware of all the havoc she was causing, Omar was glad to do it.

"Mama," Zeina said. "Tell him that's not true."

Salma didn't respond and Zeina began crying again.

Mustafa sat up. "You have no heart," he said to Omar while rubbing Zeina's back.

"Fuck you," Omar said. "You're always defending her."

"Mama," Zeina said, before she began weeping. "I hate this, Mama."

Omar began to feel bad but didn't apologize. "Stop fucking crying," he said. "You're acting like she's dead or something."

"Please just sleep," Salma mumbled into the pillow.

"Don't mind him," Mustafa said as he hugged Zeina.

Zeina peeled Mustafa's arms off her and ran out of the apartment, barefoot despite the cold. The roof was her designated crying spot; she would return in thirty minutes.

"You're horrible," Mustafa told Omar.

Mustafa always took Zeina's side, as if he were her twin and not Omar's.

Salma turned to face them, and Omar was shocked. The previously pink spots on her face were turning purple and there was a lump on her hairline, where she had bled. "Enough now," she said. "I want to sleep. Where'd she go?"

"The roof," Mustafa said.

Salma sat up. "How could you say that to her?" she asked Omar.

They were right. To blame Zeina for the bruises on their mother's face was far too malevolent. Perhaps Omar would apologize when she returned, though she would probably forget it all by tomorrow morning.

"Sorry," Omar said.

"Go get her," Salma told Mustafa.

Mustafa left the apartment to climb the ladder that led to the roof.

Salma reached for Omar's hand. "Come," she said.

Omar sat beside her.

She ran her fingers through his hair and kissed his forehead.

"It's no one's fault but his," she said. "All right?"

"He feels bad, Mama."

"And what do you think I feel?" she asked with a high-pitched voice trying to maintain composure.

Omar was on the verge of tears when Mustafa barged into the apartment.

"Mama!" Mustafa yelled, breathing frantically.

Salma stood up as quickly as possible.

"She's not up there," Mustafa said. "She went downstairs. I saw her running down the road."

Salma slapped both sides of her face. "That fucking bitch," she said, before searching for a veil and a jacket to put on. "Have I not had enough?"

Omar ran out the door. Salma yelled and told him to wait. It was almost an hour past midnight, the streets were empty and dark with everyone asleep, and that's when the monsters came out. Omar was so irritated he knew he would slap Zeina the moment he placed his hands on her. How selfish could she be? The night had already been difficult enough for the whole family.

When Abu Ahmed heard their frenzy and came out of his office, Salma spoke to him as if they were on good terms, which surprised Omar. Perhaps Zeina's little stunt would succeed in reconciling them, Omar thought, and the worst of the despair was behind them.

Part
Two

1

CHICAGO—Avel Flight School sits right outside Chicago's DuPage Airport. As a SEVIS-certified institution, more than half of the fifty-plus students who enroll in the school every year come from abroad, most commonly from India, Pakistan, and Sri Lanka.

In January 2005, the admission committee was impressed with a particular applicant from Egypt, Amir Ashraf El Kafrawy, whose level of English proficiency was a cause for concern but whose personal statement drew the attention of a number of committee members.

To Avel Flight School,

There are a few reasons that I dream of commerical pilot's license. In this letter, I want to organize them in the order of time.

The first reason I become interested in flying was pigeons. From a very young age, my grandfather and I feed and looked after the pigeons that he raised on the roof of our building. He taught me everything he knew about them. How long their eggs take to hatch. How long they take to learn how to fly. One of my best memories is watching baby pigeons jump from one side of our roof to the other side of the roof only a few weeks after they born.

One day, my grandfather told me that pigeons were used to send messages across towns in Egypt and Jordan hundreds of years ago. I didn't believe him. He told me wait one month and he would show me. A month passed. We went up to our roof and he had binoculars. He put one of the oldest pigeons we had, Gerges, into a cage. He gave me the binoculars and pointed me to a building on the other side of our neighborhood. He said he would now take Gerges to that building and tell it to go find Amir. I laughed. When I realized he wasn't joking, I almost cried. I thought my grandfather was going crazy. I was seven years old.

He left me and I wait. I was surprised, half hour later, as I look at the building with the binoculars, because he was walking on the roof carrying Gerges. He took Gerges and threw her into the air. I couldn't follow her with the binoculars. She was moving very fast. A few seconds later I saw her. She was like small dot but she got closer and closer until I was sure it was Gerges. I jumped and laughed and screamed until Gerges's babies around me became afraid. When she arrive on our roof, I found a piece of paper tied to her leg. It was my grandfather had written something. "Only idiots don't believe their grandfathers."

For some time I thought my grandfather was a magic man, until he told me that a pigeon can only fly back to its home. He never told Gerges to find me. He had trained Gerges to fly to our roof from shorter distances. It didn't matter. I still felt wow about Gerges and all birds. They have wings and can roam through the sky, which make birds God's greatest creatures.

Later that year, my grandfather and I went to Cairo Airport to get my aunt and cousin as they arrive from America. I remember hiding under my grandfather's arm as a humongous ship flew over our heads, so big and loud I thought it was only a meter away. When I asked my grandfather how many people were driving it, I couldn't believe when he said only one pilot and his assistant. I said there is no way that is true. It must be at least ten, I said. He said only idiots don't believe their grandfathers. He said that for long time.

Achieving flight is one of mankind greatest accomplishment. All my life, my dream has been between being a commercial pilot and a pilot for the Egyptian air force. I have chosen commercial because Egypt is not at war and the pilots in the air force don't fly a lot. I would like to spend the rest of my life flying to different corner of the world all the time. The opportunity to see whole world and live in the sky would be greatest gift I could dream of.

God bless you, and thank you for your valuable time.

Eight months later, Amir landed in Chicago with a student visa and made his way to the school, where he formally met Scott Maher, the director of the school at the time.

Maher's first impression was that Amir was quite timid. "I had interviewed him over the phone and we spoke extensively, but when I first met him in person he barely said a word."

After being shown around the school's premises, Amir was taken to his residence down the street, which he would be sharing with another newly admitted student, Prathit Kedia.

Within days, Prathit's relationship with Amir took a turn for the worse. Prathit took issue with Amir's cleanliness levels, with many arguments revolving around the state of their bathroom or kitchen. Likewise, Amir was continually irritated by their fellow classmates— all of whom were also Indian—who came to their home on a regular basis.

"We asked if we could switch into other residences, but there were no options available," Prathit told me. "So we were stuck together."

Currently a cocaptain for Air India, Prathit was boarding a flight at Jakarta International Airport when he discovered that the man behind the New York subway shooting was his former roommate. "I kept reading the name over and over again, and I thought maybe it's someone else. When I saw his photograph, it really broke my heart."

During his time at Avel, El Kafrawy said and did nothing to indicate that he had a radical worldview and showed no particular interest in either politics or religion.

Why, then, was El Kafrawy expelled from Avel three months after enrollment?

Before the facility pays for students to take the official FAA written examination, which grants them official approval to begin flight training, the students must pass three consecutive practice tests with a minimum 90 percent score.

In early December, most of the students who joined the school at the same time as El Kafrawy had already passed the official exam and begun flight training. Amir, on the other hand, was stuck on the practice tests, failing to score more than 90 percent on more than one in a row.

During a meeting with Maher, Amir requested that he exempt him from the prerequisite and allow him to take the official FAA exam, which he was confident he would pass. When his request was refused, he asked Maher how much money he wanted for the exemption, despite being behind on his tuition.

"I'd never experienced anything like it," Maher told me. "It took me a moment to realize... this kid just offered to bribe me. I thought, *Is he out of his mind?*"

The final violation came the next day, when Amir was caught by a supervisor trying to use prewritten notes to cheat on his practice exam. When the supervisor asked him to hand over the notes, he refused, and when she reached for the practice exam on his desk to declare it void, he grabbed her arm with force and shoved her away.

Amir was expelled from the facility minutes later and given twenty-four hours to evacuate the apartment he had been set up in.

PEORIA—Saleh Hesham is a second-generation Egyptian American who grew up in Peoria, Illinois. Every summer, his family would go to Cairo and spend at least a couple of months living with Saleh's grandmother in the neighborhood of El Haram.

On the street below his grandmother's apartment, Saleh would spend hours every day hanging out with other boys from the neighborhood, one of whom was Amir. Over the years, the pair became friends, and when Saleh learned during the summer of 2005 that Amir was going to move to Chicago for flight school, he gave Amir his American number and invited him to come down to Peoria for a weekend.

Shortly after his expulsion from Avel, Amir arrived in Peoria the day before Christmas, looking to find work somewhere in the central Illinois city, where one in every ten people are Muslim. He told Saleh that his family had failed to come up with all his tuition, and so he had given up on the prospect of finishing flight school. Instead, he wanted to find a cash job and save money for a few years, before returning to Egypt.

Back in Cairo, Amir's family protested the idea, urging him to return to Cairo and go to college. But Amir's mind had been made. "It's a common dream here," Tamer Younes, one of Amir's cousins with whom he had grown up in close proximity, told me. "Go abroad, make dollars, and return to Egypt with enough money to live for years. Amir became convinced that he could return with enough to start his own business."

Within days, Amir was set up in low-income housing in the northern borough of the city, where he began work as a clerk at El Badrawy's Deli and Supermarket, which was run by Saleh's uncle-in-law. Regular customers at El Badrawy's described him as a reserved cashier who checked them out with no problems or memorable interactions.

Amir became acquainted with thirty-eight-year-old Cecilia Ruiz, who lived down the hall from him. The pair worked similar hours and found comfort hanging out each night. "He was a nice dude," Cecilia told me. "His English wasn't that good, but he was always telling stories. Egypt this, Egypt that. He was a good listener too."

On May 3, 2007, Amir and Cecilia were walking down East McClure Avenue when a police officer, Robert Landlorf, stopped them curbside under what his commisioner stated last week was "reasonable suspicion that they were in possession of controlled substances." Footage of what followed was recently released by the Peoria Police Department.

Officer Landlorf parks his car as Amir and Cecilia walk down the sidewalk, their backs turned to him. He sounds his siren, so they stop and face him as he exits his vehicle. "How you guys doing?" he asks, and Cecilia responds with "We're all right."

Amir steps onto the street and Officer Landlorf asks him to step back onto the sidewalk. He asks them for identification, which Cecilia immediately provides.

Amir had never come in contact with U.S. police. "Is there problem?" he asks the officer as Cecilia hands over her ID.

"Let me see some identification."

"I left at home," Amir says.

"Sorry?" the officer asks.

"He left it at home, he's saying," Cecilia says. "His English isn't all that good."

"Right. What's your name?"

"Amir."

"You an American?"

Amir shakes his head.

"Where you from, then?"

"Egypt."

"Egypt?"

"Yes."

"That's a long way from here."

"We were just walking home from the zoo," Cecilia says. "We both live down on North Sheridan."

The officer inspects Cecilia's ID before he hands it back to her. "So here's the deal. I thought I smelled something when I passed you guys down there on Wisconsin. So what I'm going to do is pat you guys down and find out if you're carrying something you're not supposed to be carrying. All right? You got nothing, you'll be on your way in a minute."

"I mean, we weren't doing anything," Cecilia says.

"I'm going to have to search you," the officer repeats.

"Okay," Cecilia says.

The officer steps behind them. "Now, I'm going to ask you to walk on over there to my vehicle."

Cecilia begins walking, but Amir doesn't move. "Sorry," Amir says. "What is the problem? I don't understand."

"Just be cool," Cecilia says. "It's fine."

"But what did we do?" Amir asks with an irritated tone.

"I just explained everything," the officer says. "Now walk."

Amir takes two steps, then stops and quickly turns toward the officer, who reacts by drawing his pistol. "What the fuck are you doing? Put your hands up."

"Sorry," Amir says, his hands raised up. "What I do?"

The officer instructs Amir to put his hands on his head, get on his knees, and lie on his stomach, all of which Amir does promptly. The officer dispatches for help, points his weapon at Cecilia, and instructs her to walk over to Amir and do the same. Though they're too low on the ground to be captured by the dash cam, we can see the officer approach them as he holsters his gun and handcuffs them. "You had to make me do this the hard way," he says.

Backup arrives and a search uncovers seven grams of marijuana hidden in Amir's crotch, which explains his nervousness moments prior. He's arrested and placed in a police car while Cecilia is released.

At Peoria's Third Precinct, Amir is charged with possession of a Schedule I Controlled Substance, a crime for which he can be sentenced to one year in prison and/or a maximum $5,000 fine. He is jailed for nine hours before a judge declares him a flight risk and sets bail at $4,000. Short of a few hundred dollars to post his own bail, Amir uses a bail bond agent for a $450 nonrefundable fee. Once home, he consults with a few criminal defense lawyers. He pays $1,200 up front to be represented by Allen Yates, who manages, through a plea deal, to guarantee no imprisonment if Amir pleads guilty and pays a $1800 fine for his crime. Amir makes the deal and walks away a free man. Almost all the money he had spent more than a year saving, $3,450 of it, is gone within two weeks of his arrest.

"We would've been fine if he had just played it cool," Cecilia told me. "If it had been a regular pat down, they probably wouldn't have found it. It really depressed him."

After the arrest, Saleh's uncle-in-law began to notice a shift in Amir's demeanor. "He began to ignore tasks. Gave customers attitude. I had to warn him several times."

Amir stopped spending as much time with Cecilia, though he continued to buy marijuana from their dealer, and spent most of his time alone. Alaa Monir, who shared Amir's night shift at the deli, claimed that it was in the summer of 2007 that Amir began to garner an interest in politics. "He began talking about Bush and Guantánamo and Reaper drones. He spent a lot of time on his phone reading about it."

In early October, Amir quit his job at the deli and didn't bother collecting his paycheck for the last two weeks. On October 31, he landed in New York and spent a night with another cousin, Sherif El Sherbiny, then a sophomore at NYU. The two had also grown up in close proximity but had drifted apart over the years. "I noticed right away that he had changed," Sherif told me. "We grew up somewhat religious, but he had become far more conservative than anyone in our family. He talked about the devil's lure and the flames of Hell and it was all a little weird. But I couldn't have imagined that he had actually become a violent person. There was no indication of that at all."

The next morning, Amir made his way to Paterson, New Jersey, where he joined Ramzi Abouzeid in an apartment on 34 Palisade Avenue.

An American citizen, Ramzi Abouzeid was born in 1978 and raised in Jamaica, Queens. In 1995, he moved to Beirut to study engineering at the American University. He dropped out two years later and cut contact with his family. A video recorded in 1999, recently published by the *Sunday Times*, identifies a young Abouzeid standing behind Alaa Seif-Eddine during a martyrdom message. Abouzeid reentered the

United States on September 17, 2007, after more than a decade away. It's still unknown how Abouzeid and Amir came into contact, but it's likely to have occured online. The pair moved into a two-bedroom apartment and paid the landlord a whole year of rent in cash. During the twenty-five months between Abouzeid's arrival in the United States and the attack, a sum total of $276,700 was laundered through a jewelry store he opened in Fairview, New Jersey, with sources traced to Yemen and Pakistan.

Amir's only contact with his family was with his parents, and he never informed them of his permanent move to the East Coast. In an interview broadcast on Egyptian television, his father expressed regret for having sent his son to America. "I'm sorry for failing Egypt and the world," he said as he addressed viewers. "But it's difficult for a parent to suspect his own child of such horrible things. On the phone, my son sounded happy."

Perhaps this perceived happiness can be explained by Amir's heightened sense of significance, which is reflected on the note that was found in the Paterson apartment.

> *In the name of God, Most Merciful, Most Compassionate.*
> *My name is Amir Ashraf El Kafrawy. I am a soldier of*
> *God. With His guidance, this morning of October 8th, I*
> *will make the world a purer place.*

Investigators continue to uncover details regarding the internationally coordinated plot. The search for Ramzi Abouzeid, who fled to Islamabad three nights before the attack, will probably go on for years. Whether such an attack is preventable, and how so, is the question that encompasses the focus of scholars, academics, imams, and law enforcement officials worldwide. It is an infinitely complicated problem. What confused me most about Amir El Kafrawy's journey, however, were the moments before he entered Chambers Street Station, which were recorded by security cameras.

It's 8:16 A.M. A Friday morning. Amir walks down West Broadway wearing a thick winter coat and a brown backpack, both of which he's using to conceal and carry thirty-five pounds of explosives. Two blocks from Chambers Street Station, he enters a 7-Eleven and purchases a bag of dried peas. Down the block, he opens the bag and begins to toss peas onto the sidewalk for a pair of nearby pigeons. He gets down on his knees and watches as more pigeons gather. Dozens of pedestrians pass him, a few glancing over and appreciating the sight of a young man feeding pigeons so early in the morning. Once the peas are finished, the pigeons slowly begin to leave and Amir gets back onto his feet. He approaches Chambers Street Station, swipes his MetroCard with the confidence of a native New Yorker, and boards the southbound 1 train.

All the acquaintances, former friends, and family members I interviewed were quick to mention Amir's lifelong obsession with birds and pigeons, which seemed to have survived his radicalization. I've watched the footage many times, Amir extending his hand toward the desperate beaks before him, moments before committing mass murder, and it continues to shock me. How can a young man have compassion for a flock of hungry birds, but none for several hundred humans?

2

On January 10, 2006, Omar woke up earlier than usual, only an hour past noon. Mustafa was still in school and Salma had yet to return from work, which meant Omar was free to begin the day with his favorite ritual. Sitting on his bed, he extracted one of the dark brown soba'as—hashish fingers—in his cigarette pack. He tore off a piece, used a lighter to melt it onto some tobacco, rolled the blend up, and took that long drag that welcomed him to the new day. After smoking the whole joint, he put some water in the kettle and then masturbated over the sink in his bathroom with the help of a video he had saved on his new Siemens phone. Then he sat on his bed, opened the window beside him, and sipped on his tea as he watched the road below, where leaves and plastic bags were being carried along by strong winds. He would sit there and get high for hours on end, if he could, but there was work to do and money to be made. Omar was almost sixteen years old now, a man entirely responsible for himself, so he changed into his black jeans and left the apartment.

Omar worked right outside the western border of the eshash, on a dusty narrow road commonly referred to as the Road of Blessings, where hundreds of civilians drove by every day in search of the hashish that he and his dealer friends sold.

There was a sophisticated system of operation for the always-booming business at the Road. Throughout the day, every customer was tended to by whoever's turn it was to sell. By midnight, each of the dealers had sold more than fifteen soba'as, generating around a hundred pounds of income after dues were paid to superiors—more than the average civilian in Ramlet Bulaq made after a week of modest halal work.

Quitting school and working at the Road instead was, by far, the best decision Omar had ever made. He had been selling for just over a year and had already saved eleven thousand pounds. In three or four years, he would have six figures accumulated, which would be enough to leave the business and start a proper, legal one to sustain him for the rest of his life.

It had been a few years now since Omar had begun to understand the intricacies of Cairo's social dynamics. It was simple. In Cairo, there were two types of people: the bashas and the ghalaba. The bashas lived in luxury; they ate meat every day, learned languages, traveled the world, swam in private beaches, and shopped in towers like the ones outside Ramlet Bulaq. Meanwhile, the ghalaba served the bashas; they cooked their food, cleaned their toilets, guarded their properties, and drove them around. And despite the possibility of becoming an improved ghalban, like, for example, a restaurant manager instead of a waiter, a ghalban rarely ever became a basha. Indeed, his circumstances saw that he would always speak and act like a ghalban, an inferior to the basha, because he had been raised and educated by fellow ghalaba. The rich got richer, the poor survived, and Mubarak's government did little to equal the playing field.

If Omar had remained in school, he would have eventually worked as some front desk operator or shop attendant, making just enough money to pay rent and get married, so he could conceive a few more ghalaba for Cairo to abuse. But he had quit school two years ago and was following a plan that would absolve him from the fate of the cursed masses. After saving enough money working at the Road, he would be able to start his own business. What sort? He didn't know. Dozens of ideas inhabited his mind at all times. Perhaps he would sell satellite dishes or trade motorcycles or give driving lessons; it would depend on what people needed most when the time came. He would work every hour he was awake, save as much money as possible, and spend it all on expanding his business. He would never call another man "basha."

When he arrived at the Road, Omar was surprised to find that the entire labor force was already there, all nine dealers, among whom he was the youngest, sitting in the circle of plastic chairs that they chained to a light post every night. He greeted them and sat down as Belya attempted a magic trick with a deck of cards.

Belya was Omar's best friend. He had introduced Omar to the benefits of dealing and taught him everything from rolling joints and counting money to soba'a storage and customer manipulation. He had also been the one to acquaint Omar with Abu Ahmed's history as a drug lord.

Your father was what we call a ghost, he told Omar almost two years ago, as they sat under the Embaba Bridge and ate sunflower seeds. *The highest rank in the business. He smuggled drugs without touching them. A few of his men would go out into the desert on motorcycles to meet the Bedouins. And the Bedouins, they would come out of the desert at night, driving with their headlights off. People say the Bedouins can see as clearly in the darkness of the desert as you and I can see each other right now. Your father's men would meet them, exchange bags of money for bags of bricks. Powder, of course. Not hashish. And then the Bedouins would disappear into the desert. Then your father's men would bring the supplies back, sell them to the people like my brother, who gave it to dealers around town. Dealers with cars and everything. Heroin is where the real money is. By the time it reached places like Zamalek, it would be sold for ten times the amount your father bought it for. And he had an office, didn't he? I heard of his office many times.*

A customer arrived in a red Toyota and, as per the rules, Omar joined the rotation and sold him two soba'as. Most of the time the customers were young middle-class men looking for a soba'a or two at most. Occasionally, a wealthy man, driving a Mercedes or a BMW, would arrive and demand a whole brick, instantly ending the workday for some of the dealers. And then on rare and special occasions, a group of young women would drive by, and since the only ones courageous enough to drive into Ramlet Bulaq without a man were either belly dancers or prostitutes, Omar and the dealers got to enjoy a minute or two of red lips and improperly covered breasts.

Omar hated how powerless he was against his lust for women. Despite masturbating every morning, his sexual angst harassed him as persistently as Ramlet Bulaq's stubborn flies. Two months ago, he was introduced to a woman in the eshash who flawlessly sucked and swallowed for an affordable fifty pounds. Ever since then, he had gone to her every week, and she was hurting his savings so badly that he sometimes seriously considered reporting her to the police.

Back at the congregation of dealers, Belya failed to perform the magic trick again and again, so much so that the failure itself began to feel magical. The dealers laughed as he swore that, this next time, he would get it right. The sun was on the verge of setting on the other side of the Nile, and the wind was lifting enough dust off the ground to give an elephant a bad cough.

The dealer in turn, Menawy, tended to a Hyundai, and the customer rejected what he had to offer.

"I don't like it," the customer said. "Doesn't smell fresh."

"Oh, I have the freshest stuff you can find," Belya said as he approached the car.

"Oh no, but I have that *good* stuff," Awad said.

The conflict that was about to ensue outside the man's car had little to do with money. By refusing to buy Menawy's soba'a and deeming it subpar, the man provoked a contest and appointed himself as the judge of who really had the best hashish. The dealers belonged to different sects of Ramlet Bulaq's drug business, reported to different drug lords with different suppliers, and had their unique ways of presenting their product, sometimes wrapping it in foil, other times putting it in glass containers.

Omar personally found that customers enjoyed symmetry and malleability. Every night, he spent hours honing his soba'as, making sure every side was straight and every corner a right angle. Afterward, he laid them bare on a napkin as he took a hot shower, so they could soak in steam and become pungent and moist.

Omar was confident in the aesthetic of his hashish. He pushed his way to the customer's window and told him, calmly but with conviction, that this little soba'a that Omar was holding was the best anyone could find on this side of the Nile. "It'll help you love your wife better," Omar said. "A splendid soba'a for a splendid man indeed."

When the customer took it, bent it from each edge, and placed it under his nostrils, he was beginning to look like he had been convinced. He caressed it with his fingers and the other dealers slowly accepted defeat—all except Menawy.

"You just sold a turn ago," Menawy told Omar.

Omar put his hand on Menawy's shoulder. "The man has decided, my friend."

"Fuck you," Menawy said as he pushed Omar.

Omar looked at the ground and took a deep breath. He had been in enough fights over the years to know they weren't worth the stress. "All right," he said. "I'll forgive that one."

Menawy pushed him again. "Or what?"

The dealers got in between them. "Easy."

Omar chuckled. "Just tell him not to touch me again."

The customer took three bills out of his wallet. Just as Omar reached for them, Menawy snuck up behind him and grabbed the money out of the man's hand.

"What the fuck do you think you're doing?" Omar asked him.

The customer drove away.

Menawy took out his cigarette pack. "I'll give you a soba'a, but the money is mine."

Omar chuckled. "Are you fucking stupid?" he asked as he grabbed the collar of Menawy's shirt. "Give it!"

The dealers separated them.

"Khalas ya Omar," Belya said. "Relax."

Omar unshackled himself from their grip. "Tell him to hand it over!" he yelled. "Or I swear on my mother's life I'll kill him."

"Kill who?" Menawy responded. "You're a fucking kid!"

Menawy was three years older than Omar, taller and sturdier, but Omar wouldn't hesitate to fight him with a hand tied behind his back. Because where Omar excelled was in his carelessness; despite his young age, he genuinely felt he had nothing to lose.

He tried to run through the dealers and slap him.

Belya grabbed him. "Relax."

Omar ducked and pushed Belya away. "Tell him to hand it over, or I swear I'll—"

"What?" Menawy asked, as he pretended to struggle against the boys holding him away. "Tab kosomak a'ala kosokhtak! Fuck your mother and your sister!"

Everyone went silent and looked at Menawy.

"Idiot," Belya whispered.

Salma still spoke about Zeina quite regularly. She spoke about the girl's personality as if she were still around and prayed for her return as if it had been six days, not six years, since Zeina had vanished.

Nevertheless, Omar hated being reminded of his sister. He seldom allowed the images to resurface: Salma weeping so loud that the whole street gathered under their home. Salma smacking the cement walls until her hands bled. Salma stalking one of Abu Ahmed's cell phones, waiting for a call from Alia or Mazen, hoping that Zeina had somehow gone to them. Abu Ahmed almost killing Am Kahraba out of suspicion. Omar running around the masaken and the eshash, on the first and second and third and fourth day, burning with the hope that he would turn a corner, find Zeina, and make everything all right again. Omar knowing, despite Salma's denial, that it was all his fault. Mustafa making stray dogs smell Zeina's clothing, hoping they would lead him to her, while Salma went to the local police station every week to beg for a search team.

Everyone in Ramlet Bulaq knew of Omar's ongoing family tragedy. No information regarding Zeina, who Omar was certain had been kidnapped and murdered, had surfaced to this day. Salma still donated ten chickens a month to a local orphanage in Zeina's name, hoping to pay God for the girl's return. Mustafa had been permanently damaged; he had no friends, not a single one, and passed most of his time either studying or reading at home. Omar knew that people sometimes told his family's tragic story over biscuits and tea. None of his friends, however, had ever asked about Zeina. None had ever mentioned her in front of him until now. And though Omar suspected, by the shock on Menawy's face, that Menawy might have forgotten, Omar wasn't sure. And if there was a chance Menawy had been aware of just how much he could humiliate Omar with an insult directed toward Omar's sister, then Omar would have to make it the biggest mistake of Menawy's life.

Nothing could be done to stop Omar from extracting his matwa from his back pocket and trying to slice Menawy's neck open, like one does to a goat on the first dawn of Eid. He flipped it open behind his back with such speed that no one saw it, not even Menawy himself, then ran around the boys between them, leaped forward, swung the knife, and landed the blade right above Menawy's left eye.

Menawy screamed and grabbed his face. Three of the dealers tackled Omar to the ground. When Omar saw blood pouring through

Menawy's fingers, he yearned to cut him more and leave him blind and deformed for the rest of his life, so his family could know what it felt like to grieve for years.

"I'll kill him!" Omar yelled as he jerked his limbs, trying to break free. "I'll fucking kill him!"

But Menawy was gone within seconds. He was forced onto the back of Ronaldo's motorcycle, which took off down the road, as three dealers jumped onto Mido's and followed them.

"I'll fucking kill him!" Omar yelled. "Let me go!"

"Khalas ya Omar!" Belya and Awad yelled as they pinned Omar down on the ground, looking at him as if he were living his last moment in their grip.

Omar couldn't recall how long he was pinned against the concrete before he began to calm down. *I'll kill him,* he kept thinking, and then: *What in the world did you just do, you fool?* Blood had poured out of Menawy's left eye. Menawy worked for Abbasy, one of Ramlet Bulaq's oldest and most unforgiving drug lords. Whatever damage Omar had done Abbasy was likely to inflict on Omar. And the lord Omar worked for, Tito, would not only accept the verdict but maybe even encourage it, to teach Omar a lesson.

"Let me up," Omar said. "It's done."

"You're fucking insane," Belya said.

"Let me up!"

"You stabbed his eye," Awad said.

"I'm calm. Please. Let me up."

They slowly released their grip on Omar's limbs, both of them, and allowed Omar to stand up. He was light-headed, terrified by the thought that he might have jeopardized himself in irreversible ways. He walked over to the circle of plastic chairs and sat down. The sun had set and Riyad was tending to a customer.

"You stabbed his eye," Awad said again.

"I wish I had stabbed the other one," Omar responded.

Belya laughed.

"It's not funny," Eissa said. "This is why people go to Meet Okba. Someone was driving in and saw us. They turned around. And what's Abbasy going to do? He's not going to be happy about this. And what if—"

"Khalas!" Omar yelled, before feeling a jolt of pain in his lower lip. He touched his mouth and saw blood on his fingers.

"You're going to need stitches," Awad said.

"How did it happen?" Omar asked as he used his cell phone screen as a mirror.

"I don't know," Awad said.

Belya continued laughing and Omar joined him.

"I'm fucked, aren't I?" Omar asked.

"Of course," Belya said. "And then you say you're not like your father."

"Fuck off," Omar said.

Belya often said those words. He had also witnessed Abu Ahmed's arrest in the *eshash*, which happened on the fourth day of the search for Zeina.

Omar had accompanied Abu Ahmed and his men that first week, as they walked around Bulaq and Shobra and Embaba from morning to midnight, showing people a photograph of Zeina that Salma's boss had taken. Though no one had reprimanded Omar, he was aware that he was at fault for the horror that had suddenly befallen his family. *None of this would've happened if it weren't for you*, he had said to Zeina. And he resented not only himself for being so malicious, but Zeina for being so sensitive, and Abu Ahmed for laying his hands on Salma, and Salma for having agreed to that stranger's visit, and the stranger himself for intruding on their family's business, and the whole damn country where Zeina was still missing.

Nothing besides kidnapping could explain Zeina's lengthy absence. She hadn't gone searching for Mazen or Alia. She hadn't turned up at any radio or police station across town. Her photograph had been published in the newspaper and broadcast on television, courtesy of Salma's boss, and yet no one had seen her. But instead of staying at home with Salma and Mustafa, Omar had insisted on going out and searching with Abu Ahmed every day, hoping he had been wrong. Perhaps they would finally turn into the right street, ask the right pedestrian, and be led to Zeina's whereabouts.

Omar had a feeling Zeina had been taken far away, so when Abu Ahmed informed the search group that they would be going through the eshash again, he was tempted to protest. He couldn't imagine that anyone from the impoverished neighborhood was clever enough to kidnap and hide a girl for four days, nor that anyone would have the nerve. The search group had already entered every single hut, had interrogated innocent people, but Abu Ahmed insisted on searching the eshash again, perhaps because he knew something Omar didn't.

Omar had quickly come to understand that his father was, indeed, a drug smuggler as Mustafa had previously hinted.

The seven men who formed the search group had swords and long matwas tucked into their belt buckles as they entered the eshash. People moved to the edges of the alleys and opened the doors to their homes without being asked. It was the last day of Ramadan and the neighborhood was more crowded than usual: women were cleaning their huts to prepare for the celebratory breakfast on the first day of Eid; men were coming home with more money than usual—a result of the increased tipping for the holiday. Children were thrilled with the Eid lamps and fresh clothes a European organization had distributed around the neighborhood.

For the first time since Omar could remember, the eshash wasn't deluged with the smell of donkey shit. And he was glad to disturb the widespread joy; people needed to be reminded that Zeina might be out there, praying for someone to find her, when, in fact, her neighborhood's residents were preparing for pathetic festivities.

The group had just turned into an alley when Omar saw Am Kahraba lying on the ground, looking at the wall beside him and laughing. Omar hadn't seen him since Zeina's disappearance but knew that the man couldn't be the culprit. Am Kahraba was insane but had a child-like innocence. Everyone from the eshash knew it.

Am Kahraba noticed the search group and pointed at Abu Ahmed's sword. "Ali ibn Abi Taleb!" He stood up and approached Abu Ahmed. "Wow," he said. "In the name of God. You must be a man of great honor."

Abu Ahmed looked up and down Am Kahraba's figure. Flies were buzzing around Am Kahraba's long, thick hair, and his toenails had grown so long they curved around the bottom of his toes. Omar could smell him from a dozen feet away.

"Have we talked to him?" Abu Ahmed asked his men.

The group responded with a negative.

Abu Ahmed grabbed Am Kahraba's abscess-covered arm. "Have you seen my daughter, you crazy man?"

Am Kahraba looked away in contemplation, as if he had information that might suffice.

"Answer me," Abu Ahmed said as he tapped Am Kahraba's face.

Passersby began to gather and watch the exchange.

"I've been looking for my daughter for six hundred years," Am Kahraba said.

Omar closed his eyes in shock.

One of Abu Ahmed's men held Abu Ahmed's arm. "Boss, this man is harmless. He's crazy. Let's move on."

"He's right, Baba," Omar said.

Abu Ahmed stared at Am Kahraba without looking away. "He understands what I'm saying," he said, before cupping his hand on the back of Am Kahraba's neck. "Don't you? My daughter, you mother-fucker. She's pale. This tall."

Am Kahraba smiled. "Pale?"

Abu Ahmed punched Am Kahraba's chest with both fists. "Aiwa, pale!"

"Oh!" Am Kahraba remarked with delight, stumbling backward but not reacting to the punch. "My daughter is pale too!"

"He's an idiot," one of the spectators said from the gathered crowd.

"He doesn't know what he's saying," someone else said.

"He's crazy," a woman said. "Don't mind him."

Abu Ahmed pulled his sleeves up, looked at Omar, and ordered one of his men to take Omar home.

Dozens of people had gathered in seconds, adults and children alike, and the stray dogs began to bark as the hostility spread. Abu Ahmed inspected the blade of his sword as one of his men took Omar's hand and led him out of the crowd. The man forced Omar away so quickly that Omar had to jog to keep up. A group of boys rushed past them excitedly, as if approaching a stadium hosting a championship final. Right before they turned a corner, Omar looked back and, through the gaps between the legs of the spectators, saw two of Abu Ahmed's men bringing Am Kahraba to his knees.

A young woman walked away from the scene with her hand covering her mouth.

"What's he going to do?" Omar asked his escort.

The man didn't respond, but people like Belya recounted the images to Omar many times, over the years. The blood squirting out of Am Kahraba's bare back as Abu Ahmed slashed his sword across it again and again. Abu Ahmed yelling questions. Am Kahraba barely making a sound, holding a firm smile on his face as he stared at the people watching. The police, who had done almost nothing to help with the search for Zeina, arriving at the scene in three cars, dispersing the crowd with gunshots, and arresting Abu Ahmed and his men.

A month after Abu Ahmed's imprisonment, Salma, Omar, and Mustafa made the two-hour journey to Tora Prison, where they stood in line for another hour and had the sweater Salma had knitted for Abu Ahmed confiscated, only to be told, once inside, that Abu Ahmed didn't want to receive them. And though Salma returned to the prison two more times, in the hope that Abu Ahmed would see her, Omar and Mustafa didn't bother putting themselves through the humiliation and hadn't seen the man since.

It was regrettable that Omar sometimes proved capable of similar violence, but he was nothing like his father. He would never assault a woman, much less the mother of his children, as Abu Ahmed had done several times, and surely if he ever went to prison he would allow his family to visit him. Surely, he would help them with money (which Omar knew Abu Ahmed must have stored somewhere), rather than count on his wife to sustain them so the money could still be there when he was released in thirteen years. Perhaps Omar had inherited his father's temper, yes, but unlike the old man, he had values. In his eyes, his attack on Menawy was justified. The only problem, of course, was that everyone would disagree.

When Omar first decided he wanted to work at the Road, he had to choose among three different bosses to deal for: Maradona, Abbasy, and Tito. Belya's boss, Maradona, had a reputation for being fair and taking care of his dealers. He also had a minimum age of sixteen for his dealers, which meant Omar, who was fourteen at the time, would be automatically turned away. Omar was encouraged to approach Abbasy, who had once worked under Abu Ahmed as a teenager, but he took the highest commission of his dealers' profits: forty-percent against Tito's thirty-five. Omar was only interested in making as much money as possible, so in the end he decided to work for Tito and quickly became glad for it. Tito was not a bully like most people in the business, but logical and calculated in all his decisions. Omar was quick to gain his trust with timely payments and honest profit reports, and they had barely had any trouble since their partnership began.

After getting three stitches on his lip at a clinic in the masaken, Omar returned to the eshash to tell Tito about what had happened.

The contrast between the inside of Tito's hut and the alley outside never ceased to confuse Omar. Whereas the alley was covered with dust, trash, and animal feces, the floor of Tito's hut was covered with clean red carpeting. The black sofa facing the television had a stack of perfectly folded blankets on one of its armrests. And unlike most homes in Ramlet Bulaq, Tito's hut neither smelled like an accumulation of food and smoke nor contained any flies or mosquitoes, both of which were remarkable and curious achievements.

After opening the door for Omar, Tito turned around and walked back to his living area, where the sixty-inch television displayed a virtual golf course that Tito inhabited for hours at a time through his PlayStation 2.

Tito picked up his controller, turned around, and looked at Omar, who had followed him to the living area. "You've lost your mind, haven't you?" Tito asked.

Omar was relieved that Tito had already heard of the incident. "I'm sorry," he said. "Just let me—"

"Take them off, you animal!" Tito yelled as he pointed at Omar's shoes.

Omar remembered the no shoe policy and quickly skipped to the front door. Tito had a way of making him feel like a deranged animal.

"So you don't know?" Omar asked as he removed his shoes.

Tito didn't respond. He was on the sofa, adjusting the angle at which he would tee off the ball on the television.

Omar sat beside him. "I have something to—"

"Shut up for a second," Tito said. He squinted his eyes and then finally hit the ball, which flew through the virtual golf course and landed inches from the hole.

"Motherfucker!" Tito yelled. "So close."

He finally looked at Omar.

"Abbasy is on his way."

Instantly, Omar's mouth became dry.

Tito grinned, patted Omar's back, and then pointed at the pot of opium tea on the coffee table in front of them. "Help yourself."

Omar mostly avoided drugs besides hashish. Growing up in Ramlet Bulaq, he had witnessed the brutality of addiction firsthand. Overdoses. Deaths. Perfectly fine men turned wicked, making their children beg for drug money. Nevertheless, he granted himself a pass, since the circumstances at hand were by no means regular. He had no idea to what extent he had hurt Menawy or to what extent Abbasy would want to hurt him. Maybe some poppy tea would help relieve his anxiety.

He poured himself a mug while Tito resumed his virtual golf. The tea was only warm, so he drank the whole mug with a few gulps and waited for the high to kick in.

He watched Tito navigate the virtual golf course for a few minutes before the Madonna poster above the television grabbed his attention. Omar had seen it hundreds of times, over the years, but was now reminded of just how breathtaking it was. Golden-haired Madonna had her hands on her hips, elbows pointing outward, as she looked at the top left corner of the frame with her blue eyes, while red lipstick shone on her soft-seeming lips. A tremendously fine woman. The photograph's true greatness, however, lay in her sheer lace blouse, underneath of which was *nothing* but her perfect breasts. Omar felt heavier and heavier on the sofa as he fixated on them. He was absolutely certain that, with no hesitation, he would give up anything he had—his friends, savings, family, and left arm, if asked—just to serve this goddess before him for the rest of his life. To do anything and everything she wanted from him. To make her coffee, do her laundry, and even clean her toes on a daily basis if she so pleased.

When Abbasy knocked on the door and called for Tito, Omar had no idea how long he had been staring at the poster.

"Go, open," Tito said.

Omar looked at him and shook his head. He was high and tranquilized but didn't want to be the one to welcome Abbasy into the home.

Tito sighed and went to open the door.

"Ya Tito!" Abbasy exclaimed.

The men hugged and Omar stood up.

"Shoes off," Tito said.

"Don't worry," Abbasy said. "I know."

The two men exchanged small talk as they walked into the living area, followed by Abbasy's right-hand man. Omar looked at a point between the floor and Abbasy's face. He was terrified. Abbasy was a lunatic with a reputation for enjoying conflict; a couple of months ago, he was shot and almost killed in Embaba after being caught having sex with a friend's daughter. He had several scars on different parts of his face and wore shirts a few sizes too small, which forced his belly to stick out from underneath his shirt and hang over the waistline of his pants.

He walked in and put his hand out. "Omar, son of Abu Ahmed."

Omar shook it.

Abbasy looked at Tito and laughed. "He's shitting himself, isn't he?"

"Never," Omar said, confident that he could conceal his worries. The truth was that Abbasy, Tito, Omar, Belya, and everyone involved in the drug business felt fear. What distinguished them was how well they pretended not to.

Abbasy laughed as he and Tito sat on the sofa. Omar sat on the floor and Abbasy's friend stood at the kitchen.

"What would you like to drink?" Tito asked.

"Nothing at all," Abbasy said.

"Tea? Coffee? There's poppy tea."

"I'm trying to stop," Abbasy said.

"You sure?"

"Yes, yes. Besides, I need to be somewhere. I'm only here to discuss an urgent issue," Abbasy said as he grinned.

Tito lit a cigarette. "Right."

"What the fuck is this?" Abbasy asked as he looked at the television.

"Golf," Tito responded. "Try?"

"No thank you," Abbasy said. "You're so fucking strange, brother."

"Your mother is strange."

"People play *FIFA*. War games, maybe. But golf?"

Tito laughed. "Which people?"

"Right, Omar?" Abbasy asked.

Omar forced a smile.

"Omar, son of Abu Ahmed, is in a whole well of trouble," Abbasy said. "Isn't he?"

"He is indeed," Tito said.

Omar took a deep breath. If Abbasy continued hinting at the issue without addressing it, just to relish in Omar's nervousness, Omar might just stand up, smash the teapot on his head, and then flee the neighborhood forever. "I don't mean disrespect," Omar said, "but will you get on with it, please?"

Abbasy pretended to laugh, then quickly straightened his expression. "You couldn't disrespect me in a million years, you son of a bitch. You understand?"

Omar looked down at his lap.

"You understand?" Abbasy asked again.

"Yes, sir."

Tito smiled. "Easy."

"Fucking kids these days," Abbasy said.

"How bad is it?" Tito asked.

Omar felt his heartbeat in his neck.

Abbasy took a cigarette out and lit it with Tito's help. "He's in Shobra," he said before he took a drag. "He's just had his eye surgically removed."

Omar was so shocked that he released a brief wail.

"He'll be getting a glass one as replacement," Abbasy continued. "Now..."

Omar began planning his escape. He would go home, pack his money and clothes, then flee to Alexandria and find a place to hide and work. He would arrange for his family to know of his whereabouts and come visit him.

"Look at me," Abbasy said.

Omar did as he was told.

"You know, if you weren't your father's son, I would've come here with six men and told you right away to pick which eye you want to lose."

Tito laughed.

"You'd have no problem with that," Abbasy told Tito.

Tito shook his head.

"Because an eye for an eye," Abbasy said.

"Is the first law of the business," Tito continued.

"And we're talking about an actual fucking eye here," Abbasy said.

"Do you know what he did?" Omar asked, louder than he had intended. "He knew exactly what he was doing."

"So you go and blind him?" Abbasy asked.

"Can you just for one second imagine how—"

"I couldn't care for a second about your sadness," Abbasy said.

"You cut a man who never touched you," Tito said. "You should be grateful he's being kind to you."

Omar took another deep breath; irritating Tito would only worsen the situation. "All right," he said. "I appreciate it."

"Sixteen thousand pounds," Abbasy said.

"What?" Omar asked.

"For the cost of the surgery and the missed shifts," Abbasy continued. "In my hands by the end of the week. Saturday night."

"How am I supposed to—"

"I don't care. Rob a bank. Sell your kidney. It doesn't matter to me."

Tito picked up the controller and resumed the golf. "Well, that's that."

"And if I can't?" Omar asked.

Abbasy shrugged. "Then I'll pick the eye myself."

Omar quickly brainstormed. He had nine thousand pounds saved—two years of work drained away because of a moment's anger. The remaining seven thousand he could borrow from Tito and pay him back through higher commission for as long as it took. How long would it take? He would need Mustafa's help calculating. Surely it would take at least three years. Three whole years of reduced profits on top of the two years of savings. Was his eye worth that much?

"And I have one condition," Abbasy said.

Tito was adjusting his swing angle on the screen.

"Yabny," Abbasy said as he nudged Tito. "Pause this shit. I'm talking to you."

Tito paused and put the controller down. "Khalas, we get it. Sixteen thousand."

"I said I have one condition."

"Yes," Tito said.

"You don't lend him the money."

Omar puffed. "Why would you make that—"

"Shut the fuck up!" Abbasy yelled.

Omar looked down. "Sorry," he said again.

Salma had been right. *Keep hanging out with the dogs and they'll eventually eat you alive,* she had told him again and again. With time, she always proved to be right.

"Understood," Tito said. "You have my word. I wasn't going to anyway."

"All right," Abbasy said. "Now go," he told Omar. "We have other business to discuss. No one will be touching you. If anyone threatens you, come and let me know."

Omar stood up.

"Understood?" Abbasy asked. "Saturday night."

"Understood," Omar said.

"Be smart," Tito said as Omar put on his shoes. "Use your brain and you'll be fine."

Omar walked out of the hut. Down the alley, he picked up an abandoned bicycle and hit it against the ground multiple times, until people came out of their huts and watched him. He had been aware of how much trouble his temper could put him in, and yet he had failed to control it. Now, he had two options: either he escaped Ramlet Bulaq and didn't return for years, or he robbed someone. The former would have been a viable choice if it weren't for his family; the latter would put him at risk of going to prison.

3

My first night back in Cairo, I deactivated my social media and bought a new Egyptian number, which I gave only to Taymour and Carmen. I ignored the countless interview requests I received in my email, aiming to seclude myself until the event became old news. I was, however, checking the internet on a daily basis, determined to learn as much as I could about the aftermath of the attack.

It was all extensively reported. Standing at a gate in Newark Liberty International Airport, a woman from Fort Lee, New Jersey, was informed by a CNN broadcaster that both her daughters, who lived together and commuted to Wall Street every morning, had passed away. In Manhattan's Beth Israel Hospital, a woman birthed a son and lost her husband, who was only dropping into his office for a quick meeting. In Bradford, England, a sixteen-year-old named Kassem was cornered in an alley and jumped by members of the English Defence League, which put him into a coma. In Victoria, Texas, a man opened fire on a group of men walking out of a mosque, killing three and injuring thirty. In Jalalabad in Nangarhar Province, a group of jihadists celebrated the subway attack, hugging and shooting bullets at the sky. Less than an hour later, a U.S. Army drone disposed of the whole block, killing the jihadists along with every woman and child in their vicinity.

Our family also suffered. Only twenty people—distant relatives from Denshawai—showed up to Amir's funeral three days after the attack; the hundreds of friends and workmates that our family had combined didn't show up, which was just as understandable as it was humiliating. Youssef, Mohamed, and Enas's friends from the block were ordered by their parents to cut ties with the Salama family. Uncle Ashraf underwent four days of questioning and was forced to partake in a nationally televised interview. Khalto Heba fainted upon seeing Amir's face on the news, withdrew into her bedroom, and thrust her head into a wall so hard, a week after the attack, that she fractured her skull and knocked herself out.

I went to a pharmacy a few blocks from our home and bought ten blister packs of Xanax. I couldn't drink while at home, it was haram, and there was no way I was going to survive the turmoil in sobriety. I had taken Xanax recreationally a few times and noted the similarity to alcohol—the separation it created between the world and my feelings. Thankfully, all I needed to get it without a prescription was a few hundred pounds in the local pharmacist's pocket.

The pills were my only defense against the memories that sprouted from every corner of my surroundings. A cockroach sprints across my kitchen and I'm ten years old, standing behind Amir as he stomps it and laughs. I clog my toilet and remember Amir doing the same, shit smelling so foul that my mother couldn't fix the clog without gagging and running out of the bathroom, and us boys possessed with laughter. The sheikh calls for prayer, says, *God is great,* and I wonder if those were Amir's last words.

The pills didn't spare me such thoughts; they spared me the capacity to react to them with the emotion they warranted. A milligram on an empty stomach had me feeling as sorrowful about the whole incident as one would feel about an overcooked steak. I would think about it all and feel *slightly bothered*. I would consider the fact that, essentially, one of the primary forces behind Amir's disintegration was a lack of love, and I had contributed. I had jumped at the first opportunity to cut ties with him and never stopped to consider that I was one of his only friends. I would contemplate the fact that I was, in essence, a selfish person; that at some point in my life I became solely concerned with my need to be *cool* and *liked* and *respected*. To be accepted and embraced as *one of their own* by the more exclusive Cairo circles. I would lie in my bed, think of it all, end with an *Oh well,* and then turn to my side and fall asleep.

I was lucky to have my mother react to the incident as she did. Together with my grandmother and aunts, she constructed a compelling narrative. They made a mistake allowing Amir to go to America, they admitted, but they had only wanted to fulfill his wishes. Unfortunately, and for reasons only God was aware of, Amir fell into the wrong hands and was tricked into committing a gruesome crime. He lied to the family about his whereabouts and sentiments, and there was no way for them to have known. He was brainwashed by *professional brainwashers*, a term coined by Khalto Nermeen ten days after the attack, as I sat with her, her daughter Habiba, Khalto Randa, Ma, and Uncle Ashraf in Khalto Heba's hospital room.

Khalto Heba had been vomiting regularly ever since her self-inflicted concussion. She was deep in morphine slumber on her bed, after getting an MRI of her brain, while Uncle Ashraf sat on the arm-chair beside her, legs sprawled out in front of him. The sisters and their mother had worn black since I returned with the news of Amir's death. Only Khalto Nahla, who had gone to stay with her mother-in-law for some time, because she thought we were at risk of attack, stopped wearing black when she discovered what Amir had done.

I had just finished reading the *New York Times* article about Amir's last few years, for which I had been interviewed over email. After two days of watching over Khalto Heba, Teta had returned home a few hours ago to get some sleep, which meant we could discuss the situation without running the risk of propelling her into a panic attack.

"May you rest in peace, Baba," Khalto Nermeen said as she looked up. "God knows if you were here, you would've stopped this."

Unlike most of the fallacies assembled by different members of the family, this one might have actually been true. My grandfather had been the only person who loved Amir enough to pay him enough attention. Every day since the attack, I thought of the Friday after Amir threw hot coal onto Farida, when my grandfather asked me to accompany him to the fruit market and stressed the importance of forgiving Amir. *There's something called Selat El Rahem,* he said. *The duty of the womb. I understand that you're upset, but Amir is your family. It is your duty to forgive him because he is also of your grandmother's womb.* I was annoyed that I had been forced to exit an online *Call of Duty* game, so I nodded my head without offering much of a response.

I couldn't determine whether it was delusional to think that I could've saved Amir from his fate, if only I had remained his friend.

"He was so weak," Khalto Nermeen said. "And the people that got a hold of him, that Ramzi, they took advantage of that. And they're not beginners. They've been doing this for decades. They're *professional brainwashers*."

Uncle Ashraf, who hadn't said a word in hours, rested his head on the edge of his seat's backrest and closed his eyes.

Khalto Randa nodded. "I'm still going to pray for him," she said. "They put the virus in his head. I think we should all pray for him."

"We should also pray for all the people he killed," Habiba said, which instantly silenced the entire room.

We sat in silence for some time, each staring into the emptiness between us, digesting the details brought forth by the article. I searched my memory for any additional warning signs I had missed, perhaps an anti-American monologue when Amir was fourteen or a troubling fascination with war.

Like many Egyptians, I had been invested in the Israeli-Palestinian conflict in the early 2000s, had followed the second intifada on television and expressed hatred for Israel. I couldn't remember Amir caring half as much.

"I think I'll call the man," Khalto Nermeen said.

"Who?" Habiba asked.

"The head of the school. In Chicago. I need to know more."

"I don't know," I said. "I don't think that's a good idea."

Ma stood up. "I'm going to go get us food," she said. "It's time to eat."

"Do you need help?" Habiba asked her.

"No."

Ma left the hospital room to go to the cafeteria downstairs. A nurse walked in, checked Khalto Heba's monitor, and walked out.

"I keep thinking," Khalto Nermeen said, "what it would've been like if I had gone to visit him. If he would've snapped out of it."

Khalto Randa shook her head. "I don't think you would've even recognized him. The Amir we know and the one who did this are two different people entirely."

I was no longer able to believe in this narrative. The way Amir had behaved at the flight school, he had behaved in our building years earlier. There was continuity in his story, roots to his problems that we had failed to take seriously.

"I don't think that's true," I said. "It would be nice to believe, but it's not true."

"Enough of it," Uncle Ashraf said as he opened his eyes. "Nothing we can do to change it now."

I huffed. "Of course you would say."

"Sherif," Khalto Randa said.

"I just can't understand," Khalto Nermeen said.

"What did you say?" Uncle Ashraf asked me.

I pretended not to hear him.

"I used to change his diapers," Khalto Nermeen said, before beginning to cry for the third time in the past hour. "He was the size of my hand."

"You!" Uncle Ashraf demanded as he sat up. "I asked you a question."

"What?" I asked.

"What did you say to me?"

Silence took a hold of the room.

"Forget it, Ashraf," Khalto Randa said.

"I said of course you would say that," I said.

"Sherif!" Khalto Randa yelled.

"And that's supposed to mean what?" Uncle Ashraf asked as he raised his voice.

I shrugged.

He approached me.

I stood up. If he laid his hands on me, I wouldn't hesitate to defend myself.

Habiba covered her ears. "Please stop."

"Do I need to bring back your manners?" Uncle Ashraf asked as he pointed his finger in my face. "Did you forget how to speak to your elders?"

Khalto Randa and Khalto Nermeen got in between us.

"You're waking her up," Habiba said as she pointed at Khalto Heba.

"Nothing we can do to change it now," I said. "But what about back then?"

My mother hit me often as I was growing up. It was part of our culture; it was reflected in the films and books and plays; it was witnessed in the streets and playgrounds and sports clubs, parents smacking their children into good behavior. I had always thought it was perfectly acceptable, until I moved to America and was told that child beating can cause *extensive psychological damage.*

The only thing I recall my beatings damaging was my inclination to disregard my studies, disrespect my elders, and neglect all forms of personal hygiene. Not only were the beatings vital to my development, but they also formed some of my funniest memories with my mother. It was always a thrill to run circles around our dining room as she tried to get a hold of me and smack me with her wooden slipper. The only thing I feared more than the slipper's underside was her devilish ear pinch, which often brought me to my knees. Sometimes, if I did something especially unforgivable, she would combine the two forces, pinch my ear *and* smack me with the slipper, as I stood there thrusting my hips back and forth, like Michael Jackson, timing every thrust with every swing of her arm, so I could minimize the damage to my butt.

When I told a few American friends about my defensively useful M.J. thrusts, they found it all but funny, and my friend Meghan went as far as saying, *I think you were physically abused.* Meghan was from the Hamptons and had never been anywhere east of Palma de Mallorca, so I wasn't surprised by her comment. But I disagreed. There were other methods of teaching discipline, yes, but a controlled degree of physical disciplining was the one my mother's lineage had always used. For my American friends to call it abuse was dramatic, and I could only wonder how they would react if I described what I had seen being done to Amir.

The first time I saw it was only months after I had moved back to Cairo. My mother was at her clinic, which meant Amir and I were free to kick our feet up in my living room and do whatever we wanted. We had ordered McDonald's, a couple of Big Macs and McFlurrys, and were shouting *kosomak, kosomak, kosomak* repeatedly as our *Mortal Kombat* characters kicked each other's heads.

Our landline rang, so I paused the game. Uncle Ashraf needed Amir for an errand.

I accompanied Amir downstairs, because if he went alone, it was likely that Uncle Ashraf would tell him that that was enough playing for the day. Uncle Ashraf, like many parents, routinely gave out such verdicts without offering an explanation.

He was lying on the sofa, wearing a dark blue tracksuit, eating dates and watching music videos on the television. I was always intimidated by the man; he was rather short, perhaps only seven inches taller than me, but three times thicker in every other dimension. His arms were so bulky that when he ate at my grandfather's dining table he often left thick sweat stains on the tablecloth.

"Take my keys and fetch my cigarettes from the car," he told Amir. "They're in the glove compartment."

Amir took the keys from the coffee table and walked toward the front door.

"Don't forget to lock the car behind you," Uncle Ashraf said.

"All right," Amir said.

"Sherif," Uncle Ashraf said. "Make sure he doesn't forget."

He was the only member of our family who didn't call me Sheero.

"Okay, Uncle."

Outside the apartment, I walked down some steps and realized Amir wasn't following me. I looked back at him. "Yalla?"

He held the keys up. "I want to check on them," he whispered, referring to the various breeds of bird living on our roof.

I walked back up. "What?" I asked. "No."

"Really quickly," he said. "Two minutes."

Like many former peasants, our grandfather never adopted the idea of buying packaged meat at the supermarket. What had the animal been fed? What conditions had it lived in? Had it really been slaughtered in the merciful manner instructed in the Quran? He couldn't trust the corporations or local butchers, so he built a farm on our roof instead, where he bred and raised his own chickens, pigeons, and ducks. Most of his grandchildren, myself included, found it disturbing that the chickens we ate on Fridays had been the ones to wake us up during the week with their clucking. I stepped onto the roof soon after my arrival in Cairo and decided that it smelled like diarrhea. Amir, on the other hand, was Gedo's designated assistant breeder. He thought of the animals, which he personally assigned names, as an extension of the family, but somehow had no trouble holding them down as my grandfather sliced their necks open when it was time for slaughter. He helped track their food consumption and was especially obsessed with the pigeons. *Zoozoo flew for the first time today,* he would sometimes tell me. *Baadoones flew away and hasn't come back since Tuesday.* On one occasion, he went as far as pointing at one of the cooked pigeons on our dining table and saying, *That's definitely Scooby, the biggest one.*

Since Gedo had been on a trip to Denshawai and had asked an employee to feed the pigeons daily, Amir hadn't had a chance to see the birds for almost a week. Now he had the keys to the roof and was insisting on giving them a visit.

"All right," I whispered as we walked up the stairs. "I'll just wait for you at home."

"Come with me," he said. "It'll only be a minute."

"No. I hate it up there."

"You don't have to come outside. Just stand by the door and keep an eye out."

"I don't want to."

"Last one is a donkey?"

Though Amir was more than a year older, we were roughly the same size and equally fast, so we often expedited journeys up and down the staircase by announcing that whoever was last was a metaphorical donkey. He started running up the stairs and I quickly followed; I had lost the last three races and was desperate for a win. I was right behind him as we turned onto the sixth floor of our building, past Khalto Nahla's apartment, and ran up the last set of stairs. We had both been climbing two steps at a time the entire race, but for some reason, as we approached the last three, he tried jumping them all at once. He tripped over the last step and fell stomach-first in front of the roof's entrance. I smirked as he fell—the donkey he had just made of himself!—and saw the keys launch out of his hand and slide across the marble, toward the gutter under the roof's door.

Before I could react, the keys were swallowed. We heard them knock against the metal three times, each time making a sound more distant than the one prior, as they found their way to the underground sewage system.

I slapped my forehead and looked back at Amir, whose eyes spread with horror.

"Yanhar eswed!" He stood up and ran to the gutter, where he fell onto his knees and stared into the darkness. "Oh no! Oh no!"

"Does he have extra keys?" I asked.

"Oh my god, no!" He stuck his hand through the space between the bars.

"Amir, it fell. What are you doing?"

"I don't know!" he yelled. "He's going to kill me!"

"Shhh," I said. "Khalto is going to hear you."

He groaned. When he took his hand out, it was smeared with brown goo, which he rubbed on his pants. He stood up and began to jump on the spot, as if desperate to use a restroom. "No, please," he said as he stared at the gutter. "Please!"

"Where's your mother?" I asked, certain that his punishment would be less brutal if Khalto Heba was around.

"She's at the nady. Can we tell him it was you?"

"What? No!"

"He's going to kill me," he said. "Can you at least go tell him? I'll hide until Mama comes home."

"You want me to go downstairs and tell your dad you lost his keys?"

He ran his hand through his hair. "He's not going to do anything to you."

"No way."

"Khalto would kill him if he did anything to you."

He was right. My mother, the dentist, had authority in the family. She had probably loaned Uncle Ashraf money in the past, and if he ever mistreated me, he ran the risk of forgoing benefits.

Still, I wasn't comfortable telling him that his keys were in the sewers.

"I'm scared," I said. "I'm sure he has extras?"

"I don't know."

"I'm sure he does."

"I don't think so."

Khalto Nahla opened her front door. "What are you doing?"

I grabbed Amir's other hand and led him down the stairs. "Nothing," I said.

"Were you guys on the roof?" she asked.

We passed her. "No, we weren't," Amir said.

"You were, weren't you?" she asked as we walked down to my floor.

"How could we go on the roof if it's locked?" I asked.

She didn't respond and closed the door. Rhetorical questions sometimes worked wonders with the less intelligent adults.

We walked down the stairs in increments of five or six steps, separated by pauses for prayer. "Yarab, please," Amir said, as he looked up at God, who was beyond the many layers of concrete and seven skies above us. "Yarab, please make him forgive me."

"I'm sure he will," I said.

"Say yarab!"

"Yarab! Ameen."

Once we made it to his floor, Amir rang the doorbell and stood behind me. We stood in silence for a prolonged moment, then I rang it again.

"Don't you have the keys?" Uncle Ashraf yelled from inside.

My legs began to tremble. Uncle Ashraf's yelling alone was enough to dread; it often exited his mouth alongside viscous chunks of saliva.

His arms were the first things I looked at when he opened the door.

"Uncle, Amir dropped your keys in the gutter upstairs," I said in a hurry.

"What?"

"The gutter under the roof's entrance? He tripped. It was a mistake. Maybe you have extras? Please don't be angry. We only wanted to—"

"What'd you say?"

Amir held both of my shoulders. "I'm sorry, Baba."

Uncle Ashraf looked at me. "Go home," he told me.

"Uncle, he really didn't mean—"

Uncle Ashraf reached behind me, grabbed the collar of Amir's shirt, pulled Amir into the apartment, and pushed the door behind him. I put my hand out to keep the door from closing and followed them inside. Uncle Ashraf led Amir past the dining table and into the living area, still holding the collar of his shirt.

I stopped beside the dining table, on which there was a scattered pile of papers with a National Bank of Egypt logo on the corner. On the television, Amr Diab was surrounded by dozens of belly dancers as he sang "Nour El Ein."

"Habiby!" Amr sang. "Habiby! Habiby, ya nour el ein!"

"What were you doing upstairs?" Uncle Ashraf asked calmly.

Amir's chin dropped to his chest and he started crying. "I'm sorry."

Uncle Ashraf released his grip on Amir's shirt. "Look at me."

Amir did as he was told.

"What were you doing upstairs?" Uncle Ashraf asked.

"I wanted... to check on the pigeons."

"Oh," Uncle Ashraf said in a sarcastic tone.

Amir didn't speak. He looked down again.

"Habiby! Habiby! Habiby, ya nour el ein!"

"I mean, of course," Uncle Ashraf said. "Your beloved pigeons. Forget your father and his cigarettes. I've been sitting here with my lighter, waiting for you, but who cares? The pigeons are what matters."

Amir's crying worsened, and I wanted to tell him to relax. Uncle Ashraf was clearly not reacting the way we had feared. He hadn't so much as raised his voice.

"The wall," Uncle Ashraf said.

With the instant obedience of a low-ranked army officer, Amir walked to one of the walls and stood with his nose inches from it. It seemed unnecessarily callous, but at least he wasn't being smacked or whipped with a belt.

Uncle Ashraf walked into the hallway that led to the bedrooms. I realized I was standing in the dark and that Uncle Ashraf wasn't aware that I was in the apartment.

I heard a door being opened and closed.

"Amir," I whispered.

He looked surprised as he turned and looked at me. "Go," he whispered, and he pointed at the front door and faced the wall again.

"Habiby! Habiby! Habiby, ya nour el ein!"

I was about to slip to the front door when the door in the hallway opened and closed again. Uncle Ashraf approached the living room and I ducked behind the dining table. He emerged from the hallway holding a few big papers with strips of tape hanging from each corner, which I quickly identified as Amir's posters. Around his bedroom, Amir had hung up posters exhibiting different types of birds, with a description of each breed written below the photographs. He had bought them from a pet store last week after saving up for months.

"Turn around," Uncle Ashraf said.

As soon as he faced his father, Amir began to cry again, and I almost wanted to protest. Surely it was a fair punishment to have his bird posters confiscated for some time. They were, after all, just posters, and losing his father's keys was a crime that warranted some degree of punishment.

On the television, Amr Diab was sitting beside a fountain, singing alongside two blond women dressed in red gowns. "Habiby! Habiby! Habiby, ya nour el ein!"

Uncle Ashraf made Amir hold one of the posters, then fetched a metal trash bin from beside the sofa, which he placed on the floor between them.

"One by one," he said. "Unless you want to make it worse."

"Baba, please," Amir begged. "I bought these with my money."

"Do you want to make it worse?" Uncle Ashraf asked.

Amir shook his head.

"Then yalla."

I wanted to somehow send Amir a message and tell him to have no fear; I could buy him replacements.

Uncle Ashraf, whose back was facing me, lifted his arm again and gave Amir something that was not one of the posters. "Yalla," he said again.

"Habiby! Habiby! Habiby, ya nour el ein!"

"Yalla!" Uncle Ashraf yelled, so loud that I squatted down completely.

I stood back up, just enough to peek at them, and saw Amir ripping one of his posters with all the strength in his arms.

"There goes your hummingbird," Uncle Ashraf said.

Amir threw the poster into the bin.

"Habiby! Habiby! Habiby, ya nour el ein!"

Uncle Ashraf handed Amir the second poster.

"They were expensive," Amir said, his voice breaking.

"Yalla, don't waste my time," Uncle Ashraf said.

The music video ended, and Amir proceeded to rip all six posters apart while Uncle Ashraf watched. When Amir tossed the last poster into the bin, Uncle Ashraf fetched the mug of tea on the coffee table beside him and poured it on top.

He lifted Amir's chin with his hand. "From now on," he said, "when I ask you to do something, you go do it. You understand?"

Amir nodded, and then Uncle Ashraf giggled, as if to ensure that Amir felt humiliated. A knot tightened around the inside of my chest and I was overcome with fear. In my eight years of life, I had never considered that real people, not just the characters in comic books and movies, could actually derive pleasure from hurting others.

"Can I go to my room?" Amir asked in a calm and collected tone.

"Have you apologized?"

"You apologize!" Amir yelled, all of a sudden kicking the metal bin on the floor. "I hate you!"

Amir began running toward his room inside the hallway as Uncle Ashraf followed him and took his belt off.

"You hate me?" Uncle Ashraf asked.

"I'm sorry!" Amir yelled, as he entered his room and closed the door behind him.

They were out of sight, but a loud bang, along with Amir's scream, told me that Uncle Ashraf had either kicked or punched the door open.

"You hate me?" Uncle Ashraf asked again, before swinging his belt and making a whipcrack against Amir's body.

"I'm sorry!" Amir yelled again, this time louder and with a sob.

I tiptoed toward the entrance of the dark hallway, at the end of which was Amir's bedroom, half open and dimly lit. Uncle Ashraf's back was facing me. Beyond him, Amir stood in a corner, his hands on his face and his leg lifted to protect his torso. With the next swing of Uncle Ashraf's belt, I couldn't help but close my eyes and turn away.

I tiptoed to the front door as Amir's cries echoed across the apartment and silently made my escape. Upstairs, I lay in bed for some time, replaying the images in my head over and over again, and wondering if it was possible that Uncle Ashraf had had a spare set of keys. Eventually, I realized I ought to try to forget, so I ate both the McFlurrys we had put in the freezer and began to play *Mortal Kombat* alone.

The next day, Amir came over, and we didn't speak of any of it.

Outside the hospital room, Khalto Randa convinced me to return inside and apologize to Uncle Ashraf. He was a human being whose son had just killed himself as well as multiple innocent people. He had spent days being questioned by Egyptian police. He was suffering too.

Inside, I approached him and offered my hand.

He told me to go away, so I moved to the other side of the room.

After lunch, my mother and I decided to go home. She would nap for a few hours and then return to the hospital. I would look for flights back to New York.

We sat in silence as she drove through the heavy traffic.

"Why didn't anyone take him to a doctor?" I asked.

She took a moment to respond. "Your gedo tried to convince Heba several times."

"Were there other incidents?"

"Yes. A few."

"A few?"

"Yes," she said. "One time your uncle Hamza made fun of him. I don't remember for what. And we all laughed. And then Amir keyed both sides of his car the next day. He had to have been seven or eight."

I shook my head. "We should've known."

"What?"

"We should've known he wasn't ready to go abroad."

"Only God knows everything, my son."

I sighed.

"You're not convinced?"

I didn't respond.

"Habiby, your faith in God is the most important thing you have."
I nodded.

The truth was that my faith, what little of it had survived New
York, had recently dwindled to nonexistence. I had questioned the
teachings of Islam for years, but until this past week, I had clung to
the idea that perhaps there was a God out there, orchestrating a reasonable and moral plot. But the fallacy could no longer stand. The
world was only chaos and absurdity. Dozens of human beings had
died because of Amir, a boy who used to speak to me extensively
about Zinedine Zidane and Batman and birds, how Alpine swifts can
fly for six months without stopping. Whatever God was capable of
such odds was not the one I had been promised.

"Only God can control everything," she said.

"I know," I said.

One day, I would sit my mother down, list everything I didn't believe
in, and brace for a slap or an expulsion from her life.

Last summer, she had caught me eating pistachios when I was
supposed to be fasting during Ramadan. "I can't understand how
my own son could do this," she said. I told her it was a particularly
difficult day and I had succumbed to my hunger, when in reality
I hadn't fasted since the tenth grade. Every Ramadan since, I had
snuck many a snack to the bathroom and ate them quickly while I
ran the sink.

I began to sweat and turned the air-conditioning up to its maximum
level.

"It doesn't really work," she said.

"You should fix it."

"I did. Several times. But it keeps failing."

"Maybe it's time for you to buy a new car," I said. She had owned
her Opel Astra since 2002.

She snickered.

"What?" I asked.

"Cars are expensive, you know."

I was offended. "We *have* money."

She laughed.

"Do we not?" I asked. "You're a dentist. And there's Pa's money."

"Pa's money isn't going to last forever," she said. "And the money I make I'm going to need for when I'm old."

"I'll take care of you when you're old," I said.

She smiled in a way that suggested she thought I was naive. Egypt's economy was suffering. People graduating from the best universities were limited to entry-level positions that paid no more than the average taxi driver's salary. Also, the money we had inherited from my father had been cut by a third during the past few years, on NYU's tuition, my rent, and the additional two thousand dollars a month I spent being foolishly extravagant.

But I had faith. I was on the verge of obtaining a degree in finance from a great American university. I had good connections in Cairo; I had been well educated.

I only needed to assume responsibility once and for all.

"How much is a new car?" I asked. "A Corolla or something."

"No less than a hundred thousand," she said.

I pulled out my phone in order to make a calculation I knew would fill me with shame. I found my cocaine dealer's number and scrolled to the very top of our texts, which started during the spring of freshman year. Every time I wanted to buy cocaine from Pat, I texted him the same thing, *Snow White is playing,* followed by the address, usually my apartment or Taymour's. I scrolled down our chat history and counted the number of times I had told him Snow White was playing. Ninety-four. Usually Taymour and I split two vials, meaning I spent an average of eighty dollars every time. The last number on the calculator, after converting the dollars to Egyptian pounds, was forty-five thousand. Here was my hardworking mother, wiping the sweat on her forehead as she drove through traffic, while I had spent her dead husband's money, half the price of a new car, on *just* cocaine.

Although I didn't believe it possible, I understood, in that moment, that if my father was somehow watching us, then he must be disgusted with me too. When I thought of him, I remembered a man with proper values. I remembered being driven to a classmate's home in Oakland, a fat kid I bullied during the school day, and being forced to apologize. I had been told countless anecdotes about my father's good character. How he would put his entire life on pause to aid a friend in need. How he paid off Khalto Nahla's hospital fees when Mariam was born prematurely and on the brink of death. How he defied his mother, the most important person in his life, and insisted on marrying Ma because he loved her, because despite the fact that she was from a lower social class, he was confident that she was no less equipped to raise his children. And she hadn't been. And I needed to prove him right.

4

Arriving home from his private biology lesson, Mustafa was relieved to find that his mother was yet to return from work. Salma was his angel, the only reason he was still alive, really, but her concern for him often became insufferable. If she was home, she would keep him from taking a nap by walking into the apartment that he now shared with Omar (formerly their father's office) and nagging him, all because Mustafa's sleeping was apparently *excessive* and *problematic.*

It was true; Mustafa loved sleeping. He slept ten hours each night and then two or three hours in the middle of the day, not because he was somehow not well, as Salma repeatedly worried, but because he simply enjoyed it. To sleep was to relax and be at peace. Why should anyone impose restrictions on such an activity?

As soon as he changed into his pajamas, he tucked himself under his three blankets and turned from side to side, in search of a position to settle on. Before he could fall asleep, however, he heard someone walking up the stairs with a pace that sounded like Salma's.

"*No,*" he whispered to himself. "*Please no.*"

"Mustafa!" Salma called from the staircase. "Come help with these bags!"

Mustafa sighed. He could either go outside, help his hardworking mother, and lose any chance of taking a nap, or pretend to be asleep and hope she would leave him alone.

He didn't move.

"Yabny!" Salma called, her voice getting louder as she climbed the stairs. "Anyone there? Yarab. Almost there. Six more."

Eventually, Salma reached their floor and walked into her apartment across the hall. Mustafa could no longer relax, knowing that she would soon—

"Mustafa," she said as she walked into his apartment.

He had his back to her. *Please,* he thought. *Please go away.*

"Mustafa," she said. "Are you sleeping again? I need your help with something. You won't believe what happened. I went to the market and—"

"I'm sleeping!" he yelled.

"Well, wake up!"

"No."

"Yabny, I don't understand. Do you not care about your health? At all? Every single day the same argument. Every single day. And why should I care, anyway? You know what, I shouldn't. So I can live in peace. Sleep twenty hours a day if you like. Spend your life in bed. But then who will look after me? No one at all. How can they look after me if they can't even look after themselves? And..."

If anything was going to rob Mustafa of his sanity, it was going to be one of these rants, during which Salma rambled uncontrollably and repeatedly told herself that she ought to care less, when, in fact, both she and Mustafa knew she would always care.

"Mama."

"And if I get old, God, please take me earlier rather than later. Neither of them will look after me. How can they look after me if one is a thug and the other sleeps half the day? No, I'll take care of myself. I'll take care of myself like I always have. Like I have since the day he left me, my dear father, may God bless him in Heaven."

He kicked the blanket off him. "There. I'm up. Khalas? I'm awake."

She paused and took a few breaths. "I'm stupid for caring."

He stood up. "No," he said. "You're not."

"Have you prayed?"

"Yes," he lied.

She looked up at him; she was a foot shorter. "Are you sure?"

"I swear to God I did."

"All right," she said. "We can't expect God's mercy if we're not loyal to Him, my son. We can't expect your sister to be brought back when your brother doesn't even—"

"Mama, I know. I swear. We talk about this every day."

She nodded. "All right."

Six years had passed since Zeina had left their lives. Dozens of people had searched. Her photograph had been published in multiple newspapers. An intifada had broken out in Palestine. Iraq had been occupied. Omar and Mustafa had grown two feet taller. The neighbors living beneath them had had four children. And yet Salma still clung on to the hope that, miraculously, a seventeen-year-old woman would arrive at their door, one day, and they would be thrilled to discover that it was Zeina. As if the girl had run away, gotten lost, and failed to remember where she was from, or kidnapped and held hostage for six whole years.

It was impossible for Zeina to still be alive. Mustafa had assured Salma of this several times, over the years, but it only depressed her, and she continued to pray for Zeina's return every day. She was incapable of letting go of the hope that, once upon a time, he had suffered from too.

Indeed, it had been the mystery behind Zeina's whereabouts that devastated Mustafa the most. The constant and relentless longing for her return that almost drove him mad. For weeks after her disappearance, he heard Zeina's voice coming from a distance, only to run up to the roof or go downstairs and discover that he had imagined it. And when he looked back on the dismal experience in its entirety, he was always especially touched by his unsevered conviction that God would eventually help.

On the third day after Zeina's disappearance, Mustafa woke up and found Salma sitting cross-legged on the floor, dressed in a black gown and veil, and reciting chapters of the Quran. All the screaming and sobbing the first night had taken her voice and he could barely hear her. The foul stench emanating from the sink, which was overflowing with dirty dishes, had gotten worse, and there were no less than a dozen flies circling the apartment.

"Where's Omar?" he asked.

"Went with your father," Salma said with what little voice she had.

He closed his eyes and rested his head on the pillow, to try to fall back asleep, but the thoughts had already kicked off: Zeina was still out there, somewhere, suffering under a monster's hands. *Please!* Mustafa could hear her yell in his mind. *Someone help me!* Last night, he had overheard Salma whispering to one of the neighbors, who came upstairs to console her, about the illegal organ trade: how street children had been abducted in different parts of the city, given anesthesia, robbed of their kidneys, and then released to return to their lives; how children can live with only one kidney; how Salma hoped whoever had taken Zeina would at least spare her life and bring her back. And it was not only these kidney robbers he hated with all his will; he was beginning to resent God too. He knew it was haram to have such feelings for God, but what God was doing was no less awful. Salma, Mustafa, Omar, and many neighbors had spent hours praying for Zeina's return. And yet God had fixed none of it. He had allowed Zeina's abduction; He had known just how much agony it would put the whole family through; He had *created* child abductors and put Zeina in their hands.

Mustafa left the bed and walked across the apartment to sit beside Salma. His legs were weak under his weight and he felt as if the floor were slanting to his right. His body was famished, but the idea of eating did not interest him in the least; to sit down and have a meal would be to act like everyone else, like the fruit vendors and neighbors and prayer-calling sheikh, who had helped with Zeina's search the first day and then resumed their regular schedules, as if she had been found.

Salma's pale face was shining with sweat under the cold light bulb hanging from the ceiling. She placed her cold hand on Mustafa's neck, pulled his head into her chest, and kissed the top of his head. She smelled rotten.

"Mama," Mustafa said, "do you know why God hates us?"

Salma sighed. "He does not hate us," she said with her low, hoarse voice.

"Then why is doing this?"

"Glory be to Him, the Most High, said, *It is possible that you dislike something and there is good in it for you, and it is possible that you like something and it has evil in it for you, and God knows and you know not.* And so we just have to trust Him, my son."

He contemplated her words for a moment. "How could this be good?" he asked.

She kissed his forehead and rubbed his back. "Just pray," she said.

"And He'll bring her back?" he asked.

Salma returned her hands close to her face and continued reciting verses. She probably wasn't telling him the truth. God probably hated them and this was only the beginning; perhaps next week Mustafa would wake up and discover that Salma and Omar were gone as well. What could His reasons possibly be? The only thing he could think of (with regard to himself, at least) was the pen case he had stolen from one of his classmates at the end of the last school year, and surely that wasn't a big enough crime to have Zeina taken away from him.

"Maybe He's punishing Baba," he said.

She didn't respond.

"Mama," he said again. "Are we being punished because of—"

"Enough, my son," she said.

Abu Ahmed was a drug dealer, Mustafa was sure of it, and the whole family was being punished because dealing drugs was haram.

Mustafa was tired of praying. For three days now, he had begged God for Zeina's return, for the sound of her voice as she walked up the stairs, for one more hug, and nothing had yet changed. Maybe God was too busy, he realized. That wasn't supposed to be the way God functioned, but there was no other explanation for His unresponsiveness.

"Mama," he said, "do you think God can't hear us?"

Salma's chin had dropped to her chest and she had fallen asleep.

He heard the candy vendor's horn in the street below. "Cotton candy!" the man called. "Balloons! Cotton candy!"

When Zeina came back, Mustafa would buy her as much cotton candy as she wanted and never allow anyone to upset her ever again.

He brought his hands to his face. "Please, God," he whispered, before having an idea, one that might finally lead to a breakthrough.

He stood up and became light-headed again as he fetched Salma's handbag to take some money. She would refuse to let him go downstairs, so he didn't wake her up. He put on his shoes and jacket, opened the door, and then slowly closed it behind him. His legs struggled to support his weight as he tiptoed down the stairs, and he realized he hadn't left the building since the search on the first day.

Outside, his eyes were assaulted by the sun, and someone placed his hand on his shoulder. He turned and saw that it was Am Ibrahim, who lived on the second floor.

"Where are you going?" Am Ibrahim asked.

Mustafa pointed at the candy vendor walking toward them. "I want to get a balloon."

Am Ibrahim looked confused. "A balloon?" he asked.

Mustafa nodded.

Am Ibrahim signaled for the candy vendor. "Does your mother know you're down here?" he asked.

"Yes," Mustafa said.

The candy vendor approached them. "How are you, Mustafa?"

"I don't want candy," Mustafa said. "I'll get some when Zeina comes back."

The vendor smiled. "I'll be right here."

"Give him a balloon, please," Am Ibrahim said.

The vendor filled up a blue balloon with the gas Mustafa and Zeina sometimes inhaled to make their voices squeak. Am Ibrahim took it and Mustafa extracted the one-pound bill from his pocket.

"It's on me," the vendor said.

Mustafa took the balloon. A group of four teenagers sitting on the trunk of a car watched him. "Hello," one of them said, as if they were his friends.

Mustafa took two steps toward his building's entrance, then turned around and approached them. One of them hopped off the car and hugged him.

"How are you?" the boy asked.

"Can you guys go look for Zeina?" Mustafa asked.

The boy hugged him again. "All right," he said. "We will."

"Inshallah, she'll be back soon," another said.

"What's this for?" the third boy asked as he looked at the balloon.

"Please go," Mustafa said, before he turned around and walked away.

Upstairs, Salma's torso had dropped to the floor and she was snoring. Mustafa released the balloon from his grip and watched it levitate to the ceiling. He extracted a notebook from his schoolbag (which he hadn't touched in days) and ripped out a blank page.

Dear God, he wrote with the most exquisite handwriting he could compose.

I am writing you this letter so this will reach you quickly.
God, my sister Zeina has been gone for almost four days.
God, I want to tell you that Zeina is not a sister I find
annoying. I miss her so much. I am scared that I will never
see her again. I also want to say I'm sorry for stealing Ye-
hia's pencil case. I will never do anything like that again.
If this has been my punishment, I have learned my lesson.
I don't know what Baba has done, but we don't deserve
this. Please, God, I beg you. I love my sister very much...

Mustafa folded the sheet of paper as many times as he could. He stood up and opened the third drawer of the dresser, Zeina's, and started crying when he was struck with her smell. Every time he thought he had exhausted all his tears, a new thought, sight, or smell proved him wrong. He searched for a hair band and found a pink one, but that was Zeina's favorite, so he continued rummaging through the clothes until he found a black one, which he used to tie the folded letter to the end of the balloon string.

Thankfully, the balloon still levitated toward the ceiling.

"What are you doing?" Salma asked.

Mustafa jumped with shock.

"What are you doing?" she asked again, still lying on the floor.

"I'm going to send God a letter," he said.

She stared at him for a moment and then closed her eyes.

He turned around and approached the window.

"The roof," she said. "The roof is better."

She was right. There was a ledge right above their window on which the balloon might get stuck.

Halfway up the ladder that led to the roof, he heard Salma erupt with sobs, but she really ought not to. God must be busy with the millions of millions of prayers He received daily, and hopefully this handwritten letter would grant their case some expedition. He walked to the edge of the roof, made sure that the hair band was tight around the letter, and then released the balloon. He watched it levitate into the sky as it got smaller and smaller and the wind carried it toward the Nile. He tracked it until he no longer could and was certain it had reached enough altitude for one of God's angels to receive it. There was new hope now, and when he looked at the road below, he wasn't disappointed to find that the group of teenagers was still there, doing nothing to search for Zeina. The only help he needed was God's.

Of course, that was all six years ago. Now, Mustafa had lived long enough, and read enough Marx, Russell, and Camus, to know that not only was there no God, but life had no meaning; it was replete with unexplainable suffering and injustice, and people's attempts to believe otherwise were pitiful and absurd. He never confessed to such beliefs (God forbid Salma discovered that he was a disbeliever) but had found great relief in them. Only when he began to accept that no one and nothing—not a single civilian or government official across Egypt, nor any imagined deity in the sky—cared about his sister's abduction and murder, his mother's grief, or anything at all did the profound shock he felt toward life begin to dwindle.

Suicide was never a viable option, unfortunately, since it would only put Salma and Omar through more agony than they had already endured. During the darkest periods, Mustafa had fantasized about dealing with this conundrum by killing not only himself but the rest of his family as well. A year after Zeina's disappearance, he used to construct meticulous plans for how to kill them all and put them at peace.

Mustafa had had no choice but to go on living, and though today he wasn't exactly *thrilled* to be alive, he had come to find life manageable. The world wasn't terrible in all departments; it was meaningless and absurd, yes, but never boring, and he enjoyed learning more and more about its infinite peculiarities. He read the newspaper every day. He borrowed books from the Cairo library, anything from the Old Testament and Nietzsche's *Thus Spoke Zarathustra* to *The History of Ancient Egypt* and *The Behavior of Felines*. He had a collection of more than a hundred comic books stacked under his bed, went to the cinema whenever he could assemble enough money, and spent so much time navigating the internet at a café in Rud El Farag that the owner had stopped charging him, in exchange for Mustafa's help with errands.

Still, Mustafa would never go so far as to claim he was *happy*. There was no doubt in his mind that if he was ever given a button to end human existence, he would slam his fist on it as quickly as his skinny arm allowed. His only experience of joy came through good literature, through the pages where he momentarily became the jubilant protagonists. He had never gotten high or fallen in love. He had a couple of acquaintances from school, yes, with whom he shared notes and study tips before exams, but he wouldn't exactly call them his friends. Indeed, his best and most reliable friend was himself. And though sometimes, perhaps once or twice a month, he would experience an unexplainable dump, during which he would become so unreceptive to pleasure that he couldn't enjoy a chocolate bar or get out of bed, he didn't think he was depressed, as Salma often claimed. Not like the characters from Shakespeare's or Dostoyevsky's books, those terribly dismal bastards.

Mustafa would describe himself as *sufficiently content*. If he was left alone, he could usually fill his time and go to sleep without being too mortified by his life sentence inside the prison of human experience. He had a plan for how to spend the rest of his time too. He would continue scoring high grades on his exams and attend Cairo University for a lucrative but also tolerable field. Then he would graduate with honors, find a decent-paying job, and make enough money to move out of Ramlet Bulaq. He had no interest in the luxuries of the rich people who lived in neighborhoods like Zamalek; he did not want a beach house, Mercedes, or big backyard to sunbathe in. All he wanted was a spacious apartment where he could spend most of his time without having to ever leave. Realistically, the apartment would need four rooms. The first he would make into Salma's bedroom, the second into his own. The third he would make a library, with hundreds of books stacked along the walls, a computer with an impeccable internet connection, and a big chair for him to relax and read on. The fourth room would be a living room with a big sofa, a flat-screen television, and a DVD player, so he could watch as many films as he pleased, sometimes a few in the same day.

The only thing Mustafa struggled to envision with regard to his future was Omar's place in it. He couldn't imagine what sort of person

Omar would become. He couldn't even be sure that Omar would still be alive. And even if Omar survived and left the drug business in good health, as he supposedly planned to, Mustafa wasn't sure that they would remain close. With every month that passed, the two became more and more unalike and spent less and less time with each other.

Nevertheless, Mustafa could still read Omar with great ease. Mustafa was lying on his bed in the corner of his apartment, reading Mahfouz's *Midaq Alley*, when Omar walked in without whistling, singing, or announcing his arrival in his usual theatrical way. And Mustafa instantly knew that something wasn't right.

Salma had returned to her apartment across the hall.

"What's wrong?" Mustafa asked.

Omar lay on his bed, lit a cigarette, and stared at the ceiling.

Mustafa walked over and saw that Omar had stitches on his lower lip.

"Omar," Mustafa said. "What happened?"

Omar finally looked at Mustafa. "I need money," he said. "The four hundred you owe me."

For more than a year now, Mustafa had continually borrowed money from Omar's ever-growing savings: three pounds for a glass of mango juice; ten pounds for a spontaneous trip to the cinema; thirty pounds for new bedsheets. Omar had been glad to help Mustafa and ease their mother's financial stress. He had done it under the assumption that one day, when Mustafa became successful, it would all be repaid.

Today, Mustafa had nineteen pounds in his wallet.

"How am I supposed to do that?" he asked.

"I don't know," Omar said. "Figure something out?"

"You owe someone? What happened?"

Omar nodded.

"How much?"

"A lot," Omar said.

Mustafa sat beside him. "What happened?"

Omar barely took a breath between the long drags he was taking from his cigarette.

Mustafa sighed. Both he and Salma had warned Omar against his lifestyle countless times. "How bad?"

"Bad."

"Shit, Omar. I hope no one's going to come here and—"

"Of course not," Omar said. "Just... try. Will you?"

Mustafa noticed the scratch marks on Omar's arms. He became curious but not enough to inquire; he had a feeling the answer would only lead to a night of heightened anxiety.

"What's going to happen?" Mustafa asked. "If you don't come up with it."

Omar shook his head. "I have to. I will."

Mustafa sighed. "You have your savings."

Omar stood up and flicked the cigarette out the window. "Just give me as much as you can by Saturday," he said before he walked into the bathroom.

Mustafa returned to his bed and contemplated the problem. He could certainly find a way to make four hundred pounds, perhaps by working for Nader at the internet café full-time, but it would be impossible to do it in three days.

Mustafa was averse to stress, so he picked his novel back up. Surely if he failed to assemble the money, Omar would have no choice but to forgive him. It wasn't his fault, after all, that Omar was involving himself with savage people and calling them his friends.

Mustafa devoured a whole chapter on Zaita, a character whose profession it was to physically cripple people so that they could become sympathetic and successful beggars. And then Mustafa had a thought: What if something besides disability could inspire people to give him money? Perhaps he could find a crowded spot downtown and outline his family's tragic history on a piece of cardboard.

"Fuck it," he said to himself. "Whatever."

Omar was back on his bed, staring at the ceiling.

Mustafa closed his book. "I don't think I'll be able to pay you that much."

Omar looked at him. "At least two hundred?"

"I have nineteen pounds."

"Well, figure something out!"

"Why don't you just take the money out of your savings?" Mustafa asked.

"I will," Omar said.

"So?"

"So what?"

"Why do you need me to?"

"At least just ask Mama for a hundred or two," Omar said. "Give me *something*."

"You're telling me on three days' notice?"

"All right fine," Omar said. "But I'm not lending you money again. Ever."

"That's fine," Mustafa said. "I don't need it."

Omar snickered. "Yes, sure."

Omar often patronized Mustafa for having less money. One day, when the roles were reversed, Mustafa would remember to do the same.

Salma walked into their apartment and was surprised to find Omar home. "Oh," she said. "Look who's here."

"Hello," Omar said.

Mustafa realized he hadn't seen Salma and Omar interact in weeks. Omar always woke up after Salma left for Zamalek and returned home after she had gone to sleep. It was lamentable that his relationship with their mother was far less intimate than Mustafa's; sometimes it felt as if Omar were an orphaned cousin whom Salma had sworn to take care of. Still, the distance that had grown between them was far easier for Mustafa to handle than the hostility their relationship had once entailed.

When Omar first stopped going to school and dealing hashish, it only took weeks for Salma to find out, which led to daily fights for months on end. Fights that often brought them to tears and prompted Salma to expel Omar from their home twice, only to send Mustafa out to fetch him hours later. Fights that Mustafa eventually became so accustomed to, he would sometimes be lying on his bed, doing the Sudoku in the newspaper, while Salma told Omar, loud enough for the entire street to hear, that she hoped Omar would get arrested and imprisoned, like his father, so he could learn his lesson. That she ought to have known how much of a burden Omar would become when he came out of her womb crying with such devilish persistence. That she ought to have tossed him into the Nile right then and there.

Today, Salma had mostly accepted Omar for who he had insisted on becoming, with his financial independence sitting at the root of the peace agreement.

"How are you, Mama?" Omar asked.

"Have dinner with us," Salma said.

"I will."

Salma looked at Omar's stitched lip and sighed. She appeared on the verge of asking what had happened but began to pick up clothes from the floor instead.

"What's with arguing about money?" she asked.

Omar and Mustafa looked at each other.

"Nothing," Mustafa said.

"He needs money," Omar said. "I told him to ask you instead of me."

Salma stopped cleaning. "Is that true?"

Mustafa sighed. "Yes."

"How much?" Salma asked.

Mustafa was about to say eighty when Omar said, "A hundred and fifty."

"A hundred and fifty!" Salma said. "For what?"

Mustafa couldn't think of anything that would cost so much. Salma had already paid for a whole semester's worth of private English and biology lessons to ensure that he did well on his sanaweya a'ama exams.

"He has something on his peepee," Omar said, "that needs an expensive cream."

Salma looked at Mustafa for confirmation. He wasn't as shameless as Omar and never lied to Salma about anything besides his religious beliefs. The narrative was already half developed, however, and if Salma had a hundred and fifty pounds to spare, then perhaps it was worth the misdeed.

"It's true," Mustafa said.

"Tab stand up and show me," Salma said.

Omar laughed.

"No way," Mustafa said.

Salma approached Mustafa's bed. "Stand up, son. I'm your mother."

"No way!" Mustafa yelled as he turned away from her.

Omar's laughing escalated as Salma tried to turn Mustafa around.

"Mama, stop!" Mustafa yelled again, mortified by the thought of exhibiting his hairy genitals to his mother. "It was a joke. There's nothing."

Salma was silent for a moment before she smacked Mustafa's head. She had gained considerable weight over the past few years; she took a while to walk up the stairs to their floor and could no longer climb the ladder to the roof. But the swing of her arm had retained all the power it had always possessed.

"You're lying to your mother now?"

"No, Mama. I'm sorry. I just need some money."

She smacked his head again and Omar continued laughing.

"A hundred fifty for what? *Ha?* I'd think you wanted it for something filthy, but don't I know my son? He only wants to sleep with his stupid comic books."

"Oh!" Omar yelled.

Mustafa stopped laughing and looked at Salma with contempt. He was sick and tired of Omar's and Salma's comments about his lack of interest in sex. Why couldn't they drop it? He simply wasn't like everyone else; he felt no impulse to touch someone in such peculiar ways, not women, like he ought to want, or men, like Salma had feared, or himself, like Omar did in the bathroom daily. Even when he ejaculated in his sleep, it was always during a dream that had nothing to do with humans; last time, it happened during a dream inside the world of Lord of the Rings, as he stood in an Ent's cold shadow and heard its breathtaking, world-shaking voice. And though he had experienced the serenity that followed orgasm, he found semen, and the way it erupted out of him as he slept without permission, rather disgusting.

Salma and Omar had made such an issue out of the subject that Mustafa had feared something was wrong with him. And it was only when he researched the topic on the internet that he came to learn that it was common and perfectly fine. He was asexual, yes, and what an advantage it would give him. Unlike most people, he wouldn't have to waste thousands of hours searching for a partner, trying to court her, and then pleasing her with time, energy, and money for decades to come.

Still, it angered him when Salma mocked his manhood.

"Again?" he said. "Again you're going to start with that?"

"Khalas," Salma said. "I was joking."

"Enough of it," Mustafa said. "I told you I hate that. I've told you so many times."

"But you don't need money?"

"No thank you," Mustafa said.

Salma nudged his shoulder. "Are you sure?"

"Yes."

"Are you mad?" Salma asked.

"No," Mustafa said.

"Oh no," Omar said. "God forbid he gets mad."

"All right," Salma said. "Anyway. Dinner will be ready soon."

She returned to her apartment. Omar giggled in the aftermath of the exchange but quickly resumed staring at the ceiling with serious contemplation. There was finally some silence, and Mustafa managed to read two chapters of the novel before Omar walked over to Mustafa's bed.

"All right," Omar said as he sat beside Mustafa's feet. "Listen. You won't need to pay me back, but I need your help with something."

Mustafa closed the book.

"I'll need you tomorrow night," Omar said. "To come to the Road."

"Why?"

"It won't be much. But I need to come up with this money and—"

"Yabny, don't you have—"

"They need sixteen," Omar said.

"Sixteen what?"

"Sixteen bitches," Omar said sarcastically. "What would it be? Sixteen thousand."

"Yeah, right," Mustafa said as he sat up.

Omar looked away from Mustafa.

"*Sixteen thousand?*" Mustafa whispered. "What the fuck did you do?"

"It doesn't matter," Omar said. "I don't want to get into it. But it's someone big. And if I don't come up with the money, I might have to leave."

"What?"

"Go somewhere for a while."

Mustafa closed his eyes and fell onto his back. "We told you," he said as he grabbed his face. "So many times."

"I know. But I have a plan, brother. You just have to help."

Mustafa opened his eyes.

"All I need is one car," Omar said.

Mustafa had been rather accepting of Omar's foolishness, over the years; he had learned that criticizing every decision Omar made was only going to ravage their brotherhood. Still, he would never help him steal a car.

"You're on your own," Mustafa said.

"What do you mean I'm on my own?"

"This conversation is pointless."

Omar moved closer on the bed and put his hand on Mustafa's arm. "Listen," he said. "Just listen to me? Please. I have a whole plan. It's a bait and mug. You won't be at any risk. Nothing will happen to you if I get caught. And I won't even get caught. I have a whole plan that'll work. I know it will, but I need someone to help me."

"Ask your friends," Mustafa said.

"I can't," Omar said. "They'll ask for a share. And I can't have anyone know."

"You want us to both go to prison so Mama can finally—"

"Just listen," Omar whispered. "Listen to the plan and then say no. Please?"

Mustafa didn't respond.

"All right," Omar said. "So. We stop working the Road, all of us, usually around midnight. After that, so few customers come by, if any, that it's not worth continuing. But sometimes these customers come late, they find no one, then they leave. But this is the plan. All you have to do is sit on a chair, where we all usually sit, put a cap on your face, and pretend to be sleeping. That's literally all I need you to do."

Mustafa wanted to laugh and tell Omar that he was wasting his time, but he couldn't remember the last time he had seen so much worry in his brother's eyes. And if Omar was really at risk of being hurt, so much so that he would have to leave the city, wasn't it Mustafa's moral duty to help him?

"The customer will honk at you," Omar continued, "call for you from his window. But you stay asleep. See, the ones that come that late are usually drunk and desperate to smoke. So, whoever it is, he'll get out of the car and walk over to you. Hopefully. To wake you up. As soon as he does, you count to five, and then there's this hole in the wall that separates the Road from the eshash. You just escape into the eshash without showing him your face and go home. That's it. There's zero chance you'll be followed."

Mustafa began to understand Omar's preposterous plan. After Mustafa fled, Omar would approach the man in question and mug him, probably with his matwa. Then he would take the man's car and drive somewhere where he could sell the car at a discount to a dealership.

"The train tracks," Mustafa said. "It's dark there. And so you don't take any roads anywhere and come across a checkpoint."

Exuberance spread on Omar's face. "Yes!" he said as he grabbed Mustafa's shoulders. "You fucking asshole! Yes!"

Mustafa shook his head. "I didn't say I was going to help. But if you're actually thinking of doing this you should be smart about it."

"Yes, yes. I know. But... I beg you, brother."

"What about God?" Mustafa asked. "Do you not care what *He* thinks?"

Omar shrugged. "I have to survive."

Mustafa scoffed. For reasons he would never understand, Omar had held on to his faith. And if Mustafa ever tried to probe, by mentioning the free will paradox or bringing forth evidence of man's biological evolution, Omar would become annoyed and order Mustafa to stop. And it was not only the willful ignorance that drove Mustafa mad but the psychological dissonance too. If you asked Omar whether he believed a crime like the one he was plotting right now might lead to an eternal afterlife in Hell, he would nod, and yet here he was, plotting it, which had to be evidence that he didn't actually believe it. His true beliefs, it seemed, were too scary for him to uncover, and Mustafa sometimes struggled to be impervious to such ridiculousness.

"Please don't start with that," Omar said.

"What if there's someone else in the car?"

"I'll be watching from close by. If there is, I'll come and sell them what they need."

Mustafa thought in silence for a moment. He couldn't envision waking up tomorrow and thinking, *Today I will help Omar rob someone*, before having his mug of tea. Still, he could help Omar brainstorm the plan.

"It needs to be an automatic car," he said.

Omar's smile grew bigger. "Yes," he said. "So, you're in?"

Mustafa felt the hint of a rush he hadn't felt in years. How heroic would it be to help his brother in need? Omar often accused Mustafa of not having testicles, because Mustafa didn't belong in a crew, play sports, or spend half of his time fantasizing about women. But it was stupid to equate manhood with such activities; it was, however, going to be a testament to Mustafa's character if he helped save Omar from trouble.

It wasn't only the risk involved but also the moral ramifications that kept Mustafa from giving Omar his word. Mustafa was a nihilist, yes, but not one without morals. Stealing a man's car and causing him to fear for his life, if only for a few minutes, was the sort of crime that made the world a more wretched place.

"How are you going to do it?" Mustafa asked. "No matwas."

"Pepper spray. Blind him, then steal the keys. Maybe he leaves it in the ignition. That would be perfect."

"And tell him the police will have no problem finding the car."

"What?"

"After you spray him," Mustafa said. "Tell him he'll find the car tomorrow."

"All right, sure," Omar said. "Oh, and you have to go around the eshash. As you go home. Not through them."

"I didn't say I was going to help," Mustafa said. "I'm only helping you think."

Omar smacked Mustafa's leg. "Come on. I need my brother."

Omar was in the habit of abusing those words: *I need my brother.* The last time he used them was a couple of months ago, when he asked Mustafa to take a look at his hemorrhoids and describe their size and color, so Omar could understand how grave they were. Mustafa agreed and regretted it within an instant.

"What about all your friends?" Mustafa asked.

"We're not supposed to mug anyone at the Road. It hurts business. That's why I need you. I can't trust anyone else."

Mustafa thought in silence for a moment. Realistically, there was little to no risk of getting arrested for him and Omar. Everyone knew how little Bulaq police cared about what occurred in the eshash. When they found the abandoned car the next day, they would be incapable of investigating who was behind the theft, since they had no fingerprint database like Western countries. They wouldn't even bother to investigate, like they hadn't bothered to search for Zeina for more than one afternoon, as long as the person mugged wasn't some sort of basha, which wouldn't be likely. The only room for error was in the mugging. What if the man closed his eyes before Omar could spray him? What if he ducked and tackled Omar to the ground? For the first time ever, Mustafa was glad that Omar was an experienced and developed fighter.

"I don't know," Mustafa finally said. "I'll think about it."

5

Surprisingly, the bouncers of the United States gave me less trouble than they usually did at JFK Airport, despite my publicized association with Amir. For the first time since I began at NYU, I wasn't taken to the secondary inspection room, where I usually waited as an officer confirmed that I wasn't *the* Sherif El Sherbiny. At baggage claim, I wondered if it was because I had been assigned a marked profile of my own. How deep into my personal life had they peeked? *Here he is, the day the Knicks lost to the Lakers, purchasing two hot dogs before the game. Here he is sucking tequila out of his girlfriend's belly button in Cancún. All clear.* I had always been opposed to the idea of surveillance, but maybe it wasn't so wrong after all. I had just been spared unnecessary interrogation, and maybe, with less restrictions, they would've stopped Amir.

I took the subway instead of a cab into Manhattan, to mark the beginning of my transformation into a thrifty and responsible man. From now on, I would scrutinize every purchase I made and try not to waste any more of my family's money.

I was surprised when my phone rang only ten or so minutes after inserting my American sim card. I hadn't told anyone, not even Carmen and Taymour, that I was returning. It was an unknown number.

"Hello."

"Hi! Is this Sherif?"

"Yes?"

"Hi, Sherif. This is Adam Bowman from ABC News."

"Oh."

"Welcome back," he said, as if we were old friends. "Do you have a minute to chat?"

The train approached.

"No," I said. "I don't, actually. I'm not willing to talk and I'd really appreciate it if you didn't call me again."

"Oh. Well, we—"

I hung up.

As I rolled my suitcase onto my block, I saw Agim, the old Albanian American doorman who had watched the FBI escort me out of the building, push the revolving door around and around. Over the past few years, Agim and I had developed a kinship. On holidays I gifted him wine bottles and cigarette cartons; in return, he ignored most of the noise complaints he received from my neighbors on weekend nights.

"Sheero," he said as I approached. "Welcome back."

"Thank you."

"Long flight?"

"Very."

I walked into the building and he followed me inside.

"Hey," he said quietly. "Listen. There's... been reporters. Coming here."

I nodded. "Okay, cool."

"What should I say? If they come back?"

"That I'm not here? I don't know."

He nodded. "All right, sure."

"I'm sorry," I said. "I'm asking you to lie."

"No," he said. "It's fine. They're a bunch of entitled fucks anyway."

"Cool," I said. "Thanks, Agim."

He nodded and looked at me, clearly burdened with a thousand questions.

"Anything else?" I asked.

"Oh," he said. "No, not at all. Welcome back."

I waited for the elevator beside a young woman and her son, who was carrying a basketball he couldn't help but dribble.

"Danny," the woman said. "Stop that."

She reached for the ball, but it fell to his feet and rolled over to me. I grabbed it and offered it to her, and she took it from my hands without thanking or looking at me, which was strange, since white people usually thanked you for just about anything.

"I want to play," the boy said.

"Not here."

The elevator arrived and I followed them inside. I pressed for my floor, the seventeenth, and they pressed for the penthouse.

She stepped to the back corner of the elevator, pulled the boy close and placed her arm across the front of his torso. I stood with my back to them.

The elevator stopped on the second floor. My veteran neighbor, Stanley, dragged his laundry basket inside. He had a mole on his nose and his ears were the size of my whole hand. He reached for the button to our floor, saw that it had been pressed, and then looked up to see who of his neighbors was present.

"Oh, fuck me," he said upon seeing me.

The elevator doors shut, and I pretended he didn't say anything.

A moment passed before he turned and pointed his thick finger at me. "Listen here, boy. You stay away from me, yeah? You don't look at me. You don't speak to me. You don't come into the elevator with me. You understand?"

From the corner of my eye, I saw the woman tighten her grip around her son.

I continued to pretend the man wasn't addressing me.

"Do you understand me?" he yelled.

"Mom," the boy said.

"Don't worry," she said.

I looked at the boy, then back at the man. "You're scaring the kid," I said.

"No, *you're* scaring the kid," he said. "You're scaring *all* the kids. You and your fucking type. I fought for this country, so we could feel *safe*. For freedom. And you're bringing fucking jihadists into this country? Into this building?"

"Sir," the woman said as she covered her son's ears. "Please."

For a fleeting moment, I felt as if it was my duty to apologize. It was no longer the case that I had nothing at all to do with the tiny minority of Muslims who were radicalized; I had, indeed, unknowingly hosted one in this building two years ago, and if there was anyone Stanley had the right to blame Amir's actions on, it was the young man he was yelling at right this second.

I watched the number above me. Eleven floors to go.

"*I can't believe I'm going to be your wife*," Tamara said.

A silent moment passed before they both began to laugh.

A few months ago, Omar bought a beginner's English textbook with the hope of learning enough to understand Taymour's conversations. It was always frustrating to sit through conversations without having a clue what they were about. But the task had proved too difficult, and though Omar knew what *you* meant, he didn't know what Tamara had just said.

"*I also can't believe I'm going to live my whole life having only kissed one man.*"

"*That's not true,*" Taymour said. "*You made out with Amer in the tenth grade.*"

"*But I don't even remember that,*" she said. "*I was wasted.*"

"*I haven't done much with anyone else either.*"

"*But I haven't even kissed anyone else.*"

"*Well,*" he said, "*we can have you kiss someone. Maybe Aly or Sheero.*"

"*Ew.*"

"*Those are your options.*"

"*Fuck you!*"

Omar quickly glanced at them through the mirror. He knew what *fuck you* meant, but it didn't look as if they were having an argument.

A silent moment passed before Tamara spoke again. "I'm worried about these protests on Friday," she said. "What if people have a hard time reaching the wedding?"

"Don't worry," Taymour said.

"Omar," Tamara said. "Do you think these protests on Friday will be big?"

Omar thought for a moment. Did he tell the truth and risk upsetting her?

"I don't think so," he said. But it was a lie. If anything, the protests that were scheduled to take place on Friday looked as if they might be bigger than anything the country had yet seen.

"Will you be going?" Tamara asked.

"Of course not," Omar said. "How could I miss the wedding?"

"I mean if they go on for a while."

"Well," Omar said. "Yes. Of course."

In 2011, Omar spent the better part of the eighteen days it took Mubarak to step down right in the heart of Tahrir Square, where he set up tent and befriended Egyptians from all walks of life, some of whom he still called from time to time. He was blinded and choked by tear gas more times than he could remember and took a rubber bullet to his right ear, which had permanently damaged his hearing. He carried the bodies of injured strangers toward ambulances without ever finding out if they had lived; others he carried toward ambulances knowing well that they were dead. He could still remember it: the bleeding eyes and missing teeth, the men being run over by trucks and the sound of their limbs and ribs being crushed, the faces so swollen they stopped looking like they belonged to a human, the women being dragged by their hair, the mothers running into the middle of the fighting, screaming and searching for their children. And then there was the joy, the crying and laughing and dancing, the feeling that he had a family of millions of brothers and sisters. That now they could build a country that would treat their children with more love than it had treated them.

Today, Omar's hope for such change had vanished, but he would be joining the upcoming protests nevertheless, because nothing enraged him more than the way the Brotherhood had hijacked the revolution and ruined its legacy, and it was all too self-evident that *anyone* besides them should run the government.

"If we weren't leaving the country, I would go," Tamara said.

"I actually wanted to ask, sir," Omar said, as he looked at Taymour through the mirror. "If I could ask Nada for Aly Beh's number, or someone at his office."

"For what?"

"In case the country erupts again. To reschedule the meeting with Mustafa."

"Oh, yes," Taymour said. "Of course. Ask Nada."

"Thank you, sir."

"What meeting?" Tamara asked.

"His brother is meeting with Aly," Taymour said. "To see if he can work at Aqualife."

"No way!" Tamara said. "That's great."

Omar looked at Tamara through the mirror and smiled. He had interacted with her at least once a week for almost three years now; he had had dozens of conversations with her and witnessed her become emotional in the back seat several times. And yet she was still, at large, quite an enigma to him. On the one hand, he had seen her embarrassingly drunk countless times, had taken her home after sleeping at Taymour's apartment on many occasions, and was absolutely certain she was having premarital sex with Taymour. Still, he couldn't help but have the utmost respect for her. She had forced him to reconsider his beliefs and, for the first time, understand that they didn't apply to all people. Despite her many transgressions, she was a woman of the utmost class, with a character to match that of a hundred men.

"I did an internship there," Tamara said. "A training. When we were in school."

Omar smiled through the mirror.

"They're a great family," Tamara said.

"So I hear," Omar said, though he had never heard anything of the sort.

"Very hardworking," Tamara said. "Make sure he's on time. And that he's wearing something nice."

Omar looked at the mirror and saw Tamara smiling at him. "I will," Omar said, though he didn't plan on speaking to Mustafa for a few days.

What Mustafa had said earlier in the day, about wishing it had been Omar who was abducted and killed, had been wholly unforgivable. For years now, Omar had supported him with almost religious devotion. He had given him thousands of pounds with no expectation of having them returned any time soon. He had skipped naps to sit with Mustafa and provide him with what little social interaction he could. He had dedicated many of his days off to taking Mustafa out of their apartment, if not to the cinema or the corniche, then to the ahwa down the street. He had even gotten into the habit of changing Mustafa's bedsheets and always was the one to take out their trash. And he had done it all because, second only to Salma, there was no one Omar loved more. Mustafa was his twin, his other half, the first face he had seen every morning of his entire life. They had always shared everything: a bedroom, bathroom, hairbrush, shower sponge, and even the womb they inhabited before birth. It was cruel, then, that Mustafa should declare such hatred toward Omar. Omar knew the words had come from a place of despair, from a boy who sometimes went a whole week without laughing, but he wasn't going to forget them any time soon.

The next morning, Omar was thrilled to sleep in past noon, for Taymour had informed him that he wouldn't be needed until late in the evening. He woke up to the sound of a broom scraping the apartment's carpeted floor. He opened his eyes and was surprised to see that it was Mustafa, not Salma, squatted down and pushing dirt onto the dustpan. He almost made a remark but quickly remembered that he wasn't on speaking terms with Mustafa. Cleaning the apartment, for once, was not going to serve as a proper apology.

He sat up and lit his first cigarette of the day. He watched Mustafa pick up clothes from Omar's chair, fold them, and place them inside the drawers in Omar's dresser.

"You can stop that," Omar said.

Mustafa looked at him. "You do it all the time," he said, as if to pretend he was doing this to be kind.

Omar looked away. It was difficult to observe Mustafa for extended periods of time; he was like a well whose deep deposit contained all of the world's sadness. And sometimes, if Omar looked closely enough, it would ruin his mood for hours.

Mustafa's pale face was covered in acne scars. His long beard was patchy, and his curly hair, which he washed only every few weeks, was drenched with dandruff. A layer of fat protruded from the space between his shirt and his pajama pants because he was gaining weight at a pace his clothes couldn't match. His spine was significantly misaligned with his hips, from all the years he had spent in bed, and tilted so far to the left it looked like he was on the verge of attempting a cartwheel. On his face, one could always, with little exception, find an expression of rage mixed with exhaustion, similar to that of a man who, after waiting for hours for his turn at the bank, has just been told that the bank will be closing and he would have to return tomorrow. If you were to ask him how he was feeling, he would softly say something quite dismal, something like *I wish the world would burn at last.*

Omar figured there was no harm in getting his clothes sorted, though Mustafa wasn't exactly folding them with the right technique. He took a hot shower and, when he came out, found Mustafa changing his bedsheets. He repressed his urge to laugh, lest Mustafa think he was forgiven, and searched his dresser for the dark blue jumpsuit he liked to wear while at home.

Across the hall, Salma was knitting the last part of a bright purple sweater. As always, Omar was faced with two options: he could start an argument about the insanity of *still* dreaming of Zeina's return or save it for another day.

He extracted a box of Gouda cheese from the fridge and took a loaf of balady bread from the basket beside it. He realized the smell of cigarettes hadn't just followed him from his apartment.

"You're smoking again?" Omar asked her.

"Oh, enough of it," Salma said. "There are bigger problems in the world."

Omar chuckled. "What?"

"There's feta cheese with tomatoes behind the rice."

"It's like we've switched roles," he said.

Salma looked up at him. "Switched roles?" she asked. "Tab eh raa'yak? That yes, I'm smoking. A hundred cigarettes a day kaman."

Omar sat on the floor in front of her. "Your choice," he said before he began eating.

"So did he tell you?" Salma asked as she smiled.

Omar didn't know what she was talking about.

"Mustafa!"

"Aiwa!" Mustafa yelled from the other apartment.

"He's cleaning," Omar said. "I thought I was dreaming."

"I know," Salma said. "I think he's actually happy... about the job."

Mustafa walked into the apartment.

"Tell him," Salma said.

"About what?" Mustafa asked.

"That you're coming to the wedding," Salma said.

Mustafa nodded. "Well," he said. "You just told him."

Omar looked at Salma. "He'll need a suit."

"I know," Salma said. "He also needs it for the job. We'll go get one today. So he can look good and respectable. Right?"

Mustafa performed a smile.

Omar continued eating. Salma instructed Mustafa, with her head, to apologize.

"I'm sorry," Mustafa said. "You know I didn't mean it."

"What if he doesn't get the job?" Omar asked Salma. "Will you return it?"

"He'll get the job," Salma said. "Inshallah."

"And who's paying for it?" Omar asked.

Salma looked at Omar as if he had said something offensive. For almost a decade now, he had helped finance Mustafa's life: he had paid for Mustafa's clothes, doctor visits, and school supplies, all under the assumption that, one day, when Mustafa presumably got a job, it would be paid back.

"Suits are expensive," Omar said.

"Oh please," Salma said. "I'll split it with you."

Omar was only being petty. In truth, there was nothing he wanted more than to see Mustafa walking out of their apartment in a respectable suit.

"If you keep on like this, you're going to finish all your money," Omar said.

"No problem," Salma said. "Who knows how long I'll even live."

Omar sighed. Salma was only halfway through her forties but often made remarks about death. Sometimes it was as if Omar were raising two children.

"I'll pay for it," Omar said, without looking at Mustafa.

"Thank you," Mustafa said.

Omar continued eating and Mustafa sat beside him.

"I think we should go visit Baba," Mustafa said.

Omar and Salma looked at each other as if to confirm that they had heard the same thing.

"What?" Salma said.

Omar chuckled. "It actually took me a second to understand who you meant."

When Abu Ahmed refused the family's prison visits, back in 2000, Omar took it as a message that Abu Ahmed didn't care about them in the least. That he was a monster. With time, however, he realized that Abu Ahmed had probably been too ashamed. And though Omar could certainly empathize with weakness, which, essentially, was Abu Ahmed's governing quality, he had never been compelled to try to visit him again.

"Why would you want to do that?" Omar asked.

"He's going to come back," Mustafa said. "You realize that, right?"

"We'll be long gone," Omar said. "God knows I'm not staying in this shithole."

"How could you speak of your home like that?" Salma asked.

Omar shrugged. "He probably doesn't even remember our names."

Omar was surprised that he still harbored resentment toward his father. It had been months, if not years, since Omar had last thought of him.

An hour later, they walked into the clothing store in Embaba where Omar had bought his suit for the wedding, and the store clerk was quick to point out that Mustafa would be needing an XXL.

"He's not *that* big," Salma told the elderly man.

"He's as handsome as his mother," the man replied, before extracting a jacket and a pair of pants from the array of black suits.

Salma giggled at the compliment and Omar was slightly disturbed.

The clerk guided Mustafa toward the changing room.

"Yalla, go with them," Salma told Omar.

"Why?"

"He's going to need help."

Omar was tempted to protest, but Salma was right. He followed Mustafa into the changing room, hung the suit on the rail beside them, and told Mustafa to remove his clothes.

Once he was only in his underwear, Mustafa looked at Omar for guidance. "All right," he said. "What happens next?"

Omar smiled. Mustafa had always been a nerd; he could recite the biographies of the figures behind half of Cairo's street names and explain how your body fought off viruses. But in the face of straight-forward tasks, he was often helpless, thinking that there was a succession of steps he ought to take and anything else was wrong.

Omar extracted the white shirt from underneath the jacket. "Put this on," he said.

Mustafa took the button-up shirt, unfolded it, and tried to stick his head into it, as if he were putting on a T-shirt.

"All right, stop," Omar said. He undid the buttons, turned Mustafa so they could both face the mirror, instructed him to put his arms up, and guided Mustafa's hands into the sleeves.

"It's so hot," Mustafa said.

Omar forced Mustafa, whose arms were still raised, to turn around. He buttoned the shirt down and stepped back until he was leaning on the door behind him. The sleeve length, shoulder width, and collar fit perfectly, but Mustafa's mountainous stomach was threatening to launch one of the buttons toward Omar.

"Try to..." Omar said as he pointed at the button. "Just a little."

Mustafa sucked his stomach in, arms still raised.

"All right," Omar said. "Now jump up and down."

"What?"

"To make sure it's not fragile," Omar said. "Just... trust me."

Mustafa did as he was told.

"All right," Omar said. "Good."

"Is it fine?" Mustafa asked as he continued jumping, already out of breath.

Omar bit down on his lip to repress the laughter. "Yes," he said. "Now sing the national anthem."

Mustafa stopped jumping, put his arms down, and they both began to laugh.

"Asshole," Mustafa said.

"It's good," Omar said as he checked the fabric of the pants.

Mustafa threw his arms up and hugged Omar.

Omar was quite surprised; he couldn't recollect the last time Mustafa had hugged him, or shown any sort of affection, for that matter.

"I'm sorry," Mustafa said.

"It's all right."

"I'm sorry I'm such a burden."

Omar forced them to separate. "What's with you?" he asked. From the moment Omar had opened his eyes in the morning, Mustafa had acted like an entirely new person: one who might have some reason to smile. And though Omar was happy to witness it, he worried the sudden change would pass within days and he would only be disappointed once again.

"Nothing," Mustafa said.

Omar examined Mustafa's pupils. "You're not high on something, are you?"

Mustafa snickered. "No. I'm just... I'm sorry I'm such a burden."

"You're not a burden," Omar said. But it was a lie. Mustafa consistently took time and energy from Omar and didn't provide anything in return. He no longer gave Omar insightful advice, as he once used to, or accompanied Omar to get shawermas or shishas, or helped the family with money, or lifted Omar's mood. In fact, Mustafa usually made sure to annihilate Omar's good feelings whenever he could. When Omar came home overjoyed by Al Ahly's win in the African Champions League, Mustafa was quick to remind him of the seventy-four supporters who died in Port Said the year prior. *It's crazy that everyone has moved on*, Mustafa said. He was, indeed, quite the burden, and Omar couldn't imagine how it felt to be aware of that.

Mustafa tried to hug again, but Omar stopped him. "Enough," he said, as he removed the pants from the hanger. He wasn't going to allow them to get emotional in the changing room of an Embaba suit shop.

Minutes later, they walked outside to find Salma and the store clerk complaining about the recent daily power cuts. They caught Salma's eye, and she rang her tongue against the roof of her mouth to ululate.

She approached Mustafa and touched the jacket.

The store clerk was quick to point out that Mustafa looked like a groom.

"How much is it going to be?" Omar asked him.

"This one?" the clerk asked, buying time to think of an appropriate price with which to begin the bargain. "Thirteen hundred."

"Thirteen?" Omar asked, with the tone of someone who has been insulted. "I thought we were friends, my friend."

"*I swear to God*, you won't find a suit like this one cheaper than twelve."

"Eight hundred is all the money I have in my pocket," Omar said.

"Eleven hundred."

"If I could give you more than eight-fifty," Omar said, "I swear I would. Just because you're such a kind man."

"One thousand," the clerk said. "And I'll take the loss for you."

"Honestly?" Omar said. "Nine hundred is the highest I'll go."

"Fine," the clerk said. "Just because he looks so good in it."

Omar chuckled. The day bargaining was abolished would be the day Egypt prospered.

The clerk congratulated Mustafa. "Yalla, go back," he said as he pointed at the changing room. "So I can pack it up for you."

Mustafa was on the verge of turning around when...

"Wait," Salma said. "Let's take a picture."

"Mama," Omar and Mustafa said.

"With your phone," Salma told Omar. "Please."

"What picture?" Omar asked. "I'm wearing sweatpants."

"So just me and him then," Salma said as she pulled Mustafa closer.

Mustafa grinned uncomfortably, as if he were a football player too kind to disappoint a fan.

"Please," Salma said, already posing beside Mustafa.

Omar extracted his Nokia phone from his pocket.

"It's one of the best suits I have," the clerk said.

Salma held Mustafa's hand, a smile stretched across her face.

Omar took the picture. "It's good," he said as he brought the phone down.

"Please, son," Salma said. "I want one with the two of you."

Omar sighed and showed the clerk where to click on the phone screen. He put his arm around Mustafa's shoulders and smiled as the clerk stepped away from them.

"You look great," the man said as he positioned the phone in front of him.

"They're the fruit of my life," Salma said.

"God keep them around for you," the clerk said.

"They're twins," Salma said. "They only have each other."

"Khalas ya Mama," Omar said, anxious for the photograph to be done with.

It was during such moments that Omar became painfully aware of the extent to which the three of them were ghalaba: disadvantaged people whose causes for celebration extended no further than the occasional apple pie or new suit. A family starved not only of possessions but also of love, with one dead, one imprisoned, and one depressed to the point of handicap. A family taking a photograph because it would be months, if not years, before the opportunity presented itself again. And his only solace was that, one day, God might gift him a family with better luck. His dream was a wife and numerous children—an athlete, a nerd, and a troublemaker—with whom he could pose for photographs in many nice places, like the beach in Marsa Matrouh and the opera house in Zamalek.

6

As much as I was happy to celebrate Taymour and Tamara's marriage, I woke up the day of their wedding with an anxiety I hadn't felt in months. My mother had decided on becoming veiled and didn't see why she should postpone until after the wedding. It had also been somewhat reckless to invite Najla, who confirmed last night that she would be coming; the date we shared had been lovely, but she was still a stranger, and I would probably have to give her my full attention the whole night.

In the living room, Ma was walking on the treadmill she had recently bought and placed in front of the TV, to use while she watched a dubbed Turkish soap opera.

"How was it?" she asked.

"It was great."

"I'm almost done," she said. "Four hundred meters."

I watched as sweat trickled down her face and arms.

"Go, Ma, go," I said.

I approached the treadmill and increased the speed.

"What are you doing?" she yelled.

"Come on," I said. "Faster."

She began to speed walk. "I'm tired!"

"You got this!"

We watched her DISTANCE COVERED on the screen as she began to pant, putting one foot in front of the other. As soon as she reached the five-kilometer mark, she slammed the stop button, grabbed the rails, and stepped off the moving surface.

I gave her a round of applause.

She walked over to the sofa, soaked in sweat, and collapsed. I sat on the sofa across from her as she looked at the ceiling and gathered her breath. For a forty-eight-year-old, my mother was in great shape. She could live another forty years.

"Why are you single, Ma?"

She looked at me and laughed.

"I'm serious."

"What are you saying, exactly?"

"I don't know. Maybe you can go out there and meet someone."

"Yeah, right."

"You've been alone for almost twenty years. You might have thirty or even forty ahead of you. Why not spend them with someone?"

"Are you planning on abandoning me?"

"You know what I mean."

She didn't respond.

"Have you considered it?" I asked.

She pointed at the water bottle on the coffee table beside me. I brought it to her.

She took a gulp. "It's not as easy as you think," she said.

"I'm sure."

"Besides, I'm not alone. I have you. Your aunts. Mama. Why are *you* single?"

"Don't," I said.

I was yet to tell Ma about Najla. She would probably ask at least a dozen questions that I didn't have the energy to address, so I decided to simply have her meet Najla at the wedding and answer any questions after the fact.

"Sit down, Sheero," she said as she made space for me on the sofa. "I've been wanting to tell you something."

I sat and waited as she took another sip of water.

"Let's see," she said. "My wedding with your father was scheduled for July 30, 1987. I think it was two weeks before it, I got a call from your grandmother. Madame Nivine Ramez. Who I was yet to meet, by the way. Tante Nivine didn't approve of me, of course. Because of who they were and who *we were*. So your father and I actually got engaged with only your grandfathers present. So she calls me, and she says, *I want you to know that I won't be attending the wedding. And if you have any dignity, you'll call it off, unless of course you're willing to marry a man whose mother won't accept you. Goodbye.*"

"Damn," I said, though I could certainly imagine the nana I remembered, who passed when I was fourteen, making such a call.

"At first I was shocked," Ma continued. "I thought, *How could this woman be so evil?* And you know what I did? I called your father and told him the wedding was off. Of course, in the end, I loved him too much, and he promised she would be at the wedding. And she came. But it was horrible. Throughout the whole ceremony, she didn't smile once. And she gave my sisters such looks. She even asked your father to ask Khalto Heba to stop dancing like a belly dancer.

"For a while, she made me so insecure. But slowly, I stopped caring. Yes, I was a peasant's daughter. So what? We make the *best* food and tell the *best* jokes. And I should be proud of it. And so I behaved the only way I knew. If we were eating ful and eggs for breakfast, I ate with my hands. If your father was being mean to me, I would smack him even in front of his mother, because that's how my people show love. And whether or not she was going to accept me, I didn't care. But you know what? She did, eventually. Aren't people funny like that? Years passed and she began to let me in. She began to give me advice, asked to speak to me on the phone after speaking to your dad, and by the time you were born, we were quite friendly."

I nodded. "I see what you're saying, Ma. I'm doing my best."

"I know you are. And I think you're doing a great job."

I smiled.

"I like the idea of having this big wedding be my first night in a veil," she said. "Throwing myself into the deep end, you know."

"Well," I said. "I think you'll look beautiful either way."

She smiled. "Of course I will."

I still wanted to say *but. But why? But is it necessary?*

At the Marriott in Zamalek, Taymour, Tamara, Aly, and Claire were taking a shot when I walked into Taymour's suite. Tamara and Claire were wearing robes and had had their hair and makeup already done, despite the wedding being five hours away.

"You're late," Taymour said.

"How are you guys feeling?" I asked Taymour and Tamara.

Tamara shrugged. "It hasn't hit me yet."

"Me neither," Taymour said.

"Maybe because we've already taken three shots?" Claire said.

We laughed.

Tamara sat on Taymour's lap and kissed his head. "How do we look?"

"Beautiful," I said.

It was impossible not to be jealous. I feared I would never find the love that existed between Taymour and Tamara. They had their issues, of course. Tamara couldn't help flirting with strangers, which had always made Taymour uncomfortable. She liked to hike, boulder, and scuba dive during holidays, whereas he preferred to eat, nap, and watch movies; she wanted him to be balanced, but he continued to be obsessed with work. And yet the degree to which they considered each other's feelings had always seemed miraculous to me. I remembered one night, in New York, when Taymour and I were playing *FIFA* in his living room. Tamara had an exam the next morning and was sleeping in his bed. In the middle of a game, Taymour paused and made a quick trip to the bedroom. Her exam required a laptop, apparently, and since she might not find a seat beside an outlet, he thought he should charge her laptop overnight.

"You promise you'll name your first son Sheero?"

"No one said anything about any sons," Taymour said hurriedly.

Tamara glared at him. "Calm down?"

I laughed along with Aly and Claire.

Eventually, the girls left us alone and went to Tamara's suite to continue preparing. Slowly, more and more of Taymour's other groomsmen arrived at the suite: a couple of former tennis training partners; Aly's older brother, who was also the entrepreneur behind the company I worked for; and a paternal cousin.

The next couple of hours entailed photo shoots in different parts of the hotel: the suite's terrace, which offered a panoramic view of the Nile and Cairo's sprawl; the main garden, whose majestic trees had probably been around for more than a century; and the staircase in the hotel's main hall—a hall built as a palace in the nineteenth century to host Napoleon and his wife during the opening of the Suez Canal, which would now host Taymour and Tamara's wedding.

After thousands of photographs of the couple and bridesmaids and groomsmen were taken, there was the katb ketab, the intimate religious ceremony that preceded the large wedding party, during which the couple was officially married. Taymour, Tamara, Tamara's father, and an officiant sat on a long sofa in front of a table. Taymour and Tamara's father held hands under white cloth as the officiant placed his hand above the cloth and guided Taymour through his vows.

As I took pictures, Najla texted and asked if she could get my opinion on which dress she should wear.

I said yes and waited nervously. The impression she had given me throughout the date was one of a classy and cultured woman, but she was an outsider to these circles, and I worried she would choose something a little too casual or over the top, and it would put me at even greater risk of being perceived in a nonideal way.

To my surprise, she sent me two pictures so pleasing that I had to turn away from Taymour and Tamara, who were finishing up the official procedures, in order to hide the big smirk that formed on my face. In one picture, Najla stood in front of what looked like a full-length mirror in her living room, wearing a long dark green maxi dress that matched her hazel-colored eyes and dark brown hair pretty well. In the other, she wore a black wrap dress that revealed most of the length of her toned, olive-skinned legs and a fair amount of cleavage.

You look incredible in both, I sent.

That doesn't help! Which one matches the general dress code better? she asked.

In reality, neither of the dresses would stand out among the crowd; some guests would wear something as revealing as the black one and others would wear something more conservative. My first instinct was to support the green one, because it looked classier and would help my purposes of being perceived as someone who belonged. The black one, however, was the one I wanted to see her in, and as I recalled my mother's advice earlier in the day, I urged myself to stop caring. I did, in fact, belong here. Tonight was the wedding ceremony of my two best friends.

I really want to see you in the black one, I sent.

After the katb ketab was over, we returned to the suite, and I was tempted to drink from the champagne bottle Aly popped in a way

I hadn't been since New York. *It's my best friend's wedding night,* I thought, *I should be able to have a glass,* but such a thought could, within minutes, ruin all the work I had done over the past three years to stay sober. I couldn't predict whether one drink would put me at risk of relapsing, so I stepped out onto the terrace and lit a cigarette, while Aly went downstairs to meet his date, a girl he had been seeing for a few months, at the hotel entrance.

Salma had painted a picture of what Taymour's wedding would look like for Mustafa. She said vast amounts of delicious food would be served, everyone would be well dressed, and by the end of the night, most of the guests would be remarkably drunk. He was excited about the food and nervous about the collective intoxication. He had come across a drunk person only four times in his life: twice with Abu Ahmed and twice when Omar was a teenager. How would he react if, for example, one of Taymour's friends drunkenly introduced Salma as having been Taymour's maid? What would he say if someone offered him a drink and insisted on raising a glass for the newly married? The anxiety hounded him until he walked into the Marriott with Salma and Omar and joined a line of fellow guests waiting to go through the hotel's metal detector. When Salma poked a young man in front of them and said hello, Mustafa's nervousness shot up to such a degree that he considered fleeing.

The young man turned around and his eyes were startled. "Salma!"

"How are you, Aly?"

"Hello," Aly said. "It's been so long. How are you?"

The young woman beside Aly turned around and Mustafa was shocked: her dress, which from the back covered most of her legs, was split at the front in a way that exposed much of her upper thighs; what's more, a great degree of the curvature of her breasts was also exposed. In his twenty-two years of life, Mustafa had never been witness to so much of a woman's naked skin.

"This is Tara," Aly said as he gestured toward her.

Salma shook her hand. "Hello," Salma said.

Tara smiled. "It's nice to meet you."

"Salma basically raised Taymour," Aly told her.

Tara nodded with a confused expression until she figured out what Aly meant.

"Of course," she said. "How lovely."

"This is my son Mustafa," Salma said. "And you know Omar, of course."

"Of course," Aly said as he shook Omar's hand.

Mustafa put his hand out. "Hello."

Aly shook Mustafa's hand. "Hello. We'll be waiting for you on Sunday, ha?"

Mustafa grinned and looked at the side of Aly's suit jacket, unsure of how he should react and where he should place his gaze. "Yes, of course," he mumbled.

"He's very grateful," Omar said. "A little shy, but very smart."

"No reason to be shy at all. We'll see you inside, then?"

After the metal detector, an elevator took them up to the hotel's lobby, which they walked out of and into an outdoor area. As they journeyed through the walkway that separated the hotel's front build-ing from the central one, a glowing swimming pool to their right and an outdoor restaurant to their left, Mustafa pulled Omar closer to him.

"You didn't have to say I was shy," Mustafa whispered.

Omar chuckled. "You looked like you saw a ghost."

In the historic central hall, they walked up a set of stairs that got gradually narrower, until it split into two sets leading to opposite sides of the second floor. It reminded Mustafa of the staircase in *Titanic*, though that was a British ship, while this building had been designed to replicate the French palace of Versailles.

Indeed, everywhere he looked, Mustafa was given the impression that he had traveled not across the Nile but across the Mediterranean, where men and women greeted each other with lips-on-cheek kisses and it was acceptable for a woman to expose most of her legs. And for the first time in what was probably months, he remembered Zeina, who used to repeatedly tell him that he wouldn't believe just how different Cairo's rich were. Just how free. Of course, at the time, she had been a naive child unaware of the existential angst that often came with freedom and wealth, and the cultural belief systems the rich were not truly free from. He had read extensively about it and could see it everywhere around him: the exaggerated smiles and performed laughs, the women with fixed noses and cosmetically manipulated faces, the reliance on alcohol, the handbags and watches that all looked the same. To him, they appeared no more content than the average person; if anything, it was probably exhausting to have to live up to such high standards. Nevertheless, he could see why Zeina, barely a teenager, had found their lives so compelling.

The twenty-feet-high doorway they approached led into the massive wedding hall, which had to be at least half the size of a football field, with chandeliers hanging from the incredibly high ceiling and candle- shaped sconces on the maroon-colored walls. Scattered across it were dozens of round tables covered in white cloth and what seemed to Mustafa like an excessive amount of silverware.

Salma, Omar, and Mustafa hadn't taken more than two steps into the hall before a man wearing a tuxedo approached them. "Hello. Omar?"

"Yes," Omar said as he shook the man's hand.

The man greeted Salma and Mustafa with an exaggerated smile on his face. "We have your own table reserved, over here," the man said, as he pointed at a table in the corner of the hall.

The man escorted them to their table. "Should you need anything," he said. "Please let me know."

Eventually, the wedding hall downstairs had filled up with guests and my mother was minutes away, so I decided to leave Taymour and go downstairs until I was needed for his entrance into the ceremony in half an hour's time. The wedding hall was vast and there was a dance floor in the center made of glazed black ceramic. A couple hundred guests had already arrived, with almost every man dressed in a perfectly tailored suit and every woman in a dress that accentuated her best features. Celine Dion and Andrea Bocelli sang from the speakers hanging from the maroon walls.

As I walked toward Aly and his date, who were at the bar on the other side of the hall, I made eye contact with Aly's mother, who was speaking to a few other guests, and was then obliged to go over and greet her.

We kissed on both cheeks.

"How are you, Tante? You look great."

"This is Sheero," she said to her group. "Aly's friend."

I shook hands with the two men and woman.

"How's everything?" she asked me.

"It's good," I said. "It's hard to believe this is happening."

She smiled. "I'm sure. And how's work with Yehia? He says you work quite hard."

"He's taught me a lot for sure. He's such a workhorse."

"Look at your friend being all giddy," she said as she looked at Aly. I chuckled.

"What do you think of Tara?" she asked me.

"She's lovely," I said.

"And have you found yourself a girlfriend yet?"

"I actually have a date today," I said. "She'll be here in a bit."

"Oh, how wonderful," she said. "Is she pretty?"

"She is," I said. "And she shares your name, actually."

"Then she must be a sweetheart as well."

"I'm sorry," one of her friends interrupted as he stepped closer to us. "What's your name?" he asked me. "Sherif what?"

I chuckled to disguise my horror. "El Sherbiny."

"Oh," the man said as he pointed at me, the smell of whiskey on his breath passing with the breeze. "Oh! You need to come with me. Please."

I swallowed my saliva and look at Tante Najla. *What's happening?* I wanted to ask.

Tante Najla smiled. "This is Sameh, a friend of Tamara's father."

"Please," Sameh said as he grabbed my hand. "Please come with me."

"Where are you taking him?" Tante Najla asked.

"Just one second," Sameh said, as he placed his hand on my back and led me away. "Khaled will love this. Khaled!" Sameh called to his friend, who was chatting with another group we were now approaching. "Look."

Behind them, walking in from the hall's entrance, I recognized my mother wearing a beige dress and veil, with a brown fur jacket on top.

Khaled and the two women in his company turned toward us.

"Look," Sameh said with great excitement. "Guess who this is."

Maybe Amir was a subject they were genuinely fascinated by; maybe they were going to broach it in a way that wasn't degrading.

"Hello," Khaled said.

I forced a smile and shook his hand.

I glanced at my mother and saw that she was now approaching us.

"Guess!" Sameh said.

"What's going on?" I asked somewhat nervously, desperate that they get this over with before Ma reached us.

"I don't know?" Khaled asked.

I smiled uncomfortably as sweat permeated the shirt under my tuxedo. Ma was now within a few dozen feet, and I was already sorry that she would have to witness this. I would never see the point of her becoming veiled, but she looked beautiful, as always, and I hoped whatever this conversation brought didn't embarrass her.

"Sherif El Sherbiny," Sameh said with a grin.

"Sherif El Sherbiny," Khaled echoed.

"Who's related to?"

Khaled's expression morphed into revelation. I wanted to disappear.

"Abdallah's son!" he shouted.

I was so relieved that I released a quiet moan.

Ma was now among us, and I saw her react with a smile at the mention of my father's name. When I looked at her, Khaled turned to look at her too, and then they both erupted with celebrations as soon as they made eye contact.

"Amany!" Khaled shouted as he threw his arms around her.

"How are you, Khaled?"

They hugged for a moment, separated, looked at each other, and then hugged again.

"You look *so good*," Khaled said. "You haven't aged a year."

Ma smiled. "You're just saying that."

I was so confused that I looked at Sameh.

"Khaled was good friends with your father," Sameh said. "I only met him a few times."

Once they were separated, Khaled looked at me and pulled me in for a hug as well. "Oh, I can't believe it," he said. "You don't look like your father at all! You know that? Only your mother."

"I was wondering why you didn't guess," Sameh said.

"He doesn't look like him at all," Khaled said.

"Really?" Ma asked. "All I see in him is Abdallah."

Khaled smiled. "No, no. Abdallah was an ugly bastard. This one is handsome like his mother."

My mother greeted the two women in our company, who had watched the entire exchange with a smile on their faces.

"You were friends?" I asked Khaled.

He laughed and looked at Ma. "You don't tell him about us, or what?"

"Of course I do," Ma said. "Or I did, when he was a child. You don't remember your father had a close friend who lived in Australia?"

I did remember, so I nodded. "Kiko?"

"This *is* Kiko," Ma said.

They all laughed.

"Only a special few call me Kiko, by the way," Khaled said.

I revisited images of my father's funeral and the people who hugged and kissed me more passionately than everyone else. Suddenly, Khaled looked familiar.

"Yes," I said. "You were at the funeral."

Khaled patted my shoulder. "Of course I was."

Aly arrived and greeted my mother, who told him that she needed to talk to his brother Yehia because I had been working too many hours lately.

"Ma," I said.

She laughed. "I'm joking."

"We need to go upstairs," Aly told me. "To bring down Taymour."

I nodded and looked at Ma, who had already jumped into conversation with Khaled about his life in Australia. I told her that I would be back soon, and she told me to take my time. As Aly and I exited the hall, I looked back and saw her laughing rather loudly with Khaled and the two women in his company as they all approached the bar. Right now, she was one of only three veiled women in the hall, one of whom was Salma, Taymour's former caretaker. Ma wouldn't be drinking alcohol, speaking any English, or running into any cousins, nephews, and nieces. Still, her body language revealed not a drop of discomfort, and it calmed me in a way that made Najla's text—*I'm on my way*—even more exciting.

For some time, Mustafa simply watched as more and more guests slowly poured into the hall. He enjoyed people watching and noticed that each guest was following a similar routine upon arrival. First, they found a table on which the women could put down their handbags. Then they walked straight to the bar, only greeting the guests they were forced to cross paths with. They gave the busy bartenders their orders and waited. Once they got their drinks, most guests lit a cigarette and then began to walk around the hall and greet people with enthusiasm, chatting with them for a few minutes before moving on to another group of guests. By the time they were done greeting people, they returned straight to the bar for a second drink.

Mustafa was also surprised to see that none of the guests were paying for their drinks. For a moment, he was excited by the idea of, at some point during the crowded ceremony, sneaking over to the bar and ordering himself a drink. He had never in his life been drunk, and perhaps this would be his last opportunity. The only mind-altering substance he had tried was hashish with Omar years ago, which had been a bad experience that ended in a panic attack. From what he had read, alcohol was different: the grandmother of all depressants, the killer of all sorrows. Still, the stunt would necessitate being incredibly close to a large group of people, pushing his way past them, and risking embarrassment. He would order a whiskey with ice, which he knew from films and books to be a common drink, but what if the bartender asked him about the brand? In the end, he resigned himself to the impossibility of the idea and had only the food to look forward to.

Suddenly, the lights across the hall were dimmed, and guests began to line up on each side of the aisle that led from the entrance to the dance floor in the middle of the hall. Salma and Omar stood up, and Mustafa reluctantly did the same. They walked up to the line of guests and stood behind it, with Salma struggling to get a good view of the entrance, given all the people in front of them. When a massive roar of cheers exploded in the room, Mustafa looked at the entrance and saw a line of seven men coming down the walkway with a young man, presumably Taymour, following them as confetti and fake leaves were thrown onto them.

They stopped at the edge of the dance floor and stood facing the entrance.

"Is that him?" Mustafa asked Salma.

"Yes," Salma said.

A slow and gentle song was played as everyone, including Omar and Salma, turned their attention to the entrance, from which the bride would emerge. Mustafa, on the other hand, couldn't help but stare at Taymour, whom he had seen only once before, at age four or five, when Salma was forced to take him to Zamalek along with Zeina. Taymour was truly as handsome and stylish as Mustafa had imagined he would be. His suit fit him perfectly and his beard was impeccably trimmed; he also had great posture and carried himself with confidence. Though his attention was on the entrance, he kept looking around him, as if searching for someone, and whispered something to the older man beside him, presumably his father, who also began to look around the hall. Within seconds, the host who had escorted Mustafa's family to their table was summoned, and when Taymour said something into his ear, the host immediately turned and looked straight at Mustafa, through the dozens of guests between them. Mustafa quickly looked away, embarrassed for having stared at them so persistently. When he looked in their direction again, he saw that the host was quickly walking in their direction, and within seconds he was among them.

"Miss Salma," he said. "Please come with me. Taymour wants you beside him."

Salma and Omar immediately began to follow the host. Mustafa, on the other hand, couldn't so much as take one step forward. The thought of being greeted by Taymour and his father unnerved him, and to stand beside the groom, to be the center of attention of several hundred people, would be literal torture.

When Omar turned to see why Mustafa wasn't following them, Mustafa was quick to think of an excuse. "I'll go to the bathroom and come," Mustafa said, which Omar probably knew was a lie but accepted anyway.

Now standing awkwardly and pitifully alone, Mustafa had no choice but to make his way out of the hall. He planned on sitting on a closed toilet in the bathroom for ten or fifteen minutes, until the celebratory episode was over and he could return to his seat in the corner of the hall without standing out as awkward, but there were so many guests walking in and out of the bathrooms that he ultimately decided to make his way to the parking lot and find solace with some fresh air.

Right outside the hotel's main entrance, Mustafa came across a woman in a black dress who looked exactly like Zeina. She was looking down at her cell phone but looked up at him as he passed her. Their eyes met and then he quickly looked away, out of fear of staring for too long. When he was behind her, he looked back and saw her turn and glance at him as they made eye contact for a second time. She quickly looked away as well, then began to slowly walk toward the exit of the parking lot.

She was walking away and getting smaller in his vision, but he could see, from where he stood, that she had the same hurried gait that Zeina had once had.

Mustafa could only figure that the emotional stress of being at the ceremony was beginning to have an effect on him. Though it had been years, he had seen Zeina on other girls' faces before, in the streets and at markets, years ago when he still hoped to find her—when he still hoped she was alive.

Mustafa walked to a corner of the parking lot and tried to ground himself in reality. He closed his eyes, took a few deep breaths, and recalled his logical thinking. It was strange that the woman resembled Zeina so much, and she had clearly been struck by his presence enough to stare. Most likely, however, he had looked at her with a startled expression that she found threatening and prompted her to look back at him.

It was impossible for Mustafa not to pity himself. He had come to the wedding with the intention of, for just one night, acting like a normal person and making Salma happy, and yet here he was, hiding in the parking lot, hallucinating his dead sister. Within minutes, he renounced any hopes of being able to remain at the wedding any longer and decided to return to the hall and tell Salma and Omar he was leaving. Outside the hotel entrance, he saw one of Taymour's groomsmen looking around the parking lot and holding his phone to his ear.

As Mustafa passed him, the man looked at him.

"Hey," the man said. "How are you?"

"Hello," Mustafa said.

"You're Salma's son, right?"

"Yes."

"I saw you next to her," the man said. "I need to go say hello to her."

Mustafa nodded.

The man removed his phone from his ear and looked down at it. "How is it off?" he murmured to himself, before looking up at Mustafa. "Sorry. Did you happen to see a woman standing out here, just a couple of minutes ago? She's wearing black?"

"Yes," Mustafa said. "She walked that way." He pointed at the street outside the parking lot, where the Zamalek traffic was crying with sporadic honks.

The man looked at the street, then back at Mustafa. "Are you sure?"

Mustafa nodded. "She has hazel eyes?"

"Yes, she does."

"She walked that way."

"All right, thanks," the man said, before he began walking toward the street.

"Excuse me," Mustafa said, almost instinctively.

The man turned around. "Yes?"

"Sorry. What's her name?"

"Sorry?"

"Is her name..."

An awkward pause of silence took place between them.

The man appeared confused. "Najla," he said. "Why?"

"Sorry. Never mind. I'm really sorry."

"No worries," the man said before he turned around again.

Inside the hall, most guests were dancing around the bride and groom at the center of the dance floor. Foreign music was blasting from the speakers, while the lights on the ceiling pointed at the dance floor moved and changed colors simultaneously. The guests danced and drunkenly yelled the lyrics while looking at each other and holding hands with great excitement, as if in disbelief that they could recite the lyrics with such precise synchronicity.

Salma and Omar were standing just outside the crowded dance floor, clapping along to the music and watching the exuberant celebrations.

Omar saw Mustafa first. "That long in the bathroom?" Omar asked, yelling in Mustafa's ear so he could be heard over the loud music.

"Taymour wanted to say hello to you," Salma yelled to Mustafa.

Mustafa could only bring himself to nod. He leaned toward Omar's ear. "I saw a woman who looked exactly like Zeina."

Omar's smile vanished. He grabbed Mustafa's shoulders. "Are you all right?"

Mustafa wasn't all right. In fact, he was becoming certain that these were going to be some of the last hours of his miserable life.

"I guess just seeing things," Mustafa said as he leaned toward Omar's ear.

"Yes," Omar said, turning Mustafa toward the crowd and beginning to clap along once again to the music. "Just try to enjoy yourself."

"I'm thinking of leaving," Mustafa said.

"At least wait for the food," Omar said. "You won't regret it."

Soon enough, servers began to bring out trays of different dishes and place them on the long table on the other side of the hall. Mustafa was annoyed when Salma insisted that they be the last people to join the line that quickly formed on one side of the hall. He feared that, by the time they got to walk through the buffet, many dishes would be finished and gone, which would further taint what had already become a dreadful night. In the end, he found only abundance at the buffet and was shocked at all the types of food he failed to identify. A dark red salad Salma called beetroot. A black sauce pasta apparently made of squid ink. Small and shiny red chunks of meat, sitting on a bed of toast, that Mustafa thought was undercooked beef until Salma assured him it was raw tuna. Something that sounded like tartara.

Despite the foreign dishes and the confusion, the meal was one of the best Mustafa had ever had, and his taste buds exploded with a degree of delight he had experienced only on a few occasions throughout his life.

After most of the guests were done eating, they returned to the bar and the dance floor for what appeared to be a second round of festivities. Omar and Salma were happy to continue spectating and clapping along, but there was nothing left for Mustafa to do but go home and sleep, so he announced his desire to leave alone in a taxi, which, perhaps unsurprisingly, neither Salma nor Omar protested at all.

7

The morning after the wedding, Mustafa woke up earlier than usual, just after ten o'clock, and felt a degree of unwillingness to get out of bed that trumped everything that had come before it. His pitiful performance the night prior, as well as Salma and Omar's expectation that he would put on a suit and go to a job interview tomorrow morning, when in fact he had two years of university ahead of him, all came together to make him realize that it was time to end his life once and for all. That it was going to be impossible to live through one more morning like this one.

Today would provide a window of opportunity, since Salma and Omar always went to HyperOne, the warehouse supermarket from which they bought the week's groceries, every Saturday night. Now, Mustafa only needed to spend his last moments with Omar without revealing his intentions.

Omar came out of the shower whistling a tune, as usual. Mustafa was still underneath his blankets, so Omar was startled when Mustafa spoke. "What's your plan for the day?"

"Shit!" Omar yelled. "You scared me. Why are you awake?"

Mustafa sat up. "I went to bed early."

Omar opened the window and began to put on his own new suit. "I'm taking Taymour to the airport. Then we're going to Hyper at night."

"All right," Mustafa said. "What are you going to eat?"

Omar tucked his white shirt into his trousers and extracted a dark blue tie from his dresser, which he put in the pocket of his jacket. "Ful Nour," Omar said. "As always."

"I think I'll come with you," Mustafa said.

As he tied his belt, Omar stared at Mustafa for a silent moment, as if suspicious of Mustafa's behavior.

"What?" Mustafa asked.

"Nothing," Omar said. "Get up, then. I don't have that much time."

Mustafa was dressed within a minute. At Ful Nour, they snagged one of the many green plastic tables on the sidewalk, most of which were full of men hurrying to swallow their breakfast before work. Omar grabbed the busy waiter's attention and yelled for five ful and five ta'ameya sandwiches.

"Five only?" the waiter asked, making a joke about Mustafa's body weight.

Omar chuckled. "He's on a diet!"

"God bless him," the waiter said.

Mustafa smiled. "Can you tell him I want the ta'ameya without salad?"

"The ta'ameya without salad!" Omar yelled.

The waiter didn't hear him.

"Ya Bassem!" a man sitting at a closer table yelled. "The ta'ameya over there without salad!"

The waiter looked at Omar and confirmed.

"Thank you, sir," Omar said.

"Of course," the man responded.

"People are decent, aren't they?" Omar said to Mustafa.

Mustafa nodded as a tension grew inside him. He felt a duty to tell Omar his feelings—that he was terribly sorry for his inability to be better, that he couldn't have made it this far without him, that there was no better man to take care of Salma—but it would only cause suspicion. He rarely became sentimental; if he did, Omar would question the reason for it and, when he found Mustafa later tonight, suspect that Mustafa had indeed committed suicide.

Omar and Salma were going to be devastated, that was certain, but Mustafa's hope was that it was the kindest to all in the long run. He only needed them to believe that his death had been accidental. Otherwise, they would live the rest of their lives believing that Mustafa had gone straight to Hell.

"I'm really sorry for what I said to you," Mustafa said.

"It's all right. You've already apologized."

"I didn't mean it at all."

Omar snickered. "Maybe you meant it a little."

"No. Not at all. You're the closest person to my heart."

Omar laughed. "Which heart, exactly?"

Mustafa shook his head. Omar had never been comfortable speaking of feelings, neither his nor Mustafa's, and always used humor as a way to hide.

"I'm joking," Omar said.

Their sandwiches arrived. Mustafa realized he was sharing his last meal with Omar. He bit down on the tip of his tongue and stared at one spot on the table to prevent any tears from escaping.

"We should do this more often," Omar said.

Mustafa nodded, the lump inside his throat keeping him silent.

"Maybe when you start working," Omar said. "I think you'll get the job. I think Taymour Beh will make sure of it."

Mustafa nodded.

"You should come to Hyper and help us out. If you're feeling good today."

Mustafa shook his head. "I think I'll grill or something."

Omar finished his sandwiches and urged Mustafa to hurry up.

They paid the waiter and walked back toward their building. As Omar walked around his car, Mustafa was unsure of what to say or do; he wanted to do something, express affection in some way, but they only ever hugged on their birthday.

"All right," Mustafa said.

"Bye," Omar said without even looking at Mustafa.

"You know it's National Twin Day," Mustafa said.

Omar stopped before his car's door. "What?"

"It's National Twin Day," Mustafa said again. "In America."

Mustafa was lying. National Twin Day was on August 3, but Omar was unlikely to ever confirm the fact.

Omar smiled and walked back toward Mustafa, arms held up. "I know you don't like them," Omar said, referring to hugs, "but if it's National Twin Day..."

Mustafa wrapped his arms around Omar and pressed a little too tight, for a little too long, to maintain his act of composure. But he didn't care. Perhaps it was more important to express love for Omar properly, if only one more time.

"You smell like shit," Omar said as they separated.

Mustafa smiled. "Sorry," he said.

Mustafa realized Omar's last words to him were going to be *you smell like shit*—a fact that Omar might regret for years to come. But before Mustafa could say anything else, Omar was already in his car.

Mustafa walked up the stairs of his building with the pace of someone in his nineties. His sadness was not concerned with the future they wouldn't share—for truly there was none to look forward to—but with the past, with all the potential they had had and all their dreams that had never come true. The dreams Mustafa used to construct with Zeina as they lay on their roof and looked at the sky. It was regrettable that blessings like Omar had gone unnoticed for so long. Such was Mustafa's eternal curse; his demons consumed everything, every thought he had, every second he was awake. They seldom granted him the breath of air required to be grateful for anything. And though they had to be obliterated at last, it was comforting to see that, despite them, there had been love in his life.

Upstairs, Mustafa tucked himself into bed with the intention of releasing the tears that had almost escaped him when having breakfast with Omar, but in the end, none came. He only felt numb and eventually fell asleep.

He woke up a couple of hours later to the sound of Dohr prayer. He called for Salma, but no one responded, which meant she had already left for the fruit market, which she always went to on Saturday mornings. It was twenty minutes past noon.

Mustafa opened his bedside drawer and extracted the sixty-five pounds he had saved, which he would use for his favorite snacks and drinks.

At El Farghaly Fruits, he bought a cup of mango juice and drank it as he sat on the trunk of a roadside car. A cat, fast asleep on the sidewalk in front of him, was startled awake when a glass shattered across the street. Mustafa reached into his cup, grabbed a chunk of mango, and tossed it toward the cat, who was startled at first, then intrigued, then overjoyed as it proceeded to lick away.

Mustafa suddenly felt receptive to the beauty around him: the light blue of the clear sky, the enthusiasm with which Bibo served customers tea at the ahwa across the street, the meticulous production line created by ants around a chunk of food on the edge of the side-walk. And though it was tempting to be deceived by this sudden grace, he knew it was the joy of imminent death, not life, that he was experiencing. He was like a prisoner who suddenly feels nostalgic for the cell he's about to be freed from; despite the many things he suddenly appreciated about it, his desperate need to leave and never return remained with full force.

Next, Mustafa went to the kiosk down the street from his home, where he bought a Twinkie, a Mars bar, a Bounty bar, a bag of spicy Doritos, a can of Coca-Cola, a can of sour cream Pringles, and two Mega ice-cream cones of different flavors.

"Is it your birthday or what?" the teenager who worked the kiosk asked him.

"No," Mustafa said. "It's not just for me."

On his way home, Mustafa observed the people walking up and down the street, carrying workbags and groceries and babies and prayer mats, and wondered how many of them had ever considered ending their lives. How many of them felt betrayed for having been birthed and sentenced to a whole life in their human minds. Never in his twenty-two years had anyone in the neighborhood committed suicide, not to his knowledge, at least, probably because most of them believed in God.

In his apartment, he ate the snacks on his bed as slowly as he could. He started with the ice cream, then moved on to the chocolate, and finished with the chips. And as he chewed on his first handful of Doritos, he was comforted by a certain thought. For years, this had been Mustafa's only reliable source of pleasure, muffins and pizzas and spicy fucking Doritos, and whatever remnants of doubt he still had that he ought to kill himself at last were extinguished the second he recalled this wretched fact.

Thankfully, he was still able to enjoy the whole bag of Doritos.

Once he was finished, he opened his disorganized closet and extracted the boxes underneath his piles of clothes. He would need to get rid of all the journals he had kept, which dated back to 2003 and lasted up until a few years ago, when he still possessed the naïveté to believe his thoughts were worth recording. Though he hadn't looked at them in years, he knew they contained a hoard of disturbing thoughts that he would never want Omar or Salma to read through.

He extracted every single journal from the boxes, stacked them up for disposal, and then grabbed one and opened it to a random page.

August 18, 2005 was written on the top right corner.

The first line: *I am a grapefruit picked too early. I will not ripen, I will only rot, and no one will benefit but the maggots that devour me. I do not know from which tree I was stolen.*

Mustafa was nothing if not consistent. He closed the book and dumped all the journals into a plastic bag he would dispose of. He heard Salma coming up the stairs, so he quickly hid all evidence of his food binge and pushed the bag of journals underneath his bed.

"Mustafa," Salma said as she climbed the stairs. "Are you awake?"

"Yes, Mama."

"Come help me with these bags."

A few steps down, Mustafa took the bags of fruit from Salma and went into her apartment. She removed her veil as soon as she was inside.

Mustafa realized she was sweating a lot, so he fetched some toilet paper from the bathroom and gave it to her. She used it to wipe the sweat off her forehead. He stepped toward her and quickly kissed the top of her head, which she thankfully didn't find suspicious.

"What would we do without you, Mama?"

"*You* would rot away in a matter of hours," she said.

He forced a smile.

"It's so hot," she said.

"You shouldn't be carrying so many groceries on your own."

"Well, then you should come help me next time."

"Fine," he said. "I will."

She looked at him and raised her eyebrows. "Really now?" she asked.

"Yes."

"And I'm supposed to believe that? You've never helped me once."

"I know," Mustafa said, his voice breaking. "I'm sorry."

Salma squinted her eyes. "What's going on?" she asked.

"Nothing."

She approached him as he refused to meet her eyes with his.

"What's wrong with you?" she asked.

"Nothing," he said again, but, of course, she knew he was lying.

"Don't make me worried now," she said.

He closed his eyes. This was really meddling with his plan; later, both Salma and Omar would recall his strange behavior before his death. Perhaps it was delusional to hope they would believe it was an accident.

She smacked the top of his head.

"Mama!" Mustafa yelled.

"Are you going to tell me what's happening?"

Mustafa heard footsteps approaching their floor. From the corner of his eye, he saw an envelope being pushed into the apartment through the crack underneath Salma's front door and then heard more footsteps going down the stairs.

She turned around, saw the envelope, then faced Mustafa again.

"What's that?" he asked.

"Probably Omar's bank statement."

"But he always slips it under our door."

"Don't change the subject."

"Mama, I'm fine. I just feel bad that I never help you with these things. That's all."

She scrutinized his eyes for hints of dishonesty. "Are you smoking hashish?" she asked. "Don't tell me we got your brother to stop so you could—"

"I'm not smoking anything. I promise."

"Swear on your mother's life."

"I swear on my mother's life," he said. He quickly glanced at the envelope again and realized it didn't have any logo or written word on its face.

"All right," she said. "I believe you. I hope you're not lying."

He walked past her and approached the envelope.

"Now clean up the fridge," she said.

He picked up the envelope and looked at the other side, which also didn't have anything written on it. "That's strange."

"What?" Salma asked.

"It doesn't say the bank's name. Or Omar's name."

A silent moment passed. "Open it," she said.

"No," he said. "You know how he got last time."

A few months ago, Omar got into a big fight with Salma because she had opened his bank statements and asked Mustafa to read out Omar's purchases.

Salma began to remove empty plastic packaging from the fridge. Mustafa remembered the lady in the black dress. He inspected the envelope and looked up at her. "It's bothering me," he said as he ripped the envelope open.

He glanced at the corner of the paper to confirm that it was a bank statement, but it wasn't. It was a page ripped out of a notebook.

He quickly extracted and unfolded the paper, which was covered with lines and lines of written words. On the top left corner of the first page, it said, *To My Family.*

His arm dropped to his side, and he suddenly felt as though his perception of his surroundings was slowly becoming clouded. He looked down at the length of his body and then looked up at Salma for confirmation that he wasn't dreaming.

"*Bismillah El Rahman El Raheem,*" she said as she looked at him. "What's going on, my son?"

Mustafa exhaled the air he was holding in. He lifted the paper and read, but not out loud.

> *I don't know where to begin. Every time I imagine you reading this, I imagine you burning it right afterward. I imagine this will devastate Mama. Maybe it will. I guess I will just tell you the story, the truth, and see if you will find me worthy of your forgiveness. I don't think I am. That's why I haven't reached out all these years.*

Mustafa looked at Salma, who quickly released the empty egg box from her hands when she saw the expression on his face. She took a few steps backward and he rushed toward her before she could fall, then helped her sit on the bed.

"It's a joke," he said to himself. "Someone's playing a joke on us."

"Is it her?" she asked softly through her panicked breathing. He looked down at the paper.

> *A few days ago I was with a man who revealed to me that he was going to his friend's wedding. Taymour Malik's wedding. I realized I had met the man before once upon a time in a life I have done my best to forget. I went to the wedding and saw Mustafa, and I realized it's time I stop running. It's time I reach out to you. My family. My mother and my brothers. And so here it is. Written down here is as much of the truth as I can remember.*

Salma grabbed his free hand and pressed on it as hard as she could. "Speak."

"It must be a joke," Mustafa said, but the only person who could be behind a prank of this sort was Omar, who would never do such a thing.

When Mustafa looked at Salma, he saw that color was quickly abandoning her face. "Mama," he said as he sat beside her. "You need to breathe."

Mustafa looked at the letter again. It was two and a half pages long.

"She didn't even know how to write," he said.

Salma grabbed the hand with which Mustafa held the letter and brought it as close to her face as her limited strength allowed. "What does it say, my son?"

Mustafa began to read out loud.

"*First, I'd like to say that I didn't leave you because I didn't love you. I truly hated my life. I hated my father. I hated going to work with Mama every day and spending all my time shut up inside a room. I hated seeing people have everything when I had nothing. I hated cleaning after them. Watching Baba beat Mama like that, I felt like it was my fault. I wanted to get away. I found a docked felucca on the corniche and slept inside it in the cold.*"

"In the name of God," Salma began to cry.

"*The next morning I just walked,*" Mustafa read out loud, despite his growing struggle to breathe. "*Downtown, I saw a group of girls begging*" and making money on the streets. I started doing the same because I wanted to book a bus ticket to Hurghada, a place I saw photographs of in a magazine in the madame's apartment. I wanted to go there and be there for as long as I could before coming back home. I wanted a break. So I did that. A man told me about a bus station in Giza where all the tourist buses left. I remember thinking that the longer I was away, the more Baba and Mama would treat me better when I returned. That they would realize just how much they loved me. For a long time I have hated myself for abandoning you. I still do. But maybe you can understand that I was only a hurting child.

"In Hurghada, I made more money begging from tourists than I had ever held in my hand. On my first day, one European woman gave me a hundred pounds. I ate McDonald's and ice cream. It only took a few days for me to get in trouble with the police. I wasn't supposed to be begging from tourists or sleeping on the street. An officer threatened to arrest me and started kicking me in public for begging. He had told me to stop and I hadn't. One man named Ricky was walking by and got the officer to stop. Ricky was British but he spoke Arabic. He had lived in Hurghada for a decade. When he asked me where my family was, I told him I didn't have one. That I was an orphan street child and that my name was Najla.

"I know that this was quite horrible to do. I know that you were probably suffering back home, thinking that I was kidnapped or dead. Please try to understand that I was too young and hurt to care. Ricky ended up taking me to his home, which was a nice apartment right there in Hurghada, a short walk away from the sea. He and his wife, Penelope, had a daughter my age whom they had adopted from a local orphanage. They offered me food. A shower. A bed. Penelope went out and bought me clothes. They didn't explain why they were doing it and I didn't ask.

"Even Malak, the girl, welcomed me into her bedroom. On the third day I went to the cinema with her. I did it all with the intention of waking up one day and simply leaving. But the longer I stayed, the more I became attached. No one had ever treated me or looked at me the way they did. The three of them would watch me sing on our balcony, and Penelope would clap like I was a superstar. And everything changed when a few days later Ricky asked me if I wanted to sing at his pub.

"There were at least fifty people that night, and the way they cheered for me, I felt like I was in Heaven. He told me I could do it every Friday, if I wanted.

I know what you must be thinking. I thought of you. I loved you. I did. All I remember thinking was that I knew exactly where you were and that you wouldn't be going anywhere. So I wanted to take my time. I wanted to make the dream last as long as possible. I almost called once, but I didn't have the courage to face your anger. Eventually, within a month or two, Ricky and Penelope asked me if I would like to become Malak's sister. If I wanted to have papers. A name.

"I wish I could describe to you the way they celebrated me. It made me sick to think that I would have to go back to living under Baba's ceiling. To sweeping the floors of rich people in Zamalek. I missed you. I swear I did. But I had felt more free in a month than I had felt my entire life. So I said yes. And they took me to a local orphanage, where I lied and said I had no idea who my parents were, that I had lived in the streets of Cairo and begged my whole life, that I had recently arrived in Hurghada on a bus. I was registered as an orphan and officially adopted. My name became Najla Tamer Amin. They give orphans fake names of their choosing when they don't know who the biological parents are.

"Penelope began to homeschool me so I could eventually join Malak at school. I began to read. And write. I swam in swimming pools. I sang for people every week and Ricky even paid me an allowance for it. Within a year, I was in school. I made friends. I wore makeup. I was gifted a keyboard and had my own piano tutor come to the house twice a week. But the secret I was keeping began to haunt me. I began to dream of all four of you every night in ways that were horrifying. I had episodes of hysterical crying. I started realizing all the pain I had probably caused you. I started realizing that you probably thought I was dead. At fourteen I started smoking hashish on a daily basis. I caused Ricky and Penelope a lot of trouble and heartbreak. To have such a secret, another name, and not be able to tell anyone was horrible, but I can't imagine that it compares to what you endured. Please believe me when I say that it took me a while to begin understanding just how much pain I must have caused you. Before that, I was blind to the reality, too busy being seduced by my new life, too busy collecting the debt on everything I believed I had been entitled to. I even convinced myself that Mama and Omar hated me and that you, Mustafa, were the only one who cared, but that you would also quickly forget me. I know now that this was not true.

"*I ended up graduating from school and singing around Hurghada in restaurants and bars and hotel lounges. I made enough money to be able to live on my own. Malak went to the Netherlands for university. Eventually, I told the three of them the truth and it caused a storm. Ricky and Malak forgave me. Penelope couldn't. She insisted that I return to you, and when I insisted that I wasn't ready, she wanted me out of the house. Ricky didn't. It burned their marriage to the ground. They ended up getting a divorce, and she returned to Spain. She's still there and we don't talk.*

"*I teach piano lessons and sing at events for a living. Crossing paths with Mustafa has forced me to accept what I've been running away from for so many years. The truth. That you are my family. My mother and my brothers. That you deserve to know what happened to me. That you deserve an apology, even if you won't accept it. Please know that this is not my first attempt to reach out. A few years ago I took a taxi all the way to Bulaq, and when we turned into our street I became so terrified I urged the driver to turn around. I couldn't even glance at our building. I am still terrified now of the horror this will cause you and the hatred you will feel for me. I've sat down to write this letter more times than I can count. For years, I told myself that it was better for you to think that I was dead than to be told this horrible truth. Maybe I was right.*

"*My address is 22 Syria Street, in Mohandesin, right above Gigi's Hair Salon. I live on the fourth floor. If you wish to come see me, and spit on me or slap me, come. If you wish to talk, come. I'll be here. If you don't come, I'll know that you don't want to hear from me ever again. Your sister and daughter, Zeina.*"

Mustafa looked up. Salma was still there. Tears and snot were rolling off her chin, but she was barely making a sound. She had both hands placed on her chest, one on top of the other, and was looking up at the ceiling with closed eyes.

"Mama," he said. "I saw her. Yesterday."

Salma didn't move. "I waited all these years," she whispered.

Though he was mortified, a chuckle escaped Mustafa. "Yes," he said as he ran his eyes over the letter, to confirm that it was still there. "Yes, you did."

And then Mustafa lost control; what began as a chuckle of disbelief slowly turned into frantic, openmouthed laughter. He looked at

Salma, who, for more than a decade, he had cast as delusional in her hopes, and began to laugh with such intensity that he felt his skull could explode. All these years, he had been under the impression that his family had been the victim of a great metaphysical crime, that a number of arbitrary circumstances had been conjured up by the universe to allow for Zeina's abduction and murder. But, in fact, the family had only been victim to the decisions of a selfish and entitled child. Indeed, Salma had spent thirteen years waiting and praying for the return of someone who lived twenty minutes away, on the other side of the Nile, above Gigi's Hair Salon. And all Mustafa could do was laugh and laugh.

Acknowledgments

This book was born in an intro to creative writing class I took as a sophomore at NYU.

Thank you to Jocelyn Lieu and Charles Bock, my teachers during the couple of years that followed, for encouraging me to keep writing, and to Zadie Smith, with whom I took a class my senior year, for teaching me how to read like a writer.

So many friends have supported me throughout this journey.

Thank you to Mariam Fayez, who read and praised my work before anyone else.

To Camila Cury, Alexia Akbay, Alya Sorour, and Salma El Alfy, who read my manuscript and gave me feedback when it was still quite funny that I was trying to write a novel.

To Omar El Batawi, who hosted me in his apartment for months as I wrote the first draft and with whom I was not embarrassed to share that I wanted to get published.

To Aly El Alfy, who always believed I would publish this book, even when I didn't.

To Salem Salem and Karim Karim, whose families I consider my own.

I'm also indebted to many of the people I was lucky to meet and work with at NYU's MFA program.

Thank you to Joyce Carol Oates and Chuck Wachtel, whose praise kept me going. To Jonathan Safran Foer, who taught me the value of looking at my work as objectively as possible. To Nathan Englander, who challenged each word in my sentences. And to David Lipsky, who uncovered the tricks of storytelling in a way that changed my writing forever.

To all my NYU peers, especially Caitlyn Barasch, Elizabeth Nicholas, Raven Leilani, Andrea Gale, Dario Diofebi, Ethan Loewi, John Maher, Tim Glencross, and Scott Gannis. It is possible that this novel would have failed to come true without your insight. I am lucky to be friends with such talented weirdos.

To the poets: Aria Aber, Momina Mela, Maddie Mori, and Marney Rathbun, whose friendship kept me afloat during those tough New York winters.

I'm indebted to Noor Selim and Alya Sorour, the first people outside the MFA program to read this novel start to finish. Thank you for celebrating it the way you did.

I signed with my agent, Sarah Levitt, three weeks after finishing my MFA. For the eighteen months that followed, she pushed me to improve the manuscript and rewrite a good chunk of it. I complained and resisted in all sorts of regrettable ways, but she didn't stop pushing. Thank you, Sarah, for the incredible patience you showed, the faith you had, and all the effort and insight you brought to this novel. Thank you for helping make this dream come true.

I am thrilled to be published by a press as cool as Unnamed. Thank you to my wonderful editor, Olivia Smith, for believing in this book and these characters, for the invaluable edits, and for being transparent, patient, and sympathetic in such a rare and special way.

Thank you to the beautiful Sara El Miniawi, whose love and support were essential in keeping me from giving up during the most crucial of stages. Thank you for teaching me to be proud of every step and be patient with results.

Thank you to my dearest sister, Nadine, for reading all the drafts and for standing up for me and my life choices whenever and wherever I needed it. I will always be grateful for that beautiful smile of yours that I've been lucky to come home to my entire life.

Most people can imagine the shock that my parents suffered when I first announced that I wanted to dedicate myself to writing. Despite it, they funded my MFA and respected my choices. Thank you, Osama and Randa, for supporting me despite your worries, for sacrificing so much for my education, and for teaching me to work hard and persist. I am indebted to you for everything I am and have done.

Finally, I am thankful for the beloved Cairo circles, and all the wildness within.

About the Author

Doma Mahmoud grew up in Cairo, Madrid, Addis Ababa, and New York. He has an MFA in creative writing from New York University and currently teaches fiction and rhetoric at the American University in Cairo. *Cairo Circles* is his first book.